T0119772

the
cleveland
heights
LGBTQ
sci-fi and
fantasy
role playing
club

the cleveland heights LGBTQ sci-fi and fantasy role playing club

by Doug Henderson

University
of Iowa Press
Iowa City

University of Iowa Press, Iowa City 52242
Copyright © 2021 by Doug Henderson
www.uipress.uiowa.edu
Printed in the United States of America

Cover design by Holly Dunn; text design by Omega Clay

Printed on acid-free paper

Library of Congress Cataloging-in-Publication Data
Names: Henderson, Doug, 1972– author.
Title: The Cleveland Heights LGBTQ Sci-fi and Fantasy
Role Playing Club / Doug Henderson.
Description: Iowa City: University of Iowa Press, 2021.
Identifiers: LCCN 2020039792 (print) |
    LCCN 2020039793 (ebook) | ISBN 9781609387563
    (paperback) | ISBN 9781609387570 (ebook)
Classification: LCC PS3608.E525858 C54 2021 (print) |
    LCC PS3608.E525858 (ebook) | DDC 813/.6—dc23
LC record available at https://lccn.loc.gov/2020039792
LC ebook record available at https://lccn.loc.
gov/2020039793

For my mother

acknowledgments and thanks

To the MFA program at the University of San Francisco, where the first true draft of this novel was completed. To K. M. Soehnlein, Stephen Beachy, Lewis Buzzbee, Lori Ostlund, and Nina Schuyler for their workshops, guidance, and advice. To Lynne Nugent and Kate Conlow for their editorial feedback and for believing in this book. To Elizabeth Bernstein for so much encouragement, and the San Francisco Writers Grotto, where the early scenes for this novel were developed. To PEN America and the Robert J. Dau Foundation for supporting emerging writers. To the amazing and talented Bay Area Manuscript Group for workshopping so much of this novel. To the Bay Area gaming community for so many adventures, and stories, and laughs. To Melanie Samay, who read every draft and still asked to read more. To my husband and family, without whom this writing life would have never started. To my mom, for everything.

the
cleveland
heights
LGBTQ
sci-fi and
fantasy
role playing
club

the summoning

Ben stood in the basement and called upstairs, "Mom, have you seen my dice bag up there?"

"What dice bag, sweetheart?" his mother replied from the kitchen.

"My *only* dice bag." He'd been using that same dice bag since high school. "It's made of purple velvet. Ties with a string."

"Where'd you leave it last?"

"I thought on my desk but—"

"Oh, well, that explains it." His mother stepped into the doorway. She wore her glasses around her neck on a silver chain. "That place is such a mess down there, it's a wonder you can even *find* your desk."

"Mom, please, I'm in a hurry." Ben slid on his yellow windbreaker. Of course she would bring this up now, as he was rushing to get out the door. "Can you help me look?"

"It's not up here. I can tell you that."

"Mom, please, just look."

As Ben turned to continue his search, his cat, Onigiri, slipped through his legs and ran ahead of him.

Ben kicked past piles of dirty clothes, dirty dishes, and empty beer cans. He pushed aside stacks of books and comics on his desk. He dug past his pencil cup, crammed full, and moved around the dusty model of the Death Star he'd made in the seventh grade. But no dice bag.

Last Thursday after gaming he had come in through the front door, not the cellar door, because he was starving, and he wanted something to eat. He had slipped into the kitchen, warmed up some macaroni and cheese, and then crept downstairs without turning on a light. He'd dropped his backpack by the La-Z-Boy, put his books on the desk, his wallet by the empty aquarium, and his dice bag?

Ben closed his eyes. He felt through the air with his fingers and stretched out his mind, expanding it into every nook and corner of the basement, under the bed, behind the bookshelves, through the dark and musty shadows of the storage room.

"Little dice, lucky dice, where art thee? Manifest before me on the count of three. One, two, three." Ben glanced at the floor between his feet. Nothing. He looked at his desk. Onigiri looked back, blinking, as dust was settling upon the Death Star.

God, he was an idiot. What was he thinking? Magic doesn't exist. Those dice were just dumb pieces of plastic. He knew that and still he was such a weirdo all the time. No wonder he couldn't get a boyfriend. Ben collapsed onto the La-Z-Boy.

Above him, the basement door opened with a squeak. "Ben, honey, are these them?" From the top of the stairs came the sound of dice shaking in their bag.

"Yes!" He dashed up the steps and his mother dropped the velvet pouch into his hand. "Thanks. Where were they?"

"They were on the floor, next to the couch."

"But I looked there."

"Sometimes when you're in a rush, you don't see things that're right in front of your face."

"And sometimes," Ben said, "objects of power don't reveal themselves to the mortal plane unless called forth with a summoning spell."

His mother tsked. "You've been playing too many of those games."

"But, it worked," Ben said as he headed downstairs.

His mother called after him, "I only say that because I worry. You have to think about the real world too, you know. Think about your future. You're almost thirty after all."

"Mom, I'm twenty-five."

"That's almost thirty in my book."

"Mom, stop." They had already talked a million times about his future. "I'm going out the back. I'll be home later."

With that, Ben climbed up the creaky ladder, through the cellar doors, and set out.

. . .

Coventry Road in Cleveland Heights was a power ballad, a nap, a rainbow, a dull noise, a cluster fuck, a nostalgia, a dream. Coventry Road was coming and going, brick and steel and rust and graffiti and gum-stuck pavement, and tattered awnings and trash in the gutter. Mom-and-pop shops of eclectic attractions, bookstores, restaurants, head shops, and a lonely record store and noisy poetry readings and bars, taverns, pubs. Its inhabitants were, as the story goes, hippies, punks, dropouts, and deadbeats. Had the story been turned to another page, it might have read yuppies and hipsters and heroes, and it would have told the same tale.

Valerie propped open the front door of Readmore Comix and Games and pulled the large signboard in from the sidewalk.

Comics! it announced in big white letters with a yellow arrow underneath. Games, toys, collectibles, trading cards, fun!

Long into old age she would remember the sound and feel of that board scraping along the cement, so many times had she heard and felt its vibrations as she dragged it along. She propped it against the front counter with a thud.

Valerie was short, with thick brown hair that curled at the ends, especially if she didn't wash it. Although she'd switched from glasses to contacts back in ninth grade, she still felt like she had glasses-face, which is to say the kind of face that looked like it had been wearing glasses all day even when it hadn't. Working in a comic bookstore and reading all day probably didn't help.

Polly, standing behind the register with Kyle, asked, "Will someone make the call?" She was wearing her foxy nurse outfit, which was the same as her regular nurse outfit but with fox ears and a tail.

"We're closing in five minutes," Kyle yelled at the three customers still slumped around the store reading. None of them moved an inch. It was well understood amongst employees that customers had the worst sense of hearing.

"Make that four minutes," Valerie said, looking at the wall clock.

Valerie was ready to call it a day. She'd arrived a little late, just past ten, because she'd run up to the corner cafe to get a coffee and a Danish. Luckily, Kyle had arrived on time and already opened the shop.

Kyle was alright. He had worked at Readmore longer than Valerie or Polly. He had long black hair that he tied in a ponytail, and he somehow managed to be skinny and yet have a belly, which Valerie assumed was from drinking beer, because if he wasn't talking about comic books, he was talking about microbrews. He usually wore a green army jacket over T-shirts with random sayings like "Make Tea not War" or "Rogues do it from Behind," and while Valerie didn't hate those shirts, they didn't make her laugh either, which generally summed up everything about Kyle.

Aside from arguing with a customer over the near-mint rating on an issue of *The Amazing Spiderman* and trying to recommend a graphic novel with strong female characters, the day had been uneventful. Walt, the store owner, had called around three to ask if any good mail had come in, and after a brief discussion of what exactly qualified as good mail, Valerie was disappointed to learn that the party supply catalogs she so fondly flipped through did not make the list.

Valerie had only started working at Readmore at the beginning of the summer, straight out of high school. She'd decided to give herself a year off after graduating as she wasn't sure yet what she wanted to do about college. It was so expensive. And student loans were so intimidating and depressing. She had no idea what she wanted to major in, or what she was good at. And to make matters worse, her older sister Katie was studying abroad at Cambridge, sucking up all their parent's adoration and being generally impossible to compete with. Valerie decided, after several heated debates with her parents, to take some time off and decide what she wanted to do with herself.

"Would you ever have sex with an alien?" she asked Polly and Kyle. They were standing behind the counter drumming their fingers on the glass and waiting for the last customer to leave.

"Haven't we talked about this already?" Polly asked.

"Let's say you met someone, and they were cool and attractive, but they told you they were an alien. Do you think they'd be dateable or would you think they're crazy?"

"No, Valerie, no." Polly had red hair, blue eyes, and lots of freckles. She wore vintage cardigans and canvas shoes, liked indie comics, the more obscure the better, and when she played board games, she played them to win. She and Valerie had been friends in high school but didn't start fooling around until Valerie began working at Readmore.

"This question is more for Kyle than for you," Valerie said.

"Why?" Polly asked.

"I already know your answer."

"What are you saying?" Kyle asked. "You think I'm into freaky shit?"

"For the record," Polly said, "I could date an alien. I could date anyone as long as they were a nice person." She motioned toward Valerie with a flick of her hand.

"Then why did you say no?" Valerie asked.

"I said no for *you*. I don't think *you* could date one. You couldn't handle it."

"Why not?"

Polly and Kyle exchanged a look and then Polly said, "I'm going to go count down this second register." The cash drawer snapped open with a clang.

The clock struck seven and the last customer shuffled out.

"We open again tomorrow," Valerie called. "Ten a.m., bright and early." The door swung shut and the bell above it dinged.

As Kyle began counting down the last register, Valerie pulled her *Player's Handbook* and her character sheets for her bard, Theegh, out from behind the front counter. She'd been flipping through them all day.

When Celeste had first cornered Valerie back by the military strategy games and asked her to join the LGBTQ Sci-Fi and Fantasy Role Playing Club, she had answered, "I don't think so."

"Why not?" Celeste asked, giving her that quizzical look she always does. "I thought you loved D&D. Don't you wanna fight monsters and decimate the forces of evil?"

And of course she wanted to, but it had seemed like such a commitment. She'd have to stay late and hang out in the back room. And work was already so long and boring.

"But what?" Celeste asked. She clutched her medallion. She always wore these medallions around her neck, gold ones, silver ones, sometimes they had a fake gem in the center. "Don't tell me you're too cool or something."

"No," Valerie had been quick to say, insulted by the suggestion.

"Then who cares?" Celeste threw up her hands. "You don't

even have to tell people it's a queer group. Just tell them you're playing D&D on Thursdays, that's all they need to know."

"I guess, but is it really going to be every single week?"

"Look, this group is gonna die unless more people join, and then what? The city will have one less D&D group going. One less group for people who wanna roll a twenty-sided die and get their game on. And quite frankly, one less safe space for queer people to be themselves and have fun. Is that what you want?"

"No, of course not."

So, Valerie had finally given in, especially after Celeste added, "I'll let you pick a magical weapon with either a bonus to hit or a bonus to damage." And that had sealed the deal.

Before Valerie could come around and lock the front door, Mooneyham pushed it wide open. The bell dinged.

"What's up fudge nuts?" Mooneyham said to Kyle. "And lady fudge nuts," he said to Valerie. He dropped his black leather bag on the counter with a thud. "Although I understand your nuts are neither fudge nor nuts."

Mooneyham was the other reason Valerie had avoided joining the group for so long.

"I'll count down the register in the back," Kyle said as he slipped past Valerie and headed to the office.

Mooneyham tossed his suit jacket onto the counter, loosened his tie, and unbuttoned his collar, revealing his hairy chest. Mooneyham was tall, broad, and dark haired. He worked in finance and made more money than everyone else in the group combined. With a sniff, he surveyed the store and the rack of new titles. "Anything good come in this week?"

"Not really."

"God, this place sucks. Why do I come here?"

"I don't know," Valerie said.

"Of course you don't." Mooneyham rolled up his sleeves with

his thick fingers. His arms were hairy as well. "Who's bringing snacks tonight—and don't say Ben."

Valerie's hesitation was all Mooneyham seemed to need.

"Fuck! He better not bring some crazy shit like last time. Christ. I hope to god I still have a protein bar in my bag. I'm gonna get set up." Mooneyham collected his bag and jacket and made his way toward the back room, toward the curtain that hung in the doorway and separated the gaming room from the rest of the store. "In the meantime, you should consider what your nuts are made of. No need to report back to me, but it's probably something you should know, in case you ever decide to use them."

With a sigh, Valerie turned to lock the front door when she noticed some movement in the toy section, behind the stuffed dragon puppets. There was a man, dressed in black, standing in the corner.

"Hello," Valerie called out as she approached. The man was wearing a short top hat, tattered and frayed along the edges. How had Valerie not noticed this guy earlier? She must have been reading her *Player's Handbook* more often than she thought.

"Um, excuse me." Valerie tapped the man on his shoulder. "We're closed."

Slowly, the man turned. Wavy blond hair hung from beneath the top hat. His skin was pale but good looking, almost pretty, in an unsettling way. He might have been wearing makeup, but Valerie couldn't be sure in the dim light. He smiled just enough to reveal pointy incisors.

"I wish to purchase this multi-paged pictographic amusement," the man said in a low voice, as though he hadn't spoken all day. His lips moved in such a way that it was difficult for Valerie to tell if the fangs were real or plastic. His short fingernails were painted black and the edges were chipped.

"Sorry, but we already closed down the registers," Valerie said. "Come back tomorrow."

"Tomorrow?" The man's smile disappeared. "Did you say the word *tomorrow*? You apparently fail to understand the long, slow tediousness of the night that lies before me."

"Sorry," Valerie said again. "But we're closed."

"You dare deny the High Lord Varnec!" He revealed his fangs in full. They were not the cheap fakes that kids wore; they were the expensive fakes that adults wore.

"The who?" Valerie asked. "Varnec?"

"The High Lord Varnec." He tossed back his head. "Brother of Darkness, Champion of Despair." He straightened his shoulders, ascended to his full height, and glared down at Valerie with icy blue eyes.

"Well," said Valerie, "we're still closed."

Varnec blubbered before blurting, "I'll devour your soul!" He tossed his comics onto the floor, and pushed past Valerie, knocking over a spinner rack of Disney comics. It crashed to the floor as Varnec flew out the door.

"Whoa," Polly said, coming out of the office to investigate. "What the heck was that?"

"Just some customer who wants to devour my soul," Valerie said as she straightened the spinner rack. "Same old, same old."

• • •

Ben arrived at Readmore apologetic and sweating, bags from the grocery store swinging from his hands. It would be so nice if he could arrive at least once without being all sweaty, but that seemed to be impossible.

The back room was small and had no windows. The walls were covered up by shelves of books and graphic novels, the tops of which were crowded with figures and statues of various sizes: knights, warriors, and superheroes side by side, fighting monsters and dragons and each other. Once brightly colored, they now wore helmets and shoulder pads of gray fuzz.

In the center of the room two quivering card tables had been pushed together without a tablecloth, so as not to interfere with the rolling of the dice. A mismatched crew of worn and broken chairs, recruited from kitchens and dining room sets, surrounded them like a skeleton army closing in for the kill.

Old floor lamps in two corners provided warm amber light. Another lamp stood darkened and dusty in a third corner, apparently broken, although Ben had never seen anyone attempt to turn it on.

Celeste, the dungeon master, sat at the far end of the tables, peering over the top of her dungeon master's screen, a fold-out panel of cardboard with fanciful depictions of dragons and orcs and creatures unknown. The screen allowed Celeste to roll her dice in secret. Her braids were pulled back, and a large silver medallion hung against her chest.

"What's this shit?" Mooneyham asked when Ben set the bags on the table. "Dr Pepper and mini-donuts? Yes! You came through."

"I was in a hurry, so I just got whatever." Ben had a different concern now—someone new was sitting in his seat.

This new guy had short dark hair and blue eyes and wore a heavy metal T-shirt that Ben figured would have been blacker if it hadn't been washed so many times.

"This is Albert," Celeste said from the front of the table. "He's joining us tonight."

"Hey," Albert grinned, and Ben couldn't remember the last time he'd seen stubble parted by a smile quite so nicely.

There was no way, an absolute zero percent chance, that Ben was sitting next to this guy.

Ben could take the seat next to Mooneyham, but Mooneyham had already put his jacket and heavy bag there and Ben couldn't ask him to move them now. If he did, Mooneyham would say, "Why don't you sit over there?" and point to the empty seat next to Albert.

He could sit between Celeste and Valerie, but that chair was missing an arm and one of its legs was shorter than the others. It really served best as an ottoman for the person sitting across from it. Ben couldn't survive an hour in that uncomfortable chair, but if he complained, Valerie or Celeste would just point out the empty seat next to Albert.

Ben started to circle when Mooneyham said, "Would you just sit down already so we can start?"

So, Ben turned toward the only option still available: the empty seat to Albert's left.

"Hey again," Albert said, as Ben dropped into his chair. "I'm Albert."

"I know," Ben mumbled into his backpack and pulled out his pens and character sheets. "Welcome to the group."

the fellowship of the room

As Ben straightened out his character sheets, and shook his dice out of his dice bag, Celeste clapped her hands from behind her dungeon master's screen. "You should all introduce your characters. Albert, since you're the newbie, why don't you go first."

From a black folder with a sticker of a red pentagram on the front, Albert pulled out his character sheet. He had filled it out by hand and covered it in scribbles and doodles of weapons and monsters. "His name is Godson Flamebender and he's a neutral-good paladin."

"How can a paladin be neutral-good?" Mooneyham asked with a snort. "They're a holy order. Don't they have to be lawful?"

"Typically," Albert said. "He's still a goody-goody knight-in-shining-armor type, but let's just say he has fallen to certain temptations."

"What kind of temptations?" Mooneyham asked.

"Sexual temptations," Albert said.

"What? There's no sex in D&D," Ben said. "At least, none that we've ever played."

"Exactly. It's a lack of sex that's causing all his problems, especially the kind of sex he's interested in. He has to take all his frustrations out on the battlefield. Why do you think he named his pole arm 'the Rammaster'?"

"I don't know," Ben said.

Mooneyham snorted. "You wouldn't."

"What about you guys?" Albert asked. He pulled a small plastic food-storage container from his backpack, and wrapped in toilet paper inside was a small painted metal miniature of a paladin in heavy armor carrying a pole arm. He placed the miniature on the table in front of his character sheet. "What are your characters like?"

"I'm playing a wandering bard named Theegh," Valerie said, gesturing at her unpainted miniature of an elf singing and playing a lute. "And Mooneyham's a dwarf fighter named Gunther."

"A wandering bard and a dwarf fighter? That's it?"

"What more do you need?" Mooneyham asked. His miniature dwarf, no bigger than his thumb, had a giant axe, a big black beard, and red armor. It was meticulously painted, complete with a golden trimmed base with fake grass and rocks.

"Well, I always like a good background story," Albert said. "That's my favorite part."

"Mine too," Ben said.

"What's your character like then?" Albert asked.

Ben picked at the corner of his character sheet. "His name is Bjorndar and he's a druid." Ben placed his miniature on the table: a hooded half-elf with red hair, a dark green cloak, and a longbow on his back. The paint was chipped on the edges where the cloak swirled around the boots, but Ben was proud of the paint job nonetheless, since he'd done it himself. Unlike Mooneyham, he couldn't afford to pay someone to paint miniatures for him. "Bjorndar was raised as an orphan by a traveling circus, but not really a circus like we think of a circus. More like a traveling performance group. Like medieval vaudeville or something like that."

"Yeah, that sounds way better," Mooneyham said.

"Just listen," Celeste said, giving Mooneyham a look.

"One day, when he was in his teens, he went out into the woods to fetch some water from a mountain stream and there he saw a boy, about his same age, watching from between the trees. The next day, the same thing, and the day after that too. How strange, he thought, why is this mysterious boy spying on me? Until finally, he called out to the boy. Tentatively the boy came out from the trees and introduced himself. His name was Peeko. His skin was as pale as moonlight on water and his eyes were big and dark like caves just waiting to be explored."

"Yeah, we got it," Mooneyham said.

"Just keep going," Albert said. "It's good so far."

Ben's throat was dry but the Niagara Falls of his back sweat was flowing. From the corner of his eye he could see Albert's blue eyes watching him attentively, and he wasn't sure if that made telling the story easier or harder. "Eventually Bjorndar befriended this strange boy. More and more with every day he looked forward to their time together, climbing trees and playing in the river, and when the circus left, Bjorndar ran away from his family, who wasn't his real family anyway, and he stayed behind with Peeko, who took him to his home, an all-male druid retreat hidden deep in the mountains. There Bjorndar lived amongst the druids and learned the druidic arts, earth magic and all that kind of stuff. Until one day a group of marauding orcs came through and raided the entire village. Bjorndar alone survived."

"How?" Albert asked.

"I imagine he was out hunting and then came back to find everyone slaughtered. Even his dear Peeko, who by now was his lover. Of course."

"How'd he die?" Albert asked.

"I don't know," Ben said. "But they must have gutted him or done something horrific, because it sent Bjorndar into a painful and heartbroken rage. He gathered what supplies were left and went off into the woods, taking up a life of solitude. Only now, at last, is he heading out into the world to take his revenge against the orcs and find a way to mend his broken heart." When he finished, Ben kept his eyes on his character sheet. He didn't look at Albert. He didn't look at anyone.

"Pretty good," Albert said.

"I don't know," Mooneyham said. "That story makes me a little uncomfortable."

"What? Why?" Ben asked.

"'Cause it does."

"What about his?" Ben nodded toward Albert. "Flamebender the Rammaster?"

"His is sweet. A gay paladin that spears people up the butt? That's awesome."

"It's ridiculous."

"It's better than an escapee from a nudist colony."

"They're probably all vegans," Valerie added.

"He's a druid! That's how they live!"

Everyone burst out laughing. Ben stood up and announced he needed a break. Celeste quickly followed after him as Ben headed to the front of the store, near the windows and the racks of hand puppets. This was the furthest spot from the back room and there was a sense, although unproven, that the puppets would dampen the sound of any arguing.

"I don't like him," Ben said.

"He's just being Mooneyham."

"I mean Albert. He makes me nervous. He's not a good fit."

"Are you serious?"

"I knew from the beginning, with the very first glimpse. He's not like us. Just look at him. He's too good looking to play D&D." Ben paced amongst the puppets. "Who is this guy, coming in here all cool and good looking?"

"Regardless," Celeste said, and Ben could tell by the look on her face that she was trying to be patient, "he told me he loves gaming, and it sounds like he's a real geek at heart."

"Yeah, right. No geek, at heart, or at who-knows-what, has ever looked that perfect and joined a group like this."

"He's not perfect. He's wearing a T-shirt and jeans. And he didn't even bother to shave."

"Exactly! He's perfectly unshaven. If I don't shave, I look like a crazy person."

"You *are* a crazy person."

"I certainly don't look like *that*," Ben motioned over his shoulder to the back room. "I just don't get what he's doing here."

"I told you, he just moved to Cleveland and he's looking for a new group. He wants friends. Did you see his character sheet? I can tell he knows what he's doing."

Ben laughed. "Who moves to Cleveland? And people that good looking don't need a fantasy role playing club to find friends. They can be running around in the real world, having sex and breaking hearts and doing whatever they want. He should be at some party right now getting wasted and doing whatever. I don't get it. Plus, his character is stupid."

"Stop." Celeste grabbed Ben's shoulders and put a halt to his pacing. "It doesn't matter if you think his character is stupid. It doesn't matter if you think he's amazing or a dud. I just got the group back up to five members and I'm not going to let it fall apart again. Look at me. Are you listening? I'm going to ask you to pull yourself together and get back in the game. Do you think you can do that?"

There was a stack of dusty board games on the floor, and Ben found them far more interesting than looking Celeste in the eye.

Celeste was the reason Ben had joined the group. They went back to college, before she had transitioned, when she still went by Ronald. Although even then she'd begun growing her hair out and tentatively presented as a woman. Ben knew with Celeste DMing he wouldn't have to worry about anything with the group. He wasn't expecting someone like Albert to join though.

"Ben, are you listening to me?" Celeste shook him by the shoulders. "Are you going to come back to the game with me or what?"

So, it had come to this, either go home and endure a night alone with the cat or stay and endure who-knows-what while sitting next to a guy far too good looking.

"Alright, I'll do it," Ben said. "But I'm not sitting by him next week."

They returned to the back room and Ben tried to act as though nothing had happened.

"Thank you everyone for waiting." Celeste retook her spot at the head of the table and smoothed back her braids.

"For what it's worth," Albert said, as Ben sat down, "I think an escapee from a nudist colony sounds pretty hot."

Ben's face went red and he turned his focus to Celeste, who was leaning over the gridded dry-erase map that she laid out across the tabletops, one hand clutching her silver medallion against her chest. If she had also heard Albert's comment, she didn't respond, but she was smiling.

"Adventurers," Celeste said, with a clap of her hands. "Let's begin. As usual, you're at the Cod and Piece."

"What's that?" Albert asked.

"The ye old gay bar in town. You stumble into the bar, out of the cold, rainy night, shaking off your coats and boots. The barkeep, Jasper Whistletooth, leans over the countertop and says—"

the sacrifice

"Welcome back." Whistletooth quickly waved them inside. "We've been waiting for you."

Pulling open the front door unleashed a thick cloud of smoke and the sour smell of stale beer. Lightning flashed through the windows, but if thunder followed it couldn't be heard above the roar of laughter and the wave of music that came from inside the Cod and Piece. Crowds of rowdy men and women sat along wooden tables drinking and laughing. On the long bar, scantily clad men gyrated and cavorted with patrons. To the right was a large stone fireplace, burning merrily.

Near the fire, a bard dressed in colorful clothes and a hat shaped like a star played a jaunty melody on his lute. The crowd clapped in unison as he tapped out the rhythm with his foot. Beside him, a few men and women stomped and danced and sang along.

"That's Zabarini," Theegh said. "He's the most famous bard in all of Hammervale. He's played for royalty. He's traveled the world."

"Oh, of course, Zabarini," Bjorndar said. "He's huge with the gays."

"Should we get some drinks and join the fun?" Gunther asked.

"Unfortunately, there's no time for that now," Whistletooth said as he ushered them behind the bar and into a back room. "We've much to discuss."

The back room had a low ceiling, and the sounds and smells of the kitchen came through the thin walls. A large wooden table covered in maps and diagrams sat in the middle of the room. Even more maps lined the walls. The low cases and shelves along the walls were filled with books, scrolls, and small crystal scrying orbs. A mangy guard dog beneath the table raised its head as the group entered, then went back to sleep.

Whistletooth sorted through the maps on the table. "I was going to send you to the castle, but I heard it's under construction. But no problem. There are other things to explore. This area over here for instance, about a day's ride away." Whistletooth pointed to a dark green swath on the map. "Cultist activity in the forest of Mythredor has gotten worse of late. Even more concerning, we have word from several villagers that strange creatures have been lurking about harassing merchants and caravans. There is a cave in the woods that has long been used as a resting place for travelers, and rumor has it that it's been taken over. By what or whom, no one is certain. But you can bet the cultists are involved."

"You want us to check it out," Gunther said. "What should we do if we find some cultist activity?"

"Be cautious. Find out what's going on. If there are any cultist activities—put an end to them. We cannot allow the Sleeping God to rise."

"Sounds good to me," Bjorndar said. "We shall investigate this cave and return with more information."

Whistletooth nodded. "I see you now have a paladin traveling with you. A welcome addition to the party, I am sure. Should you need any supplies or provisions, be sure to speak with Alyssia behind the bar."

Without any time to waste, the party set out from the Cod and Piece and arrived to find a dark haze had settled over the forest of Mythredor.

Gunther led the way as they walked through the dense forest, keeping to the well-worn road. Theegh absently strummed his lute as he followed along. Flamebender took up the rear.

A low mist clung to the ground about their ankles. The sky was overcast, what could be seen of it through the thick canopy of leaves. As they came to a bend in the road, Flamebender saw a flash of something to his right, a glimpse of pale flesh. A shirtless young man with dark, tussled hair was running through the trees. He had a playful smile on his face, and when their eyes met he gave Flamebender a wink.

Curious, Flamebender pulled his pole arm from his back and stepped off the road and into the forest.

The music from Theegh's lute had grown louder, fuller, and richer, accompanied by a flute and drum.

"Where is that music coming from?" Gunther asked.

The party stopped to listen. Theegh stopped strumming his lute, but still the music continued.

"What happened to the new guy?" Bjorndar asked.

Gunther, Theegh, and Bjorndar were alone on the road. Flamebender was nowhere to be found, and still the strange music filled the air.

They called out for Flamebender, but there was no answer. Only the music.

"Someone is rocking out on that flute," Bjorndar said.

"How did we lose a paladin in full plate armor?"

"It wasn't my job to watch him," Bjorndar said.

"I think he lost himself," Theegh said.

The music was growing louder, closing in on them.

Theegh crept toward the edge of the forest. "The flute is so close." He peered between the trees, trying to see into the dense undergrowth. "It's just right there."

"No, don't." Bjorndar grabbed Theegh by the arm before he could step off the road. "Don't go into the forest. It isn't safe."

"Let's carry on with our quest," Gunther said. "No doubt we'll find the source of that music, or it will find us."

"What about the paladin?" Theegh asked.

"Meh." Bjorndar shrugged. "The new guy."

"I bet my beard, if we find the music, we'll find him too," Gunther said.

They continued down the road, and the music traveled with them. The haunting flute was never more than a few feet away. Theegh tried to play a counter melody, but the music of the forest changed to match his tune.

Eventually, they came to a small trail that branched to the right.

"This is the way to the cave," Gunther said. "It isn't far."

"Be on your guard," Bjorndar said as they stepped onto the narrow trail.

They crept quietly through the underbrush as they approached the dark maw of the cave.

"I'll cast invisibility and scout inside," Bjorndar said. "You guys wait here." Bjorndar mumbled a few indecipherable words and then vanished.

The music stopped.

"Oh shit," Theegh said.

Gunther did not look concerned. "Anyone who fights me is gonna go down as quickly as a keg of dwarven stout, which is to say pretty quickly."

"Good one," Theegh said. "How do you come up with that stuff?"

"I read a lot of books."

"I read a lot of comics," Theegh said.

"About dwarves?"

"No."

"There's your problem."

From out of the shadows, Bjorndar reappeared. "Flamebender is in there, unconscious," he said. "Whoever captured him has stripped him half-naked and placed him on some type of altar."

"You didn't see anyone else?" Gunther asked. "No cultists?"

"No, but there were an awful lot of hoof prints."

"Hoof prints?"

"They're too small to belong to a horse. More like a goat's."

Theegh asked, "Why would goats want to sacrifice a paladin?"

The music began playing again, this time accompanied by laughter and cheering. Rather than swelling all around them, it now seemed to come from one particular spot through the trees to their right. Without exchanging more than a look, they stepped through the forest in search of the source. They came to a small clearing with a long, wooden table filled with meat and fish, jugs of wine, and platters of fruit.

At the table sat four men, naked from the waist up. One played a flute, another a drum, a third strummed a small harp, and the fourth blew into a set of pipes that hung around his neck on a string. The lower halves of their bodies were covered in thick fur, and their feet were cloven hooves. Small horns curved from their foreheads.

"Satyrs," Theegh said.

"You mean fauns," said the one with the flute.

"What's the difference?"

"Oh my god, did you really just ask that? Satyrs are like hairy, old daddies. Fauns are like smooth, young twinks." The faun dragged a hand down his lithe, hairless chest.

"What's a twink?" Theegh asked.

"You," Gunther said.

"Never mind," Bjorndar said. "You've captured our friend and we mean to take him back."

"Now he's your friend?" Gunther said. "He was 'the new guy' just a minute ago."

"Hold on," Theegh said. "Back up. How can I be playing a twink if I don't even know what one is?"

"All twinks are playing a twink," Gunther said.

"Can we move on?" Bjorndar asked.

"Certainly," said the faun with the flute. "Madrigal dance remix!"

With that the fauns jumped into a rousing melody. Bjorndar quickly covered his ears and yelled for the others to do so as well, but he was too late. Theegh and Gunther had already started to dance. The fauns cheered them on.

Bjorndar cast another invisibility spell and watched from the trees as Theegh and Gunther shook their butts and gyrated their hips.

"Take off your shirts," yelled the fauns. "Show us your pecs!"

Gunther and Theegh removed their armor and slowly pulled off their shirts.

"Drop your pants," the fauns commanded.

Gunther and Theegh, still dancing, unfastened their belts and dropped their pants to their ankles.

"Now sword fight!" yelled the faun with the pipes.

Gunther picked up his heavy battle axe, and Theegh pulled out his thin rapier.

"That's not what I meant," said the faun, "but close enough I guess."

Gunther and Theegh clashed their weapons together with a clang, and the fauns encouraged them to fight harder and faster.

Bjorndar stealthily stepped away and made for the cave. He found the paladin still inside atop the crude altar, which was nothing more than a stone slab encircled with white candles. Flamebender was armorless and bare-chested. The fauns had anointed him in foul-smelling oils, but otherwise he appeared to be unscathed.

Bjorndar gingerly placed a hand upon the paladin's chest and felt a faint heartbeat. "Thank the Goddess, you're still alive." He tapped the paladin gently on the cheek. "Wake up good paladin." But the paladin didn't stir.

Then came a noise from over Bjorndar's shoulder. He turned to find Gunther. His eyes were wild and his face was red. The great axe was raised high above his head.

"The Sleeping God will rise!" Gunther brought the axe down upon Bjorndar's neck and sent his head flying.

• • •

"No!" Ben propelled himself backward, away from the table. "What are you doing? You can't kill Bjorndar!"

"It wasn't me." Mooneyham quickly pointed to Celeste. "I was being mind controlled."

"He was under the satyr's power," Celeste said. "And," she pointed at the green twenty-sided die in front of Mooneyham, "Gunther rolled a natural twenty, on a power attack, while you were prone. That's a massive amount of damage."

"Plus," Valerie added, "you were distracted."

"While you were feeling up the paladin's pecs." Mooneyham gave a nod to Albert.

"I wasn't feeling up his pecs!"

"You kinda were," Albert said, grinning.

"I was trying to figure out what that oil was. Whatever. This is stupid. You can't just kill Bjorndar."

"You know I love you Ben, but it's too late," Celeste said as she tipped over the figurine of Bjorndar.

"No, come on, really?" Ben looked down at his character sheet, at Bjorndar's stats and hit points and abilities. There had to be some way out. This couldn't be happening.

"Don't worry," Albert said. "Flamebender can heal you."

"Hello, my head is cut off. How're you gonna heal that?"

"And Flamebender's not even awake," Valerie said. "He's unconscious or something."

"Not anymore," Celeste said. "The horrific howl released by Bjorndar's severed head as it spun through the air, raining blood, was more than enough to wake Flamebender. In fact, Bjorndar's head landed in your crotch," she said to Albert. "So, you sit up to find him looking up at you from your lap."

"Really?" Ben said. "Seriously?"

"Oh shit." Valerie slapped the table top. "Why didn't anyone think of this? I can totally sew his head back on with the strings from Theegh's lute. They're magical even, that's gotta do something, right?"

"Perfect," Mooneyham said. "Who's got a needle?"

Silence passed between them as they looked from one to another.

"God," Ben said. "This is the worst."

"Alright." Celeste stood up from behind her screen and clapped her hands. "This is what we're doing. Flamebender, you wake up, covered in blood and oil, a severed head in your lap. You have no idea what the hell is going on. Gunther, you snap out of it, dropping the axe in horror over what you have done. And you feel shame for having fallen under the fauns' magic and, of course, for cutting off your friend's head. Luckily, the fauns have run off." Celeste reached across the table and removed the miniature fauns from the map. "Theegh, with the fauns gone, you are free to run inside the cave, where you find this terrible scene, but you don't rush to sew on any heads, because that's stupid. Sorry about it."

"We don't have a needle anyway," Valerie added.

"Whatever. Flamebender, you know from your religious readings that the only way to resurrect this druid would be to travel to the underworld and retrieve his soul from the city of the dead."

"I do? How do we get there?"

"There are many entrances. You've heard tell, during your travels, of a river that flows into a strange cave. That river will take you into the underworld."

"One second," Mooneyham said. "What about the story line

we're on now? What about the cult and the Sleeping God?"

"We'll just put that on hold and come back to it once Bjorndar's been saved."

"And what am I supposed to do?" Ben asked. "Just sit here?" He rolled his golden twenty-sided die across his character sheet and watched it sparkle under the light. "My dice want some action too."

"What about his body?" Valerie asked. "Should we leave it, or bury it, or take it with us?"

"I can cast a preservation spell on it, to keep it from rotting," Albert said.

"Why don't we take the head and leave the rest?" Valerie asked.

"Good idea," Albert said. "So how about this: Flamebender wakes up, finds the severed head in his lap, still warm. He quickly takes it in his hands and, whispering a prayer, he preserves it at death's doorstep, trapping a little piece of Bjorndar's soul in it as well."

"So, I can still see and talk?" Ben asked.

"Sure," Celeste said. "That's fine with me. This way you can still participate."

"Do any of the rest of us get a vote on that?" Mooneyham asked.

"No," Ben said.

　• • •

With a firm grip on its hair, Flamebender held up Bjorndar's head and looked into its eyes. "Speak," he commanded. "Tell me what happened here."

"This fucking dickwad decapitated me." Bjorndar's eyes turned to Gunther.

"Why would you do such a thing?" Flamebender asked Gunther, who was climbing to his feet.

Gunther said, "I'm ashamed to say it, but I was under the spell of some mischievous fauns."

"So says you." Flamebender looked down upon the dwarf.

"It's true." Theegh ran forward, huffing and puffing. "I saw the whole thing. Well, not the head cutting off part, but I saw the fauns control him."

"And where are the fauns now?"

"They ran off," Theegh said.

"Are you sure?" Flamebender asked. "They're crafty. One of them lured me in here by pretending to be a handsome squire, lost in the woods."

"They meant to sacrifice you to the Sleeping God," Gunther said. "They're cultists, I'm sure of it."

"So I too discovered once they brought me here. But first they wanted to have their way with me. Why else do you think I'm all oiled up like this? They couldn't keep their fingers off my holy musculature. It's a good thing you three came along when you did."

"Sounds like we may have missed a good time," Gunther said.

"Can we get back to the whole, returning-me-to-life thing?" asked Bjorndar's head.

"Actually, I kinda like you this way," Theegh said. "I don't feel like the most useless one anymore."

Gunther snorted. "Being more useful than a severed head isn't really something to brag about."

"Fear not, my friends." Flamebender tucked the head under his arm. "I know of a cave just a short journey from here that leads to the underworld. We shall venture to the city of the dead and make you whole again."

. . .

Ben watched as Albert spoke with such authority.

Perhaps Celeste was right. Albert didn't seem so bad after all. He certainly didn't act as though they were all a bunch of idiots. He actually looked like he was having a lot of fun.

Ben had also discovered, from the number of times the hairs

on their arms brushed against each other, that Albert was left-handed, which caused them to bump each other every time they rolled their dice. Ben had tried to move his chair away, but the tables were small and crowded and it seemed that no matter how far away he moved, their arms ended back together, touching again.

Albert didn't seem to notice or wasn't bothered by it. He was too involved at the moment in finding a practical way to carry Bjorndar's head. The room must have been too hot for him, because he kept wiping his brow with the bottom of his T-shirt, pulling it up and uncovering the fan of hair across his flat stomach. Or else, with a pinch at its center, he would quickly pull his shirt in and out, to air himself, giving Ben a short glimpse of the thin thumb of hair at the pit of Albert's neck, down to his chest and then back up again. Then to his sideburns. His eyebrows. The deep set of his blue eyes. The shape of his nose in silhouette.

On Albert's left arm, Ben saw the bottom of a tattoo, dipping from the sleeve of his T-shirt. It looked like an anchor, but he couldn't be sure.

Ben realized that not only were their arms touching, but their legs were touching too, under the table. He wanted to ignore it, to stop focusing on it and focus on the game instead. To laugh at what everyone else was laughing at and to cheer at what everyone else was cheering at, instead of joining in a second or two later to give the appearance of following along. But he didn't want it badly enough to turn to Albert and say, "Would you mind scooting down?"

He looked back over at Albert, and found Albert looking over at him, with his big grin and his teeth and his suspiciously good looks.

"Don't worry," he said. "I'm gonna bring you back to life."

God, Ben thought, *please do.*

• • •

With Bjorndar's head firmly strapped to the back of Flame-bender's pack, the group set out through the forest. They traveled from village to village. Stopping to ask directions along the way and killing the occasional dire wolf or giant bat. Until they came to the strange cave and the dark river that flowed, not out of, but into the cave. Even more surprising was the old man, sitting in a small rowboat, casting his line near the mouth of the cave.

Flamebender called to him, "Hail, good sir. Might we borrow your boat?"

"What for?" The grizzled old man looked at them suspiciously.

"We need safe passage into the cave."

"You go in there, you'll never come out."

"What do you know about this cave?" Gunther asked.

"Enough to know you won't be taking my boat in there. It'll be lost forever, as will your souls."

"Oh, but we will be taking it." Gunther pulled out his axe. "Either by force or by—"

"By gold." Flamebender put a gauntleted hand over Gunther's mouth.

"Well, if it's gold you're offering, how much've you got?"

For five gold, enough to replace the old boat ten times over, they were able to float their way down the river and into the cave. Flamebender and Gunther took up the oars while Theegh sat back and strummed his lute, conjuring a ball of light to guide them.

The tunnel wound its way down, deeper and deeper into the Earth, and just when they began to feel it would go on forever, the tunnel opened up into a cavern so large they could see neither walls nor ceiling.

"Are we still underground?" Theegh asked. He commanded the light to rise higher, but still they could not see the ceiling of the cave. They appeared to be drifting across a vast ocean. The water was dark and painfully cold.

"We must be deep," Gunther said. "We've only gone down."

The current stopped and the water became still and stagnant. The little boat came to a stop.

"If we want to get any farther we're going to have to row," Flamebender said.

"I can see something out there on the water, rising and surfacing," Bjorndar said from the back of Flamebender's pack. "It's headed our way."

With the feeble light from Theegh's orb they could see a dark mass, beneath the water, swimming quickly toward them.

"Don't look back," Bjorndar yelled. "Just row!"

Flamebender and Gunther dug their oars into the water, rowing as hard as they could. A terrible screech echoed around them as the creature rose above the water and lashed out with thick black tentacles.

"I see land," Theegh said. Under the dim light they could make out a thin shoreline. "Hurry!"

"It's almost upon us," Bjorndar said, and the creature cried again, ringing their ears. "Why aren't you rowing faster?"

"I didn't roll high enough," Gunther said.

"We're almost there," Theegh said. "Only a little more."

A thick, black tentacle lashed at the side of the boat, threatening to topple it. Theegh dodged and Gunther slipped aside as another dark tentacle tried to grab him. A third lashed itself around Flamebender, while yet another lifted Bjorndar's head from the backpack. Flamebender and Bjorndar yelled for help as they were pulled into the air.

Amid the mass of tentacles, a snapping beak rose from the water, surrounded by glistening red eyes.

Theegh struck a jarring chord from his lute as he dodged a tentacle. Gunther chopped at a tentacle with his axe as it tried to latch onto him with its suckers.

In a panic, Bjorndar's head cried madly for help. Flamebender pulled the Rammaster from his back as the creature brought them closer to its sharp beak, and with a thrust of the pole arm, he pierced one of the many red eyes.

The creature howled as red, viscous ooze spurted from the punctured eye. It lost its grip on Flamebender and dropped Bjorndar's head back into the boat with a heavy thud. Flamebender, however, fell into the dark water with a splash and sank like a rock.

Theegh grabbed Bjorndar's head by the hair and they leaped from the boat as it reached the shore. The creature reared up and lashed out. Its thick, heavy arms smashed the boat to pieces, and then it howled, seemingly in pain. Flamebender was still fighting—underwater!

With another terrible yell, the creature dove below the surface. The water turned an inky black. From the shore, they could see a dark shape swimming away, but there was no sign of Flamebender.

"He'll be fine," Gunther said. "Paladins have tons of hit points."

"But he can't swim in plate mail armor," Bjorndar said.

They watched for any sign of Flamebender. The water was still. Then, the debris from the row boat began to stir. A dark tentacle rose up amongst the floating wreckage.

"Not another one," Theegh said.

The tentacle rose higher as it came toward the shore. They watched as it flopped limply from side to side, but before they could register that something was odd, Flamebender's head and shoulders broke the surface of the water. He walked onto the shore and tossed the tentacle at their feet. It landed with a blubbery thud.

"Did I scare you?" he asked, grinning. Then he promptly collapsed.

They ran to pick him up and dragged him from the edge of the water. Once they were a safe enough distance away, they rested for a short while so Flamebender could recover his strength.

"How will we get back?" Theegh asked. "The boat has been destroyed."

"We have no choice now but to move forward," Flamebender said. He picked up Bjorndar's head and strapped it back onto his pack.

They now found themselves in a flat, barren landscape. There was no wind, no sound at all, aside from the crunch of their boots on the dry, brittle ground.

"I don't think anything has walked this way in a very long time," Gunther said.

"Then what's that?" Theegh asked, pointing.

A shadowy something was approaching from the darkness, soon joined by many somethings, coming from all sides, thin and vaporous, floating above the ground.

"Spirits," Flamebender said. "Ghosts, on their way to the city of the dead."

Fascinated, they stood and watched as a crowd of ephemeral bodies passed by, some still holding the swords and spears that must have been in their hands when they died.

"They don't seem to know we're here," Bjorndar said. "Or if they do, they don't care."

"This makes it easy then." Flamebender turned in the direction the ghosts were moving. "We only have to follow them to know we're going the right way."

Walking in step, they joined the spirit crowd and followed, across the empty expanse. A thin line on the horizon grew into a wall before them. They marched on until the smooth obsidian walls climbed dozens of feet high and they came to the spiraling black gates of the city of the dead. And there they stopped. The dark, gilded gates were open and surprisingly unguarded. The spirits moved through the gates without stopping or looking back.

"Anyone is free to enter the city of the dead," a passing spirit said. "But no one ever gets out."

Gunther looked up at the massive gates and the jagged, black walls of the city. "Are we sure we want to go through all this, just to save him?"

"Yes," Bjorndar's head said.

"That's a good point," Theegh said. "He could always just roll up another character."

"No, he can't," said the head.

"We've come too far to turn back." Flamebender planted the holy Rammaster into the hard ground. "You should be ashamed. You're supposed to be his friends, and friends don't just kill each other and travel all the way to the land of the dead only to turn back around once they've arrived."

"Sometimes they do," Theegh said with a yawn.

"Well, not this time," Flamebender said. "I do not yet know why our paths have crossed or by what higher power, but I do not believe in coincidence. We have set out to find our destiny and I do not intend to travel halfway down the path. So, we are going into this city and we are coming out in one piece, and that includes Bjorndar."

"Yay," said Bjorndar's head.

"Alright, already," Gunther said. "Of course we'll do it, christ. But maybe we should hold off until next week, 'cause it's getting kinda late."

. . .

"We can't stop now," Ben said. "We're right there."

"Dude, it's almost midnight," Mooneyham said. "Hell, Valerie is falling asleep over there."

"What?" Valerie stirred. "I'm paying attention."

"Don't worry." Celeste looked down the table at Ben. "We'll continue where we left off next week."

"But we're so close. Roll my head through the gate and I'll save myself."

"Look," Celeste said, "I hadn't really planned this encounter anyway. I was just kinda winging it, so if we stop here and continue next week, it'll give me more time to prepare."

"Makes sense to me," Albert said as he slipped his character sheet back into his pentagram folder.

"Me too," Mooneyham said, taking the miniature Gunther off the map.

Valerie had fallen back to sleep.

Ben slumped in his chair. "I have to go the entire week being dead."

"It'll go fast," said Celeste.

As their arms brushed together for the final time that night, Ben took another look at Albert. It would be a whole week before he'd see those arms, or those sideburns, or that smile that parted so easily. He watched Albert collect his things and put on his jacket, until Albert looked up and their eyes met, then Ben looked away and pretended he couldn't get his backpack zipped shut.

"God, this bag sucks," Ben said, just to make sure everyone knew he really had been trying to close his backpack and had not been staring at Albert.

"Here." Albert reached over. "Let me try." For a moment their fingers touched. The bag zipped right up. "That was easy," Albert said. "You must have loosened it."

"Or you have the magic touch," Ben said.

"I don't know about that," Albert said with a laugh.

Just then Albert's phone began to ring in his jacket pocket. "Oh shit." He looked at the number and answered the phone, turning his back on Ben.

"I'm leaving now," Albert was saying. "Keep your pants on. I'll be there in, like, fifteen minutes. Jesus, you're such a horny slut."

Ben watched, his backpack in one hand, his yellow windbreaker in another, as Albert turned and gave the group a quick wave goodbye, still yesing and uh-huhing into his phone. There was a chance that Albert might have been, quite possibly, talking to someone who could have been his boyfriend.

Mooneyham clapped Ben on the back. "Have fun being dead for a week."

thrift store hero

Gray morning gloom crept over the city.

For a moment, Cleveland Heights was frozen in the small pause that exists just before the alarm clock sounds, before cooing and snoring bodies stretch and groan into awaken-ness and go downstairs to make a pot of coffee. Everything was blue and gray and silver then, and if anyone were out and about they would easily be forgiven for whispering of ghosts or fairies, magic dust or doorways into other worlds.

The moment only lasted for a cat-stretch, and then dull white light rose up between the houses and the trees, and the alarm clocks rang. The bodies rubbed the dust from their eyes, and all thoughts of magic and dreams and living other lives seemed silly again.

Ben rolled over, his water bed sloshing beneath him, his cat, Onigiri, lying at his feet like a sack of flour. Only 7:30. Still too early to get up, but when Ben closed his eyes he only saw Albert grinning back.

Last night had been such a mess.

Ben stared at the ceiling, at the poster of Conan the Barbarian he'd hung there back in high school. Light was beginning to seep through the lacy curtains, allowing him to make out the individual skulls Conan stood upon, a naked woman clutching his leg. Such was the life of a barbarian; always some slave girl or a princess clutching onto them.

When Ben had moved into the basement, dragging most of his things from his old bedroom upstairs, he'd brought down the poster as well. Conan had hung over his bed since middle school and it had felt strange to wake up to a blank ceiling. He was happy to have Conan above him again.

Once, Artie, his best friend from school, had cut up a picture of Ben and taped his face over Conan's. In the photo Ben was yelling at the camera—"Don't take my picture!"—which looked particularly ridiculous when taped onto Conan's head. That was a dozen years ago. Artie had moved off to college and had a wife and two daughters now. The taped-on face had long since fluttered to the floor and disappeared.

How did barbarians ever find it in their chaotic-neutral hearts to save a girl, unless it was to have sex with her? Not that there was anything wrong with that, as long as she was willing and he got her permission first. But with a barbarian's busy schedule— burning down villages, slaughtering mage lords, riding on pterodactyls—there didn't seem to be much time for chitchat, and they were notoriously bad at it. "Nice loin cloth. Wanna clutch my leg?" What kind of girl, or boy even, goes for that anyway?

No, it was far better to be saved by a valiant paladin. He'd at least have a horse and shining armor, not to mention a moral code. He'd lift a boy up, look deep into his eyes and ask if he were okay. Maybe give him a rose. He wouldn't make him lie on a pile of skulls. He'd spend time with him and get to know him.

Unless he already had a boyfriend.

Ben padded over to his desk, leaving Onigiri bobbing up and down on the bed.

Onigiri was a white short-hair with one blue eye and one green, and although he was only three he was already deaf in the ear on his blue-eyed side. The vet said it was genetic; the problem with all-white cats. Onigiri didn't seem bothered. He still came running at the slightest sound from the can opener. Ben had named him after the Japanese rice ball, because as a kitten that's what he'd looked like all curled up and asleep.

Ben turned on the computer and checked his auctions.

When Ben lost his job at the library and had been unable to find a new one with his degree in history, at least not a good one that paid any real money, he'd started selling his old toys online. It had been a temporary solution two years ago, but, like moving into the basement, it had become a permanent one. If his parents pushed him to move out, or find a real job, he'd remind them that he was a victim of the new economy. There just aren't that many jobs right now. Besides, it wasn't like he sat around all day and did nothing. Some months he made over a thousand dollars.

He scrolled through his current listings. He was going to get at least ten dollars for each of the Transformers he'd posted, and the Power Rangers bath towel was going to bring in fifteen. But the Rainbow Brite comforter hadn't received one bid. He'd thought for sure it would go for thirty, maybe fifty bucks. That comforter was in perfect condition. Even the stupid Chihuahua that said "Yo quiero Taco Bell" was going to make him twenty. Did no one care about Rainbow Brite? It had to sell. If he reposted it he'd set the starting bid at two dollars. Never mind that it had cost him five.

At this rate he would make less than a hundred dollars for the whole week. He couldn't live on that.

Onigiri jumped onto the desk and rubbed against the monitor. Ben pulled the cat off and poured him onto the floor.

"I'm trying to work."

But the cat jumped right back up again and walked across the keyboard.

There must be some other things that Ben could auction. What did he have that he would be willing to give up?

There was that stack of records.

He'd been saving them for Jeff, because Jeff had bought so many of them from him in the past. But there was no way that was going to happen now. He hadn't touched them in months. He'd let them sit and collect cobwebs, like mementos of a dashed love were supposed to do. Some of them were certainly worth money to the right person. But he didn't know much about records and hadn't had the energy to price them and photograph them and post them all online, but perhaps it was time.

Ben had joined the role playing club to put the entire dark and painful summer behind him and forget about the whole thing. Forget that he hadn't found a job, despite several interviews. That he'd spent three months in the basement playing video games and gaining weight. He'd spent so much time pining over guys, and Jeff of all guys, with his thin blond hair. His cold blue eyes and tiny teeth in his round little mouth that had spat out those doom-tipped words that had pierced Ben's heart like a black arrow, "You're a nice guy, but I'm not into you."

Ben was done with all that. Done with Jeff. Done with guys. Done with wanting things he couldn't have. He was in the role playing club now, solely focused on killing ogres and rolling his lucky dice. There was no room for guys anymore. Or love. What foolish thoughts.

He picked up the records and blew the dust off. He didn't remember buying so many, but there had to be over a dozen. Some jazz, some blues, a couple of classic rock albums. He knew what Jeff liked, so he'd bought accordingly.

On Jeff's first visit to the basement, he had asked, "What do you do with all this junk?"

"I sell it." Ben wasn't simply some guy hoarding stuff in a basement; he was the LeBron James of collecting.

"Check out this Wishbone puzzle, it's still got all the pieces. Or this Carmen Sandiego umbrella." He'd jumped from one thing to the next, like a desperate car salesman. "And I have all these

Power Rangers, the real ones, from Japan, where the yellow one is actually a guy, not a girl like she is in the American version. Maybe they're not that cool any more, but still."

"I really just came here for those records," Jeff said.

So, the LeBron James of collecting shuffled over to his bookcase and sold off the jazz records he'd found at the thrift store.

"These are great," Jeff had said. "Let me know if you find any more."

Ben knew that if he was going to sell that new stack of records, he had to be more aggressive about them than he was in the past. He needed to get some real money for them. And that would mean enlisting some help.

• • •

On Saturday, Celeste walked into the Hobby House and was greeted right away by Phillip, the owner, a man well beyond retirement age, and William, Phillip's son, a man near retirement age.

"What is it this week?" Phillip asked. "Another haunted forest?"

"Nope." Celeste couldn't help but smile. "A city of the dead. A necropolis."

Phillip and William whistled, not in disbelief or wonder, but something in between.

"Sounds like a tricky one," Phillip said.

"I suppose it's no fun adventuring in someplace normal is it?" William asked.

The Hobby House was located in a shopping plaza on Cleveland's west side between a Dressbarn and a former RadioShack. The store was known for its train sets and was popular with train enthusiasts who seemed to Celeste to be in either the six-to-eight age range or the sixty-to-eighty age range.

But the Hobby House served anyone interested in models, not only trains, and so it was popular amongst war gamers as well.

Celeste had been going there since she moved to Cleveland back in college, which felt like another life entirely, but she continued to go because she still loved building models and terrain, which was useful for the games she ran at Readmore.

"I'd like to make a gate, or some kind of entrance to the city. Something imposing."

As a young man came out from the back room, William asked, "Have you met Curtis yet? He's my nephew. Just started this week. I'll let him help you out." William clapped Curtis on the shoulder and instructed him to show Celeste to the necropolis aisle.

"The what?" Curtis was tall, slightly hunched, with dark hair and dark eyes. He had long arms and big hands. He wore a blue Hobby House polo tucked into his jeans. "The medieval stuff is over here," he said, leading the way.

"I know," Celeste said, but she followed along. On days when she felt shy, or rather didn't feel like being looked at too closely, she wore her braids down and let them fall about her face. Today was one of those days.

"You been here before?"

"Yeah, all the time. I run a game over at Readmore."

"Readmore? On the east side? In Coventry? How long you been doing that?"

"Not quite a year."

"So, you're the dungeon master. You're the boss."

"I don't really think of myself as 'the boss.' My role is more to facilitate group storytelling."

"You don't torture your characters or try to kill them? Throw them in the dildo maiden or something?"

"The what?"

"It's like an iron maiden but with dildos instead of spikes."

"No, I have to say, that idea hadn't really come to me." Celeste pushed her braids aside and chuckled.

"Yeah, I guess you can't play too rough or everyone will quit."
They turned a corner, and Curtis said, "Here's the medieval stuff.
We just got these trebuchets in. There's castle walls and some
columns. Here's a drawbridge."

The white metal shelves were sparsely stocked, a simple cot-
tage, a tavern, a guard tower. There were kits for cobblestone
streets. And models for castles as well, elaborate kits that cost
hundreds of dollars.

"Thanks," Celeste said. "I'll take a look."

"No problem. And you can use that dildo maiden idea if you
want. Let me know if you need help coming up with stuff. I got
lots of ideas."

Celeste figured she could use the cobblestones to make a wall.
She picked up a bottle of glue, as well as some paint. When she
returned to the front counter, Phillip and William were in a heated debate, which was not unusual for them.

Phillip said, "I'm not in the war business; I'm in the nostalgia business. People always ask me how I can be so obsessed
with war and fighting and tanks and bombs and jets. I tell them
they're looking at it the wrong way. It's not for the blood and
violence that people want to relive these old battles; it's for the
heroism they inspire. That's what I sell them. Heroism."

"I completely agree," Celeste said, setting her basket on the
counter.

William said, "That's a load of nostalgia-laced bull-crap. Don't
you think some guys, hell, most guys, want to imagine themselves blowing things up? Half the guys in here would rather play
as the Germans or the Japanese than play as the Allies. Something about being the so-called 'bad guys' makes them feel like a
bunch of badasses. And that's what guys really want, to feel like
badasses."

"Are the two mutually exclusive? Being a hero and a badass?
In my games we like to emphasize the story," Celeste said. "I try

to give each of the players a moment in the spotlight so they can feel important, whether that means feeling like a badass or a hero or both."

"That's 'cause you're role playing," William said. "This is war gaming I'm talking about. It's different. It's straight up strategy and combat, more technical than anything else."

"But still," Celeste said, "even in a war game that feels mechanical and mathematical, don't you see a story unfolding as the battle takes shape?"

"Sure, I suppose so."

"I really think creating a shared narrative is what it's all about," Celeste said.

"That's easy for you to say," Curtis said. "You're the dungeon master. What would your players say though? Are they in it for the story or to feel powerful?" Curtis balled up his fists and flexed his muscles. "They might even say that *you're* in it for the power, 'cause you're the dungeon master."

Just then Celeste's phone began buzzing in her pocket. It was Ben.

"One of my players." Celeste gave William and Phillip an apologetic look and stepped away from the front counter.

"Hey," Celeste said. "Is this about Bjorndar's head?"

"No," Ben said. "What do you know about Albert?"

"As much as you do, I guess." Celeste walked toward the trains set up near the front windows, her fingers fiddling with the large gold medallion around her neck as she talked.

"He works at Destruction Records, right?"

"Yeah, he saw me putting up flyers there and was like, 'Gay Dungeons and Dragons? That sounds awesome.'"

"I've got these old records I thought he might be interested in, or at least he might know what to do with them."

"Why don't you go to the record store and ask him?"

There was a long pause at the other end. "Maybe I'll wait until next week. I just met him. I don't want him thinking I'm into him or something."

"But aren't you?" Celeste watched as the trains whizzed past the tiny department store and the post office.

"No. I just need help with these records. Besides, I think he has a boyfriend."

"So what? You're just showing him some records." Celeste had known the moment she saw Albert at the record store that he would bring some hotness to the role playing club. It was good for Ben to get a little shaken up. He'd been in such a rut for so long. "What does it matter if he has a boyfriend?"

"It doesn't, except that, you know."

"Boy, get it if you want it." Celeste could practically hear the gears turning in Ben's head.

"But I don't want to overstep my bounds or anything."

"By doing what?" Celeste asked.

"I don't know, going to his work and talking to him."

"I'm not saying you should stalk him or anything. Just go by there and be like, 'Hey, what's up? How'd you like the game last night?' Then when he tells you how much fun he had, because the game was awesome and the DM was amazing, you mention you've got some records you wanna sell."

"Just like that?"

"Yes," Celeste said. "What would Bjorndar do? Have some courage." There was silence at the other end of the phone. "Hello?" Celeste checked her reception. "Ben, are you there?"

"Yeah, I was just thinking."

"Trust me," Celeste said. "Just do as I say and you're not gonna go wrong."

Celeste hung up and found Phillip and William looking at her. Phillip was shaking his head.

"What were you saying about not being a controlling DM?"

• • •

Mooneyham had just returned to his desk, with a bagel in one hand and a cup of coffee in the other—thankfully someone in the office cared about other people enough to stop and get bagels—when Kevin rolled over to his cubicle.

"Mooneyham."

"Jones."

"We missed you last night. What happened? You never showed."

"I didn't say I would." Mooneyham ate a quarter of his bagel in one bite.

Mooneyham worked on the eighth floor of Patriot Bank. His cubicle was not one that faced Lake Erie, but it was only a row away from those that did. If he stood up and stretched he could see over the low partitions and out to the water and the horizon beyond. On a slow day he stood and stretched often.

"What's up with that?"

"Sorry dude, I have a long-standing commitment on Thursdays."

"A long-standing commitment? What the fuck is that?" Kevin burst out laughing. "This guy has a long-standing commitment. I've never heard of such a thing."

"You can add that to a very long list, I'm sure." With another bite, half the bagel was gone. If Mooneyham had known the day was going to be this slow he would have stayed home and had more sex. Huey had looked so inviting lying between the sheets, Mooneyham hadn't been able to resist a quickie. But they needed to find a way to have sex in the morning and still have time for breakfast.

"Okay, don't get testy, I'm just fucking with you." Kevin leaned in and gave Mooneyham several short punches on his shoulder.

"Get off of me." Mooneyham pushed him away, trying not to spill his coffee.

"Tonight, after work," Kevin said, suddenly serious. "We're

meeting. Me, you, Anthony, and Devon. We're gonna make this thing official. And then afterward Jeanette's having a party. And it's Jeanette, so you know what that means?"

"What?" Mooneyham tried to picture who Jeanette even was.

"Loose women, horny chicks, easy sex! Come on, you're single. It's totally guilt-free."

"Sorry, I got plans." He and Huey should start having sex in the shower. That would save at least fifteen minutes. Multitasking was everything. Tomorrow, he'd put some bread in the toaster, usher Huey into the shower, fuck, shave, eat toast, get dressed, give his teeth a quick brushing, and then get out the door. He may even get to work early.

"Dude, you're killing me," Kevin said. "We've been talking about this meeting for weeks."

"Alright," Mooneyham said. "I'll come out for a drink or two."

"Yes! We're gonna get you so shit-faced you won't believe it."

"But I'm not going to that stupid party," Mooneyham added, but Kevin was already wheeling himself away.

Upon getting his job at the bank, there were several things that Mooneyham always intended to do, but never did. He never joined the softball team, he never volunteered to host a potluck, and he never came out to his coworkers, all seemingly harmless acts, yet rife with the potential for disaster. Not that he couldn't handle a game of softball or a potluck dinner. He'd played lots of sports in high school and college. He was built for sports. And he enjoyed cooking. He was built for eating too. It was the social aspect of those things that turned him off. Coming out proved to be more difficult than he expected. He'd been waiting for the right moment, but the right moment never materialized, and now, three years on, he was so used to navigating the waters of straight assumption that coming out seemed like an impossibility.

Mooneyham pulled out his phone and sent a text to Huey.
Sorry working late tonight. Sad face.

. . .

On Coventry Road, Ben was looking in the windows of Destruction Records. He wanted to check out what was new and read the chalkboard in the window of the ten best sellers and the staff picks. At the top of the list was Jeff's pick: a John Coltrane album. And down near the bottom, where the handwriting was small and messy, was Albert's: Goateyes, Blodsdrape. Clearly, the two had different tastes.

If there was one store on Coventry that could compete with Readmore in terms of longevity, it was Destruction Records. They had been in business since the late sixties and helped to establish Coventry's counterculture reputation. Unfortunately Destruction hadn't aged as well as Readmore. Any attempts to branch out by selling clothing or jewelry or incense had fallen flat, and over the years the store had become less like an angry, edgy revolutionary with its fist in the air and more like a graying substitute art teacher who smelled of patchouli oil and wore too much topaz jewelry.

Through the chalkboards and posters, Ben strained his eyes for a glimpse of Albert, but he was not behind the counter.

Through an open doorway, a set of stairs led down into the basement. Above the door a sign read "Vinyl Vault" in neon pink. That was where Jeff worked.

Most people were surprised to discover that Destruction had a basement. That was where the collectible and used records were kept, in rows of long wooden bins. The vault was largely the domain of a few long-term employees, like Jeff, who referred to themselves as the Crypt Keepers. Destruction opened at ten, but the Vault often didn't open until eleven or even later when the first Crypt Keeper arrived. Until then the basement was closed off with a little chain and a handwritten sign that read "The Vault is Closed" in blood-dripping letters. The Keepers walked in every day with their coffees and cell phones, carrying their bikes over one shoulder, and went straight to the basement.

The vault was practically a separate store. It had its own cash register and computer. Its own telephone and toilet. Behind the counter was a dirty back room with cheap thrift store art on the walls. There the Crypt Keepers could sprawl out and talk about records and bands, one-upping each other with obscure music trivia. There had once been a time when Ben longed to hang out in that back room, but not anymore.

Perhaps it was Albert's day off, or he was at lunch. Coming to the store had been a long shot anyway. But before Ben turned to walk away, there was some movement in the doorway of the Vault, leading down into the basement. Albert came running up the stairs. And he was laughing. He braced himself in the doorway, and threw his head back, laughing harder. He could barely stand, he was laughing so hard. He had to put his hands over his stomach. Ben couldn't help but feel a pang of jealousy. It would be so awesome to make Albert laugh like that. Then coming up behind Albert was the familiar face of Jeff, grinning.

Of course they would be friends. Ben turned away. He didn't want to think about Jeff and Albert laughing together, having a good time, being best buds. Ben stepped into the first store he could, Albatross Used Books, and headed straight into a back corner where he pretended to be interested in women's health.

"Can I help you?" An old woman in a flowered house dress approached Ben.

"No, I'm good."

"You seem quite eager to find something."

"No, I'm just . . ." Who was he kidding? "Actually, do you have any books on magic?"

"Would that be smoke and mirrors or card tricks?"

"Druidic?"

"Hmm, we have a New Age section." She led him across the store, but when they passed the books on medieval history Ben stopped.

"This is good," he said, spying several books on the Knights of the Templar and the Crusades. He pulled out a few titles and looked for a comfortable place to sit. Nothing would clear his mind better than a little history lesson.

• • •

Later that afternoon, Valerie strolled into Readmore Comix ready to start the closing shift. The store was busy for a Friday afternoon. Walt was on a ladder, his gut hanging out the bottom of his T-shirt, taking a poster down off the wall for a customer, and Kyle was behind the far end of the counter, clutching the phone to his chest.

"Valerie," he said, "what's on the schedule tonight? Do you know?"

"Hold on, I don't remember." Valerie dashed to consult a calendar taped to the countertop.

The LGBTQ Sci-Fi and Fantasy Role Playing Club wasn't the only group that Readmore hosted. There was something different every night. A trading card game one night, a war game the next. There was a chess night and a book club night, even a knitting group. A Japanese horror movie night proved to be so popular it moved out of the back room and into a local theater. A group for sock puppets lasted one meeting.

"It's Battle Tech," he said. "Starting at six."

On the opposite side of the store Walt had taken down the Wolverine poster, and the wall looked bare now.

All the walls at Readmore were covered in posters and artwork. Most were of superheroes. Many were fantasy or sci-fi themed. Some were movie tie-ins. All were for sale, even the promotional ones.

Walt's customer didn't seem happy with the condition of the poster once it was off the wall and presented to them. Valerie could hear Walt saying, "It's vintage. It's to be expected. You could turn around right now and sell this online for twice as much."

This was Walt's usual response, and when the customer finally walked up to the register with a smile, Valerie knew the old trick had worked again.

Eventually the afternoon rush died down and Valerie found herself with Kyle, standing behind the front counter, drumming her fingers on the glass. Outside, the rush hour traffic was slowly pouring down Coventry Road, smoking and honking and puttering along inch by jerking inch, sunlight glinting off the hoods.

A few feet away, a tall, lanky customer was flipping through a black binder of trading cards. The best of the cards, the rarest and most expensive, were kept in this binder. Customers were able to page through and buy the individual cards they needed, and there were hundreds, ranging in price from five dollars to fifty. The binder was known as the Book of Rare Cards, and it was to Readmore Comix as the Mona Lisa was to the Louvre; for many, the whole point in coming.

"We don't both need to stand here and guard the book, do we?" Kyle asked. "'Cause I need to alphabetize my section. The back issues are getting out of control."

The Book of Rare Cards had been stolen in the past. The perpetrator was never caught and the employee working the counter that day was promptly fired. Walt had spent months of trading and swapping and cutting deals to build up another Book of Rare Cards. But the argument was often made, by customers and employees, that the second book was nowhere near as good as the first.

"Well, I'm not gonna guard it," Kyle said, tightening his ponytail. "My shift is over soon. What if that guy takes two hours to make up his mind? I'm not gonna get stuck back here the whole rest of the day."

The book was bound to the counter by a string, looping around the spine of the binder. But there was still a conviction among the employees that the Book of Rare Cards would be stolen again, that it was inevitable.

"It's so stupid anyway," Valerie said. "There's scissors right here, in this cup, not even two feet away. What's to stop some customer from picking them up, cutting the string, and running out the door? We should put these over here, so no one can get to them." She moved the cup to the other end of the counter, between the far register and the take-a-penny dish.

"Forget about even taking the book," Kyle said. "All someone has to do is pop open the rings on the binder and just take out the pages. Would you notice if a page was missing? I wouldn't. How often do you even look in that thing? I never do. Pages could be missing right now and I wouldn't even know."

"What I don't get," Valerie said, "is that the other end of the string isn't even tied to anything. It's just taped down to the bottom of the counter. All someone has to do is pull really hard and they could take it."

"Oh, yeah," said Kyle. "It's all about the illusion that the book is secured, when it really isn't."

Valerie expected the book to be stolen at any minute, to be taken with a quick yank and a dash out the door, but somehow the illusion held. It was amazing to her that a simple string was enough to deter its theft. Either that or, she figured, it was true; the second Book of Rare Cards really wasn't as good as the first.

Walt came out from the office. He was a short pudgy man, with gray hair and a trim mustache. He always wore a polo shirt and a lanyard from Comic-Con 2002 around his neck, the store keys dangling on the end. "Does someone want to put on the gorilla?"

The gorilla costume hung in the storage room at Readmore

Comix, and it was impossible to count the number of people who had jumped out of their skin after throwing open the door to grab a broom. On slow days, Walt would force someone to put the costume on and dance around out front, traditionally with a giant inflatable banana. The banana was long lost however, and when Valerie last asked what happened to it, Walt told her, "We no longer talk about the banana."

Why Walt thought this costume "grabbed customers" was a mystery. Kids were afraid of it, babies cried because of it, dogs barked at it. Several employees in the past, Valerie and Kyle included, feeling they were older and more mature, had taken Walt aside and explained to him how lame they thought it all was. But still, on slow days when there was nothing else to do, the tradition continued.

"Alright," Kyle said. "I'll alphabetize my section."

Walt returned to the office, leaving Valerie to guard the Book of Rare Cards. The lanky customer flipped through the pages, and Valerie watched the traffic crawl by. The late afternoon sun overpowered the fluorescent overhead lights as it crept through the front windows, past the strategy games and the chess sets. Valerie watched the sunlight slowly slink its way toward her, over the front counter, the boxes of trading cards, and the jars of dice, until finally stopping, all dust sparkles and golden shimmers, right on her lap. She gazed into it, stretched her palms through it, was tempted by its heavy promise of a warm nap. Her drooping eyelids and her drifting mind struggled to resist. But resistance was futile.

No sooner had her eyelids touched down than she felt a hand gently shaking her.

It was Polly, smiling.

"I wasn't sleeping." Valerie rubbed her eyes and stood up. The Book of Rare Cards was still tied to the countertop.

"Good thing I brought you a latte and two broken cookies."

Her red hair glowed in the afternoon sun. She wore a tight green minidress with a brown belt around her waist, black leggings, and knee-high brown boots. A little green hat, shaped like a tiny tent, sat on her head. This was her Legend of Zelda look. "If you have two broken cookies, does that make four?"

"I don't know. What a weird question."

"You're weird." The freckles on her nose scrunched together as she said it. Polly studied Valerie for a moment.

"Are you wearing the same clothes as yesterday?" Polly asked.

"Maybe."

"When's the last time you washed your hair?" She shook her head in disapproval. "Did you oversleep again?"

"Kinda. I worked late last night."

"You mean, you were playing games late?"

After Polly went into the back office, Kyle walked behind the counter and said, "You guys are so cute together. She even brought you cookies. I can't stand it."

"Yesterday she brought me a sandwich," Valerie said with a shrug.

Kyle glared at her.

"What? She did." Valerie sipped her latte.

"I hope you're having fun in the old role playing club, although it sounds like you guys stayed pretty late."

"No, we finished by midnight. It's more that I found this website. It's called Asstrobabes," she said, drawing out the word "ass" to make sure Kyle got the joke. "Let's just say it blew my mind."

"Oh, so that's why you stayed up so late." Kyle shook his fist at his crotch as though he were jerking off. "Sounds like tentacle porn. Look, if you don't appreciate Polly, someone else will." He pointed at himself and gave Valerie a sly smile.

"You're gross. Don't you have a girlfriend? Miya?"

"Do you think I'd look good in cosplay? Speaking of which . . ."

Kyle had been looking over Valerie's shoulder, and he nodded now at something behind her. Valerie turned and saw Walt approaching, and with him was Varnec, still dressed in his top hat and fangs.

Kyle must have sensed conflict coming because he slipped away just as Walt and Varnec reached the counter.

"Valerie," Walt said and pulled on his lanyard, "did you refuse to help this customer last night?"

"No."

"She most certainly did," Varnec said.

"We were closed. I didn't see him in the store until it was too late."

"You didn't see me? Am I of such average height and weight? Am I of such average appearance? The High Lord Varnec never goes unnoticed."

"I seem to remember you were hiding in a back corner."

"How dare you imply that I am a sneak and a hide-about."

"A hide-about?"

"Alright," Walt held up a hand. "Will you ring him up now please? Thank you."

"You did tell me," said Varnec, leaning across the counter, "to come back tomorrow. And thus, here I am, like a nightmare that returns every time you close your eyes." He slapped the latest issue of *Betty and Veronica* onto the glass.

"My eyes aren't closed," Valerie said. "And that's three dollars and seven cents." Valerie tried to keep her voice as smooth as possible.

With his long thin fingers Varnec slid two pennies from the take-a-penny dish and gave Valerie the exact change. "We're coming for you," he said. "You and your friends."

"What are you talking about?"

"You, all of you. Drowning in your tears."

sneak attack

Ben walked out of Albatross Used Books, into the chilly evening. Coventry Road was charmed and Ben couldn't believe his luck. He'd found, for only five dollars, a Dungeons and Dragons *Monster Manual* from 1977. It was just sitting in the fantasy section. Who would have sold it back, and how long had it been waiting there for someone like him to come along? His luck was too perfect. Ben hurried to an empty bench and flipped through the pages.

The illustrations were amazing. The gelatinous cube, with a half-digested body inside. The Owlbear, half owl, half bear. And page after page of dragons. Fiery red dragons, icy blue dragons, and valiant gold dragons. All for five bucks. He still couldn't believe it. He could sell it online for fifty, it was in such good condition, but he'd never do that. It was too precious. Man, the guys were going to freak out on Thursday when he showed it to them. What would Albert think?

Behind the gloom, the sun was beginning to set and the shop lights had come on. The strings of white lights that wrapped around the trees up and down Coventry Road twinkled against the graying sky. "Fairy lights" they were called in England, and Ben could believe, as he walked beneath them, that there were thousands of Tinkerbells lighting amongst the leaves. He could be in another world, in a story.

Young couples, arm in arm and hand in hand, strolled past. A man and a woman in matching Case Western sweatshirts jogged by. A little girl, perhaps two years old, toddled out of a cafe door right in front of Ben and nearly made it to the street before her mother managed to grab her hand. Two pairs of couples met and exclaimed, "Oh how funny. Long time no see."

The scene was so ordinary, yet under the fairy lights it wasn't hard to see the magic just beneath the surface. That the mother should catch her daughter just before the street, that the couples should meet with such serendipity, that Ben should find this book simply waiting on the shelf. All of Coventry seemed charged with chance and possibility.

It made sense now that Ben would join the role playing club and meet someone like Albert. Ben could so clearly see how it was meant to be. The most implausible things were the most likely to happen. An unnamable mechanism was at work in the universe, at once both hidden and obvious, and somehow just beyond reach, so that try as he might Ben had no way of influencing it. He could only hope it took pity on him when the time came.

A couple, not much younger than himself, sat down at the other end of the bench. They wore vintage sweaters and tight jeans. Their old shoes, of a style no longer made, had clearly been bought secondhand. They were probably out on a date, Ben thought, perhaps going to see a band at the Grog Shop. They were laughing and no doubt talking about how special the night was. How excited they were about seeing the band together. How awesome it was that they met and shared the same interests.

They were clearly members of Coventry's hip elite, clued in on trends and fashions that Ben couldn't keep up on. He lacked the interest and the skill. Yet there was something alluring about the energy they put out, the sparkle in their eyes, and the dimples in their cheeks. Ben wanted to be a part of that energy and capture some of it for himself. They looked to be having such a wonderful time, giggling between themselves.

Ben didn't have to strain hard to overhear them.

"I can't believe he's reading it in public," the guy said. "I'd keep that shit in the basement."

"If—if," the girl was giggling, "I ever catch you playing Dungeons and Dragons, I'm dumping you so fast."

"No, just shoot me. My life would be over at that point anyway." They fell into each other, laughing.

Ben closed the *Monster Manual*. He walked away from the bench, down Coventry Road, past the storefronts, beneath the fairy lights, still twinkling.

Usually, when Ben bought a new book, he couldn't wait to get into the basement, pour some hot water into his electric footbath, and read the night away. But not tonight. He climbed down the steps to his darkening room and crammed the *Monster Manual* into his bookshelf without another glance. He didn't pull out the footbath. He didn't check his auctions. He couldn't bear to know if the Rainbow Brite comforter had sold or not.

He collapsed onto his bed and lay there for some time. He didn't take off his yellow windbreaker or his shoes. He lay there, unmoving, his face in the pillows until Onigiri, purring, curled up at his side.

• • •

From the lounge on the fifty-fourth floor, all of Cleveland sparkled at Mooneyham's feet. The Browns stadium with its orange seats sat to the left, and the Rock Hall with its shining glass pyramid sat to the right. Beyond them, Lake Erie stretched out into dark infinity. Or to Canada at least.

"Someday, this will all be ours," Kevin said, leaning back into the thick leather chair.

"That's right." Anthony set his bourbon swirling in his glass. "Cleveland will belong to us."

"Fuck Cleveland." Devon was leaning against the windows, apparently unafraid of heights. "I want all of Northeastern Ohio."

Mooneyham snorted. "Even Youngstown?"

"You can have Youngstown," Devon said. "I'll take the rest."

Devon joined them at the long oak table. They swiveled in their leather chairs and watched the cars zoom up and down Euclid Avenue.

"I was serious, guys," Kevin said. "If we play our cards right—"

But Mooneyham couldn't hear Kevin finish because Anthony jumped in and said they needed to worry about Steven Powell on the Customer Satisfaction team, and Devon reminded them about Mitch Connor in Planning and Retention. And since they were considering all the possible rising stars, Mooneyham added Nancy Choi to the list.

"Guys, I know," Kevin said. "Slow and steady, like I told you. Like four turtles."

"Hold on." Anthony placed his drink on the dark tabletop. "Who decided on turtles for our mascots? What happened to sharks?"

"Sharks were too obvious." Kevin gave a wave of his hand.

"I thought we chose velociraptors," Devon said.

Mooneyham said, "More like jackasses."

"Hey." Kevin shot him a look. "You're in this too, you know. Now, I've got something for each of you." Kevin picked up his leather bag. To Anthony he gave a green stress-ball with a turtle painted on the back. To Devon he gave a bean-stuffed turtle sitting on its haunches and waving an American flag.

"I want you to put these on your desks," Kevin said. "To inspire you." To Mooneyham he gave a flat porcelain turtle.

"This is a soap dish," Mooneyham said. "I'm not putting this on my desk."

"Why not? Put your cell phone in it."

"I'm not putting my cell phone in a soap dish. Are you nuts?"

"Then use it to hold your change. I don't care."

"What's pharnuthol?" Anthony asked, reading the words printed around his stress-ball.

"It's an anti-anxiety medication," Kevin said. "But don't worry about that."

It was pretty clear that Kevin had grabbed whatever random turtle shit he had in his apartment, but still Mooneyham asked, "Why didn't we all get the same thing?"

"Because if we all suddenly put the exact same turtle on our desks at the exact same time, people would know we're in this group, wouldn't they?"

"Where's yours?" Anthony asked. "What is it?"

"Mine's already on my desk," Kevin said. "It's Michelangelo."

"Michelangelo?" Mooneyham asked. "You mean, the Ninja Turtle Michelangelo? The one with the nunchucks?"

"That's right." Kevin smoothed down his tie. "He was always my favorite."

"Why the fuck do you get to be a Ninja Turtle, while I'm a soap-dish turtle?"

Kevin couldn't get an answer out before Anthony cut in. "There are four Ninja Turtles, guys. We could each be one."

"That's even better than velociraptors," Devon said.

"I'm Donatello," Anthony said.

"I'm Raphael," Mooneyham said.

"Guys." Kevin held up his hands. "Think about it for a minute. Ninjas are sneaky. They use subterfuge and disguise." He pointed at the porcelain soap dish, as if that somehow represented a disguise. "They wouldn't suddenly announce to the world, 'Hey, we're the ninja turtles.'"

"They do on the show all the time," Mooneyham said.

"What I mean," Kevin said, "is that if we're really going to be like turtles, who are also ninjas, we have to be smarter than this. We have to hide in the shadows, with patience and cunning and wait for the right moment to strike. Now, pick up your turtles. Go on, I'm serious. I want you to hold them and really think about what they mean. What images and emotions do they stir? When you guys look at these turtles, strategically positioned on your desks, what are you going to think about?"

Anthony held up the stress-ball and said, "Employees must work hard to overcome adversity."

"Good," Kevin said.

Devon studied the beanbag turtle waving its flag and said, "Employees must have pride? Loyalty maybe?"

"Not bad," Kevin said. "Keep working on it."

They turned to Mooneyham then, who looked at the porcelain turtle and said, "Employees must wash hands before returning to work."

treasure hunters

On Sunday morning, there was a last-minute bidding war for the Rainbow Brite comforter. It went for forty dollars to a Susan Miles in Oakbrook, Illinois. Ben was relieved, not only because the blanket had sold, but because he'd begun to doubt his eye for a good find.

Now it was time to make the thrift store rounds again. The City Thrift, the Village Thrift, East Side Thrift and West Side Thrift, Goodwill, and Salvation Army. He followed a perfectly designed Euler circuit, hitting the same stores in the same order each time.

The Heartland Thrift had recently opened, and Ben had been anxious to try it out. It was the same inside as all the others though. Large and unfriendly. It smelled of chemicals and dust and decay. The lighting was harsh, row after row of fluorescent strips, and although the clothes were all hung in rainbow order it was difficult to tell the difference between black and brown and navy blue under the lights. The store was busy, and Ben had a suspicion that half of the people there were actually buyers looking to score some good finds from the Midwest and take them back to San Francisco or L.A.

Ben understood there was money to be made in old Hawaiian shirts and Levi's, but he didn't have the knack for it. That wasn't his market or his area of expertise. He would need guide books to figure out the differences in the details and styles, and that felt too much like work. He hunted for the things he was interested in: old electronics, wall art, toys.

Although the Heartland Thrift was new, everything inside felt dirty and dingy and discarded, but there was a thrill in sorting through it all; something primal was stirred up within Ben. Something left over in his hunter-gatherer nature. He always felt on the edge of a great discovery, and somewhere buried in all that abandoned junk he would find it: something special, unique, and infused with a dormant, hidden magic.

Ben saw the Garfield phone the moment he turned a corner and entered the housewares department. It was in a plastic bin, under a shelf of glass vases and jars. He swooped down like a hawk and snatched it up before anyone else could.

He turned the phone over in his hands and took a critical survey of its condition. There were a few scratches on the back of the receiver. He pulled it out of its cradle and Garfield's eyes opened. The mouthpiece was dirty, but that could be cleaned up easily. He figured he could get thirty dollars for it. But, as he continued to turn the phone over, he couldn't find a price.

He took the phone over to the skinny girl standing behind the jewelry counter.

"Can you tell me how much this is?" Let it be five dollars, he thought. Or even less. If it was ten that would suck, but maybe he could get forty bucks for it.

"If it ain't got a price, I can't sell it to you. We can't sell anything that ain't been priced."

"You can't price it right now?"

"They do all that in the morning."

"Who is they?" Someone had to be able to tell him how much the phone was.

"The pricing team, but they don't just give something a price. They've got to research it." She put the phone behind the counter in a box with some other items.

"What if I gave you ten bucks for it?" Not that he wanted to pay that much, but what if he could auction it for fifty?

"Sorry," she said. "You can come back tomorrow morning if you still want it." She turned to the other end of the counter to help a young girl who'd been calling out, "Hey, excuse me, over here."

Ben paced among the shelves of used books. There had to be some way he could buy that phone. It wouldn't still be around tomorrow. Someone else would buy it before he had the chance.

Maybe the price tag had simply fallen off. It could still be in the bottom of the plastic basket. He hurried back to check, but no. There were no price tags in the bottom. There was a black computer keyboard, however, with two price tags. One of which, the green one, on the upper-right corner, was barely hanging on, as though it hadn't been intentionally placed there but had fallen off another item, such as the plastic Garfield phone. Fifteen dollars, it read.

If he bought the phone for fifteen, he would like to get sixty-five for it, but would that be possible? People did love Garfield. But the phone wasn't in the most perfect condition. There was no doubt that it would sell though, even if it didn't sell for more than fifty. And the extra money would be nice.

His back to the store, Ben slowly, carefully, lifted up the corner of the sticker and it peeled right off.

"Excuse me." There was a new girl when he returned to the jewelry counter, and that was a relief. "Can I see that Garfield phone?"

"I don't think it's been priced," she said, but she handed it to him anyway.

"Oh, it's right here." He turned the phone over and showed her the green sticker stuck to the bottom, but she was already helping another customer and didn't seem to care.

As he walked toward the checkout line, the phone in his shopping basket, Ben debated whether or not to go through with it. Could he really rip off the Heartland Thrift? If giving them fifteen bucks for this phone was ripping them off, then yes. Fifteen bucks seemed more than a fair price, although he was still hoping to get sixty-five, or more. There might even be another bidding war, like the one for the Rainbow Brite comforter.

Ben walked up and down the rows of men's clothing, but he wasn't really looking at anything. He was too occupied with thoughts of the bidding war the phone might incite. He passed into the housewares department, and there, leaning over a table filled with boxes of used records, was Albert.

"Hey," Ben said. "What're you doing here?"

"Shopping," Albert said with a grin. "Just killing time and I need a new bookcase or two." He looked at the Garfield phone in Ben's basket. "My sister Marcy used to have one of those. I wonder where it is."

"Yeah, it's cool," Ben said casually. "But I don't think I'm going to get it. It's kind of too expensive." He could see himself at the checkout getting yelled at for price swapping, and in front of Albert. He pushed the phone onto a shelf of pots and pans, and then turning back to Albert he asked, "So, what did you think of the game last week?"

"Oh my god, it was epic. I mean, sorry about your head and all, but that game was awesome. I can't wait for next Thursday. I bet you can't either."

"No, are you kidding? I need my head back. Or, well, Bjorndar does."

"I was so stoked afterward, I told Jeff about the game and he wants to check it out too."

"Jeff? From Destro Records?"

"Yeah," Albert said. "Why? Do you know him?"

"Kinda," Ben said.

"I don't think he'll ever really join us because he's too cool. Or so he thinks, you know. He acted like gay Dungeons and Dragons was the worst idea he'd ever heard of. But I think I could persuade him, if you know what I mean."

"So, wait, are you guys dating?" Ben asked.

"I don't know." Albert flipped casually through the records. "We're more, like, just fucking to be honest. But it's coming around. We'll see what happens. I think it's hard, you know, to have a relationship with someone that's solely based on sex. I think it either becomes something more or it fizzles out, you know."

"Yeah," Ben said, nodding. "Totally."

Ben watched as a girl in her early twenties, who'd been hovering near the shelves of pots and pans, picked up the Garfield phone. "Oh cool," she said and ran over to show a friend.

"And it's cheap," the friend said.

"I hope you didn't really want that thing," Albert said as the girl dropped the phone into her shopping basket.

"No, it's okay, I guess."

"Anyway," Albert said, "sorry, I didn't mean to go into all that."

"It's cool," Ben said, forcing a smile. "I hope it works out, or something." He stared into his empty shopping basket and then put it down.

"Thanks," Albert said, returning to the records.

"Say, if you're looking for records," Ben said, "I've got some that I want to sell. Although, now that I think about it, they're not really your style. Mostly blues and jazz. Maybe some classic rock."

"I don't just listen to metal," Albert said with a grin. "I'm not a complete stereotype. Maybe I could come over and take a look?"

"Sure, if you want," Ben said. "That sounds good."

"Let me get your number." Albert pulled out his phone. "Plus, whatever I don't want, Jeff might."

"Ha! I mean, yeah, that'd be great."

• • •

Doom.

Ben stood at the edge of Lake Erie as the waves crashed around him. Cold wind burned his cheeks and spray doused his jeans, but he didn't move away. The sun was setting and the sky was as gray as the water. He'd parked his car on the edge of the road and walked out onto the rocks. He'd never been here before, on this cold, hard edge of the lake, but it felt like the right place to be because Albert and Jeff were fucking.

Why should he have expected anything different from the universe? It was funny actually, and Ben laughed into the wind before he started yelling and howling. He wiped his nose and his eyes, but he wasn't crying. It was just the cold and the wind. Why would he cry over Jeff and Albert, over his luck, or any of the other dumb things that happened to him? He should keep on laughing, because it was all one big joke.

His feet were drenched and so cold they hurt. His yellow windbreaker was not strong enough to keep him warm, and his teeth were beginning to chatter. He couldn't stay out much longer. But he did. He pressed himself against the wind until he was too numb to feel anything.

When he got home he took a long, hot shower, curled up on his loveseat with Onigiri and sent Albert a text.

Good running into you. I'm serious about those records. Let's hang out again.

. . .

Mooneyham sat with Huey at a table near the back of the Thai Garden and helped Huey cut string beans. A few feet away, the kitchen door swung open and closed at a steady rhythm as waiters and waitresses dashed in and out.

"Let's do something for our anniversary this year," Mooneyham said. He took a handful of beans from the pile. The beans were crisp and green, and even with the smells from the kitchen, Mooneyham's nose could pick up their fresh sent.

"Like what?" Huey tossed cut beans into the stainless-steel bowl in the center of the table. "We didn't do anything special last year."

"I have some ideas. Plus, the guys at work are driving me fucking crazy right now and I could use a little break."

Mooneyham and Huey cut and peeled, cut and peeled, as the wait staff bustled around them. When the bowl was full Huey called for a waitress to take it away and bring an empty one.

For most Clevelanders the Thai Garden was a dining adventure. The restaurant sat on the corner of Coventry and Mayfield Road, diagonally across from Readmore. The food was not the best representation of Thai cuisine, as Mooneyham could testify, having been to Bangkok with Huey. But as most of the customers had no idea what people ate in Thailand or Taiwan or wherever it was that Thai food came from, authenticity didn't really matter.

Huey's sister Mary had opened the restaurant with her American husband five years prior, and the place had been an immediate success as there was nothing as exotic on Coventry.

"Why are they making you crazy?" Huey asked. "Cause they make you work late?"

"It's not really work," Mooneyham said. "This is work." He grabbed another handful of uncut beans.

"This is *not* work," Huey said, as waiters dashed to and from the swinging kitchen door. "This is prep."

"You could say the same thing about the turtles then," Mooneyham said.

"The turtles?"

"Yeah, this little group I'm in." Mooneyham pulled the porcelain soap dish from his leather bag.

"Oh my god, what is that?"

Mooneyham explained the general idea, how the guys were all young executives, how they were trying to move up in the bank and decided to work together to achieve their goals.

"What are these other guys like?" Huey asked.

"I've known them for years. I can't even tell you how many seminars I've gone to with these guys."

"Are they cute?"

Mooneyham snorted a laugh. "They wear pleated pants, if that tells you anything."

Huey grimaced. "Do they know you're gay?"

Mooneyham tossed beans into the bowl. "No," he said.

Huey, his head down as he strung beans, didn't respond.

"Do you think they should?" Mooneyham stopped cutting and folded his arms across his broad chest.

"Of course it's up to you," Huey said. "But I don't keep it a secret."

"But you don't announce it either, do you? You don't say, 'Hi, I'm Huey, I'll be your gay waiter tonight.'"

"Sometimes I want to, if the customer is a cute guy."

"I'm not trying to keep it a secret," Mooneyham said. He picked up his knife and grabbed more beans. He couldn't expect anyone to understand what it was like to work at the bank with these guys. "I gotta wait until the right moment."

Huey began cutting again. "It's your decision. I was worried 'cause you were spending so many nights at work, but now I know it's with a bunch of straight banker guys, it's not so threatening."

return to the underworld

On Thursday, Ben sat next to Albert in the same seat he'd sat in before. He slipped his windbreaker over the back, and Albert slipped off his hoodie. Albert was wearing a faded black T-shirt with "Goateyes" written across the front. It was even smaller and tighter than the one he'd worn before. As they unpacked their books and dice, Ben asked, "Are we still on for tomorrow?"

"As far as I know," Albert said.

"Cool." Ben tried to sound casual. He poured his dice onto the table and carefully picked out his golden twenty-sided die.

"Where'd you get that d20?" Albert asked.

"I've had it forever," Ben said. He opened up his hand, and the die glowed in the dim light. He studied the look in Albert's eyes as the die sparkled.

"It's pretty cool. Valerie told me it's magic."

"I don't know about that," Ben said.

"Oh, god," Mooneyham said. "Just tell him the story already."

"There's a story?" Albert asked.

Ben looked around the table, and everyone was looking back expectantly. "So I got it down at Carl's Comics and Cards back in the day. They had these big jars of dice on the countertop, and I was trying to dig out the best dice, when I noticed, back behind the register, on a shelf with a bunch of books and stuff, was this golden d20."

"Separated out, like it was special?" Albert asked.

"Yeah. I was going to just buy a regular one, like all my friends had, but then I was like, 'How much is that gold one back there?' And Carl, the owner, without even looking at it, said, 'Oh that one's not for sale.'"

"Why?"

"Exactly," Ben said. "So I asked, and he said, looking me straight in the eye, 'The only way to get that die is to roll against it and win, but no one's ever succeeded.' So, of course, I said, 'Can I try?' and he rolled his eyes and sighed like, oh my god, what a waste of precious time. But he tells me the rules, best two out of three, highest roll wins. I pick out a die from one of the jars, just some regular d20, and he laughs, as though I've picked the wrong die."

"I always hated that guy," Mooneyham said.

"So by this time, there's kids all around us. Basically, everyone in the store came over to watch. So, I was a little nervous. I hadn't realized it was going to be such a big event. On the count of three we rolled, and still to this day I can remember exactly what we got. First, I rolled a five and he laughed and all the kids laughed, but he rolled a three. A three! Then I rolled a ten and he rolled a seven."

"No way."

"Yeah, the crowd went nuts."

"So, he gave you the d20?"

"No," Mooneyham said, "he changed the rules."

"Hey," Ben said, "whose story is this? He said to me, 'Let's make it three out of five.' I was like, 'That's cheating.' But he was like, 'It's my shop, I can do what I want.'"

"What a bastard."

"Totally, but what could I do? Everyone was watching and I was like thirteen. So, I just rolled again and got an eight and he got a one."

"Sweet," Albert said with a grin. "That's a critical failure."

"Yeah, the crowd went twice as nuts as before. It was like I'd single-handedly taken down a frost giant or something."

"You pretty much had," Albert said. "So, then what?"

"So, then he just threw up his hands and said, 'The die knows what it wants and goes where it wants to go.' And he gave it to me."

"That's awesome."

"It's bullshit." Mooneyham folded his arms across his big chest.

"No, really, it's true."

"I'm not saying it didn't happen," Mooneyham said. "But you pretty much implied that the die has a mind of its own, which I think is bullshit."

"Wow," said Valerie, from her end of the table. "I don't get why you didn't buy the regular die, the one that beat him. That's obviously the good one."

"I know. I did buy it. I bought a whole bunch of dice that day, but that was twelve years ago and I've since lost them all. Only this one has managed to stick around, like it hasn't yet fulfilled its destiny or something."

"Such fucking bullshit," Mooneyham said.

"You can believe it or not. I don't care."

"How did Carl even come to possess this d20," Mooneyham asked, "if it's supposed to be so epic?"

"He said he won it, just like I did, off some gypsy."

"A gypsy?"

"Yeah, at a convention."

Mooneyham laughed. "Dude, he was pulling your leg. I mean, come on, you were a kid. You had no concept of reality. He knew what a dork you were. He knew how much you wanted to believe in magic and gypsies and shit. He was playing with you. As soon as you left he probably replaced that d20 with another one just like it, ready to fool the next dumb kid who came in there."

"Maybe." Ben looked down at the golden die. The gypsy story did seem ridiculous now that he thought about it.

"Yeah," Valerie said. "Maybe he was the gypsy in disguise, trying to trick you."

"What are you talking about?" Mooneyham asked.

"Regardless," Celeste said from her end of the table. "It's a good story. And it's a pretty cool-looking d20."

"Yeah," Albert said. "But is it magical or lucky? Did that guy get it off some gypsy? Let me see it a sec." Albert picked up the die before Ben could protest, and he rolled it a few times. "Six, seventeen, ten. It doesn't seem to be weighted or anything. And it feels good in your hand. I like it."

"Just wait," Ben said. "You'll see." He turned the die over beneath the light. "This d20 is different. It has power."

"Adventurers," Celeste said, changing the subject. "When we left off, I believe you were standing outside the black gates of the city of the dead." She pointed to a spot on the map, near a large archway. "You had just learned that anyone may enter, but that no one gets out alive. Flamebender gave a rousing speech to embolden you, and now the moment has come to enter the city. Magic dice or no, are you ready to proceed?"

Celeste waited, looking the players over until she had everyone's approval.

"Then I present to you, the gates of the city of the dead!" With a flourish she placed the model gates she had made onto the map.

• • •

Flamebender, with Bjorndar's head strapped to his pack, led the way. The dreadful, moaning wind of the underworld rose up as the party joined the crowd of spirits. They passed under the gates slowly. The walls of the city were fifteen feet thick and made of dark stone slabs. Once through, they were confronted with a frightening expanse. The city of the dead was not a city. It was a giant corral, holding a herd of ghostly bodies that stretched as far as they could see. Dark clouds churned overhead, filled with fire. Great licks of flame flared and arched like fiery serpents in the sky.

"This was a mistake," Theegh said. "We shouldn't have come here."

"How are we ever going to find Bjorndar's body amongst all these ghosts?" Gunther asked.

"Fear not," Flamebender said. "The gods haven't forsaken us. They will show us the way or something."

"They better do it soon." Theegh pointed across the crowd. "With my passive perception of seventeen, I see something coming our way."

Through the ghosts, they could make out the ornate tip of a spear, bobbing up and down, marching its way toward them. There was no cover, nowhere for the party to hide.

And as the spear came closer, they saw the tiny red demon carrying it.

"The living!" it yelled and hopped from foot to foot, waving its arms in an angry dance. First there was a rumbling sound, and then the ground began to shake. Cracks began to appear, and then the ground split open, and fire and lava spewed out all around them. They couldn't keep their footing and were knocked prone. Flamebender fell with such force that Bjorndar's head was jolted free and rolled toward a fiery split in the earth.

"Are you kidding me?" Bjorndar asked, as he grabbed the edge with his teeth. Lava churned beneath him.

• • •

Valerie, part of her mind always focused on the store, was the first to hear it—a tap tap tapping coming from the front door. She stuck her head out between the curtains. "It looks like there's somebody out there. Looks like one of the guys from the Thai place down the street." Valerie could often see the waiters standing out front on their breaks.

The man was jabbing the window with a key. He jabbed even louder and faster as Valerie approached.

"I'm coming, I'm coming," Valerie said.

"Where's Richard?" the man asked, as soon as the front door was unlocked and opened. "I need Richard."

"Who?" Valerie asked.

"Richard. The big guy."

"Mooneyham?"

Before Valerie could turn and call for him, Mooneyham had come out front.

"That's Huey," Mooneyham said. "My boyfriend. He works over at the Thai Garden. His sister's the owner. What's going on?"

"Some guys want to beat me up," Huey said, stepping inside.

"What?" Mooneyham asked. "Who?"

Ben, Celeste, and Albert had all come out front, abandoning the game for a moment, and stood in a circle.

Huey gave the group a weak wave. He was still dressed in a white shirt and black pants, but he had thrown on a brown leather jacket. He was wearing a black bow tie too, a real one. Not the kind with a clip like Valerie had worn when she rented her tux for prom.

Huey said, "I was walking home from the restaurant, and these guys walked past me. They always walk past me. Or sometimes I walk past them. They go to the Irish bar down there. This time they said 'faggot' as they walked past me and they shouldered me, you know, like this." He jerked his shoulder forward, demonstrating. "They were all laughing and looking at me. I thought, oh this is it, they're gonna beat me up this time."

"What assholes. Are you okay?" Mooneyham pulled Huey in and kissed the top of his head. "Why didn't you tell me about them before?"

"They never did anything before. Just laughing and looking

at me. But now, I don't feel safe. I don't wanna walk past them again. So, I came here."

"Are you gonna be alright?" Mooneyham asked. "Do you want me to call the cops or something?"

"What are the cops going to do?" Huey asked. "Can't I wait in here for you? I can just sit and read or something."

"Sure." Mooneyham looked at the other guys for agreement. "Does anyone care?"

"I'll be quiet," Huey added.

"Absolutely," Celeste said reaching out to Huey. "I'm sorry that happened. Good to see you again. Come on back." She gave Huey a hug.

They all gave him a hug then except for Valerie, who gave him a pat on the back. "We should kick those guys' asses," Valerie said.

Albert said, "I thought this shit only happened in Detroit."

Mooneyham ushered Huey into the back room, and Huey's eyes lit up when they fell upon the gaming table. "So, is this your game?" he asked. "How do you play? Can I try it?"

Valerie saw Mooneyham and Celeste exchange a look, but Celeste said, "Of course you can. Have a seat. What class would you like to be?"

"Class? What do you mean, class?"

"Just give him a premade character," Mooneyham said, which was a relief because making a new character from scratch takes forever.

"What do I do?" Huey asked. "Can I be a wizard?" He sat down near the head of the table, between Mooneyham and Celeste. "Girl, I'm gonna cast a spell on you," he said to Mooneyham. "Your heart is gonna go bam!"

"First of all, we don't try to kill each other," Celeste said.

"Not usually," Ben added.

"And second, wizards don't make people's hearts explode. They control the elements, like lightning and fire," Mooneyham said.

"Oh, so, she can be a storm girl. Like, her name is gonna be Marilyn Monsoon and her skirt is gonna fly up every time she calls a tornado!"

"Something like that," Mooneyham said. He took the premade character sheet from Celeste and pointed out the various boxes and lists to Huey. "These are your hit points. Here are your spells. It's like a video game, but on paper."

"Why don't we just play?" Ben asked. "And maybe he can pick it up by watching everyone else."

"What are those?" Huey asked, pointing at the gate and the painted miniatures sitting on the map. So, Mooneyham explained all their characters, how they'd just started fighting a demon, that lava and fire had erupted from the ground, and they weren't sure what to do.

"What about Marilyn? Doesn't she get a figurine?" Huey pulled a Wonder Woman statue off the shelf behind him. It was at least a foot tall, dwarfing the other miniatures, and so heavy the thin card table shook when he put it on down.

"What are you doing?" Mooneyham asked. "Be serious. That's too big. Here, use this." He fished into his pocket and gave Huey a coin.

"A penny?"

"Just to mark where your character is. It doesn't really matter what you use, but that statue is distracting. Swinging that lasso above her head, come on."

"Don't tell me to come on. Use your imagination," Huey said, and reluctantly he put the penny on the map amongst the miniatures.

 • • •

Flamebender ran to the edge of the fissure and picked up Bjorndar's head.

"Thanks," Bjorndar said, spitting out bits of dirt and rock. Flamebender quickly strapped the head onto his pack. The lava began to spread from the cracks in the ground, forming a molten lake of fire. The ground they were all on broke apart, and soon they were standing on floating islands, drifting away from each other. Flamebender and Bjorndar's head on one piece, Gunther and Theegh on another, and Marilyn Monsoon on a third. The demon stood on a jagged rock in the center, cackling and hopping from one foot to the next in a little dance.

Gunther hurled a hand axe at the demon, but the creature jumped aside as the axe whizzed past and sank into the lava with a puff of sulfuric smoke. Flamebender took his shield in his arm and, winding up, let it fly like a discus. It clipped the demon on the shoulder and then circled back. Flamebender reached up and caught it above his head, but the demon seemed unfazed.

"He's too hard to hit from here," Flamebender said.

"Bjorndar was our archer," Gunther said. "We're at a disadvantage now, fighting at range." The heat from the molten lake lapped at them in oppressive waves. Their bodies were drenched in sweat. The islands were sinking and growing smaller, giving them less room to stand.

"Seems like a good time to play a song of courage," Theegh said and began strumming his lute. Music filled the heat-thickened air.

"I'm so sorry guys," Bjorndar said. "You're all gonna die trying to save me."

"Wait," Flamebender said. "We have a wizard now."

They turned to Marilyn Monsoon.

"Marilyn," they called. "It's your turn. What are you going to do?"

Marilyn threw back her cloak. She raised her arms above the fires and said, "I turn the lake to ice."

• • •

"No, actually, you don't," Celeste said, pushing back her braids. "You can't really do that."

"Why not?"

"Because I told you," Mooneyham said, leaning over and pointing a thick finger into Huey's character sheet. "These are your spells, right here, on this list."

"There isn't one to turn fire into ice?" Huey asked. "Can't we just pretend?"

"You have to choose one of these, from this list," Mooneyham said. "This isn't Do-Whatever-You-Want Land. There are rules."

Huey looked over his character sheet. "What do I choose? Help me. How about this—Magic Missile. Oh no wait, Color Spray, 'A vibrant burst of clashing colors erupts from your hands.' That sounds fun, right? Or no, how about this, Glitterdust, 'A shower of golden sparkles covers everyone and everything in the area.' Oh my god, it has to be that."

"Alright, if that's what you want." Mooneyham placed a twenty-sided die in Huey's hand. "Now, roll to see if you hit."

"Don't forget to add your bonuses," Celeste said.

"And I'm playing a song," Valerie reminded them. "That gives him another bonus."

"But if his floating rock is moving," Albert asked, "doesn't he have to make a concentration check?"

"Oh my god, it's getting too complicated. I'm just gonna roll and you guys tell me what she does, okay?" Huey sent the die tumbling across the table. "Come on Marilyn, baby. A seven. Oh, lucky. So, what happens?"

"You miss," Celeste said.

"I miss?"

"Even with your bonuses, that's too low to hit." Celeste looked apologetic.

"Can I try again?"

"On your next turn."

"So, that's it?" Huey sat back in his chair. "I can't do anything?"

"You could move," Celeste said. "But, you're on a rock, floating in a lake of hellfire, so there really isn't any place to move to."

Huey folded his arms across his chest. "This game is stupid."

• • •

The heat swelled, and the flames rose higher upon the lake.

"What were you saying about us having a wizard?" Gunther asked.

"Sorry," Flamebender said. "It's all this heat. I'm getting delusional."

"So, we're still gonna die?" Theegh asked.

"One thing is clear," said Bjorndar's head. "We've got to get off these floating pieces and onto the center rock. We can't fight him at a distance."

Before they could float too far away from each other, Flamebender, with as much of a running start as possible, used his pole arm to vault across the lava and onto Gunther and Theegh's tiny island. He landed unsteadily, and the island began to capsize, but Gunther grabbed Flamebender by the arm and they calmly waited for the island to level itself.

The demon shouted in rage. Pointing his staff, he sent a fireball hurling at them. It roared into the lake just in front of their shrinking island, and the flames flared all around.

"We've got to get onto that rock. Do you have any rope?" Flamebender asked.

"I do," Theegh said, pulling off his pack.

"Good, Gunther, tie it to an axe. If you can throw well enough, lodge it into rock, then we can pull ourselves over before this island sinks."

Another fireball landed near them, and the floating island wobbled again.

"We have to hurry," Gunther said. With three of them on the tiny island, it was sinking faster. "Do we have some way to distract that stupid demon?"

"Actually, we do," Flamebender said. He took Bjorndar's head in his hands. "I'm going to toss you at the demon."

"What? Why? I'm just a head. What am I supposed to do?"

"A bite attack. Snap at his toes. Something to occupy him while we pull ourselves over there."

"Are you crazy? What if I land in the fire? This head is all I've got left. I'm so close to being alive. I can't die all the way. Not now."

"If you die," Flamebender said, "we'll bring you back again."

"You're already trying to bring me back again!"

"No, seriously," Gunther said. "Since we're in the city of the dead, we won't have far to travel." He held up his axe, the rope tied firmly to it. "Alright, I'm ready."

"Be brave Bjorndar." Flamebender looked into Bjorndar's eyes as he held the head between his hands.

"Only because this is your idea," Bjorndar said. "Let's do it."

Flamebender gave a windmill toss, and Bjorndar's head arched through the air, howling in terror, as it dove down upon the demon. Bjorndar kept his eyes open until just before the impact, then he clamped them shut. And bit down. First onto the demon's filthy, waxy black hair, then its ear. And then, with a jarring thud, he was on the ground between the demon's feet. The smell was terrible, although it was unclear whether it wafted from the sulfuric lake of fire or from the creature's cloven hooves.

Cloven hooves! It had no toes. There was nothing for Bjorndar to bite. He rolled around the demon's feet while it danced about, trying to smash Bjorndar with the butt end of its staff. Bjorndar's mouth and eyes were filling up with grit; the taste was awful. But he didn't have to endure for long. Flamebender and Gunther were soon there, followed by Theegh, who had nearly dropped his lute climbing onto the rock.

Once surrounded, the demon didn't survive more than two rounds of hacking and stabbing. Gunther kicked its dead body into the lake of fire, and Flamebender snapped its staff in half over his knee.

"That was close," Bjorndar said.

Flamebender smiled at him. "I wasn't worried."

"You didn't have much at stake," Bjorndar said, as Flamebender strapped him onto the pack. "But I have to say, good job coming up with the rope and the head tossing. That was pretty epic."

"For us maybe, but too bad we lost our wizard," Theegh said.

"I'm sure she's okay," Gunther said. "She's happier reading comic books somewhere instead."

With the demon dead and its staff broken, the lava and flames sank back into the ground. The ghosts returned and the party found themselves again in a formless fog of souls.

"Back where we started," Gunther said.

"How will we ever find Bjorndar's body amongst so many?" Theegh asked.

The low moan had also returned, as translucent bodies floated aimlessly by.

"Hold me up," Bjorndar said. "I bet I can find it. We have a connection, after all."

Flamebender unstrapped the head from his pack and lifted it up.

"As high as you can. Careful," Bjorndar said, wincing. "Not by the hair please."

"How about this?" Flamebender pulled out his pole arm, the holy Rammaster, and impaled Bjorndar's head upon the end of it. "Is that high enough?"

"That's so wrong," Theegh said, cringing.

"It kinda tickles," Bjorndar said. "And I can see a lot better up here. Now just turn slowly in a circle. More to the left. Slower. There! Straight ahead. It's kinda ghostly, but I can see it. Do I really walk like that?"

From his vantage point, Bjorndar could spot patrolling demons as well, and something larger and far more sinister moving on the horizon. He led the party carefully through the haze of ghosts, carefully avoiding any patrols, until they came upon Bjorndar's headless spirit, its arms outstretched and its hands feeling the way.

"Halt, body of Bjorndar," Flamebender said. "Cease your senseless wandering of the underworld. We have come to make you whole and return you to the land of the living."

Bjorndar's body did not respond. It gave no sign that it was aware of their presence at all; it continued its slow search.

"It can't see or hear without me," Bjorndar said. "Quick, put me back on my shoulders so I can come back to life."

Flamebender pulled the head from the end of his pole arm and gently placed it atop the transparent shape. The head didn't fall through, but floated atop Bjorndar's ghostly body, which remained vaporous. He was not yet fully restored.

"What's wrong?" Bjorndar asked. "Why didn't it work?"

"You won't fully return to life until you escape the underworld," a passing ghost said.

"What? No one told me that."

"That's how the underworld works," the ghost said. "Only those who reach the surface can return to life."

"And that won't be easy," said another. "The way out is guarded by the three-headed Hellrebus. With a mane of vipers, it's as large as a mountain and quick as a cobra. It breathes fire and its teeth can bite though souls."

"We've seen it, moving against the horizon," Bjorndar said. "I tried to get a better look while I was on the Rammaster, but it was still too far away. I can't stay half dead. We can get out of here, right?"

A low moan filled the air, and a foul breeze swept past them, rustling their cloaks, but the ghosts did not stir.

the enemy revealed

Celeste closed her rule book with a thud.

"Thank you, gentlemen, for another great game. That will be all for tonight," she said with a short bow.

The dice had barely stopped rolling before Albert turned to Ben and said, "This calls for a celebration!"

"Why?" Ben asked. "I'm only half alive."

"That's a big deal," Celeste said. "You managed to find your body and get your head on."

Ben had to admit, it did feel pretty good to have Bjorndar's head reunited with his body, even if that body was incorporeal and couldn't really do or feel anything.

"How about we go the Cedar Lee Diner?" Albert asked.

"I dunno." Valerie rubbed her eyes. "I gotta work in the morning."

"What are you, forty?" Mooneyham asked. "I gotta work too, but you don't see me backing out."

"Really guys," Ben said. "We don't have to go out and celebrate. If people wanna go home, that's cool."

"No it isn't," Albert said.

"Actually," Huey said, sliding the books off his lap and climbing to his feet. He didn't say another word but leaned against Mooneyham and closed his eyes.

"It's cool," Ben said. "Really. We don't have to if people don't want to." Ben dropped his dice back into their velvet bag.

"But I do want to," Albert said.

"So do I." Celeste folded her dungeon master's screen back into her bag. "I didn't eat before the game. I spent so much time prepping and finishing up that gate for you all."

"It was wonderful," Ben said.

"Alright, I'll go," Valerie said. "I'm more hungry than tired anyway."

"You must be really fucking hungry then," Albert said.

• • •

After saying goodbye, Mooneyham took Huey's hand as they walked down Coventry Road. The lights were sparking in the trees, part of some neighborhood revitalization project that was just an underfunded attempt to make the street more attractive to yuppies. And it was working. Even though it was after midnight, the bars and restaurants were noisy. People spilled out onto the sidewalks and laughed and smoked amongst the skinny trees that lined the street.

Mooneyham was anxious to check out O'Malley's, the Irish bar, and see who those assholes thought they were, but Huey was dragging his feet, too tired to keep up. Sleepy and stumbling, he looked adorable under the lights. His maroon apron half hanging out of his back pocket. Mooneyham wanted to pull him tight and kiss the top of his head, but there were too many people around.

They walked another block, past the dry cleaners, the wine shop, and the women's shoe salon, all dark and empty, with closed signs in the windows. Mooneyham stopped when they were across from the Irish bar. The facade was traditional, dark green with a black sign and gold lettering—O'Malley's. The front door was open, letting music and people filter out.

Mooneyham pulled Huey onto the darkened stoop of Coventry Pets so they could watch the crowd, all men, smoking and chatting in deep, rich voices that carried across the street in an indecipherable buzz. These men didn't look tough or scary. They looked like privileged white guys who bought all their clothes at the mall.

"If you see those guys, point them out," Mooneyham said. He'd love to tell those assholes off. He couldn't fight them, but he could be intimidating with his height and size. He imagined looking down at them and saying, "Hey, fuckwads, leave my boyfriend alone." He could see the look on their faces as they realized—Oh shit, this big dude is gay.

"There." Huey nodded at three men, in jeans and polo shirts, to the left of the door. One was leaning against the building, the second was lighting a cigarette, and the third was Kevin Jones from the financial services department.

"Shit. I work with one of those guys." Mooneyham pulled Huey deeper into the darkness.

Kevin was pink-cheeked and spitting as he spoke, telling the guys some wild story. Mooneyham could hear their laughter as it echoed against the pet store.

"Are we going over there?" Huey said. "Marilyn would kick their ass."

Mooneyham didn't know what he should do now. Not with Kevin there. He could still storm over. He could yell, "Hey fuck-wads, leave my *friend* alone." This small Asian man by my side, who you harassed earlier. But that wouldn't be intimidating. He could see the confusion on Kevin's face and hear him asking, as he looked at Huey, "How do you know that guy?"

He's my *friend.*

Mooneyham looked down at Huey, who was leaning against the storefront window, trying to keep his eyes open.

"Let's go home," Mooneyham said.

They walked beneath the trees and the lights for several blocks, and when it felt safe, Mooneyham took Huey's hand again.

"Can't you come out at work?" Huey asked.

"I will." Someday. Once he'd moved up the ladder. Once Cleveland belonged to him. Once he had more power and influence and no one could look at him as just another faggot.

. . .

First the bacon, only a bite, to tide the taste buds over. Then, with the toast, poke open the eggs and let the yolk run out, as the crunchy crust of the bread softens, soaking it up, and that's the next bite, the eggy toast. Dude. It's good. Pour the syrup on the pancakes, down onto the bacon too, but not the eggs, gross. Push them aside. Quick! Make a barrier with the toast. The next bite is the pancakes; get some butter too. Take a sip of coffee. Goddamn! Pancakes and coffee! This is what life was all about.

Valerie fell back into the booth and wiped her greasy mouth with her hands. "I fucking love this place."

Celeste and Albert grunted in agreement as they dug into their food. Ben, who was broke and could only afford tea and toast until he sold a Castle Grayskull playset or some shit, didn't look like he was having as good of a time. But whatever. He never looked like he was having fun. He probably frowned during sex. Valerie didn't want to think about it.

Valerie hadn't been too stoked about coming to the Cedar Lee Diner, not because she didn't like it, but because they always went there. In a better city, there would be more late-night places open, but Cleveland was lame. At least the east side was. Maybe on the west side they had more places, but who wants to drive all the way over there at midnight? Nobody. So, everyone who's awake and hungry ends up at the same place at the same time. And the diner doesn't turn anyone away, even if they're drunk or dressed up like vampires or both.

On the way to the booth, they had walked past the vampire kids, two tables of them, dooming and glooming over their bacon and eggs. Of course Varnec was at the head of the table. Valerie had locked eyes with the creep, and all the vampires had fallen silent, glaring at Valerie as she went by.

"Your friends are here," Celeste said, as if Valerie hadn't known.

But they were so not her friends. A week ago she didn't know who Varnec was, and now they were like mortal enemies or something. Valerie had only talked to that guy twice. It was just like a vampire to hold a grudge.

Albert, Ben, and Celeste replayed the greatest moments in The Rescue of Bjorndar, but Valerie was more interested in shoveling in her food.

Ben said, "If Bjorndar had stayed dead, I would have been crushed. What can you do when you're just a head?"

"Oh, I can think of several things," Albert said, with a grin. The guys all laughed, and Ben blushed. He blushed at everything.

"Come on now," Celeste said. "I wouldn't have let you guys die. I would have stepped in before that happened. I want the encounters to feel dire and exciting, but not hopeless, otherwise they're no fun. I'm not the kind of dungeon master who's out to kill everyone."

Valerie ate her last bite of eggs as the talk got around to Albert, how amazing it was that he had found the group. Celeste and Ben agreed that it was awesome and whatever. Valerie couldn't focus on that conversation either and was starting to wonder if finishing her plate had been a good idea. A kind of comatose state was settling over her, warm and comforting, like a pancake blanket.

"Anybody here like Samuraiah Carey?" Albert asked. "They're playing on Saturday."

"I'll go," Ben said.

"You like metal?" Celeste asked, sounding surprised.

"Maybe," Ben said. "I mean, I don't not like it."

"Jeff hates it," Albert said. "So, I'm looking for someone else to go with me."

Valerie had sent a text to Polly—*We're going to the Cedar Lee. Wanna go?* And she answered—*Working on a paper. Be up late. Come over.*

Valerie was debating how she should respond. How could she go over to Polly's when she could barely stay awake? Her own bed felt like it was a million miles away.

"I need more coffee," Valerie said. She turned to find the waitress and saw two women approaching. They were from the vampire table and they were giggling and whispering to each other as they walked.

The younger one was about Valerie's age. She had pink hair and wore a black zip-up sweatshirt with cat ears on the hood. She had thick black-framed glasses and striped stockings, none of which struck Valerie as very vampirish. But when she smiled, there were her fangs.

The older woman had gray hair frizzled into a giant storm cloud about her head. Her face was powdered but that only emphasized her wrinkles. Her lips were bright red, like horror-movie blood. She wore a black dress with a silver ankh around her neck. She looked like someone's kooky mother. Valerie could imagine her kids coming home, starving, and their dad saying, "Leftovers for dinner tonight guys. Mom's out playing vampire again."

"Which one of you is Valerie?" Vampire Mom asked. As she spoke, Valerie could see all the fine lines around her lips, either from smoking or just being old, and there was lipstick on her fangs, which only made her sadder for Valerie.

She turned and looked directly at Valerie, giving her a start.

"Is it you?"

"Maybe," Valerie said, which she knew was a dumb answer, but they seemed to be playing a kind of game, like they were role playing but in the real world. Only Valerie wasn't sure if she was supposed to have a role or be herself.

"Give it to her and let's go," Cat-girl said.

Scowling, Vampire Mom handed Valerie a folded piece of paper. It was a placemat. One side advertised new breakfast specials, available anytime! Only $6.99! The other side was a letter, written in red crayon.

At last the veil has lifted. Laid bare before the House of Ruthven, your joke of a role playing club has been revealed.

All who cross us shall fall upon the thorny rose of calamity.

Thus the heralding of your torment sounds.

We shall danse to the macabre of your suffering and savor your blood upon the caliginous dawn.

Hark! The raven cries—the end, the end, the end!

The High Lord Varnec

"Is this for real?" Valerie asked. "What does 'caliginous' mean?"

No one had an answer for either question. They passed the letter back and forth, reading and rereading it.

"Are we supposed to respond?" Valerie asked. "Should I write something back, like, 'Leave us alone you sideshow freaks'?" She knew that didn't sound as threatening or poetic, but that wasn't her intention.

"What did you do to this guy?" Celeste asked.

"Nothing, I swear." If Valerie had known that little moment at Readmore would lead to all this drama, she would have simply rung Varnec up and let him pay for those stupid comics.

There wasn't anything so amazing or special about Varnec. He was a guy in a vampire costume. Maybe he could impress some goths, who romanticized their lives, but he had no power over Valerie. Valerie couldn't give a shit about that whole scene. And they shouldn't give a shit about her either.

"Look." Ben pointed out the window. "The vampires are leaving."

From where they were seated, by the windows, they could see the vampires filing out the front door. The vampires advanced upon the window, in a mob, hissing and scratching at the glass as they shuffled past, and behind them, in his top hat, stood Varnec.

Valerie climbed to her feet to get a better view, and when their eyes met Varnec smiled at her, tipping his top hat and flashing his fangs.

Valerie met Varnec's gaze and held it. If Varnec wanted to start shit, then it was on. Celeste stood and joined her, and then Albert and Ben did too. They stared Varnec down, even when other tables turned to look and their waitress asked what was going on, they didn't break. They didn't stop until a manager dashed out the front door, yelling and shooing the crowd of vampires with a clipboard. Only then did they break their gaze as Varnec and the vampires whooped and screeched and fluttered away, like bats from a belfry, into the night.

altered beast

Mooneyham sat on the RTA and counted the stops, only three more until he was downtown. The morning was rushing by. In ten minutes, he would be at the bank, walking down the aisle of cubicles and past Kevin's desk. When he saw Kevin, he was just going to say it—I'm gay.

Well, he'd take him aside first, maybe into the copy room or that little break area off the main hall, where the vending machines were. He'd be cool about it. He wouldn't just blurt it out.

He'd make some small talk, buy a Snickers, and say, "Look, you're my friend, so I want you to know this." No doubt Kevin would be surprised. He'd probably try to resist the idea at first, saying Mooneyham was too macho to be gay.

But Mooneyham would reassure him, maybe put a hand on his shoulder, look him in the eye. It would all sink in. The task would be over, and they could go about their work as usual.

Over breakfast, Huey had been in a quiet mood, but not because of last night, or so he said. But something was bothering him. He didn't want to fool around in the shower or in the walk-in closet as they dressed. And when Mooneyham kissed him goodbye, he turned his head.

"What's that all about?" Mooneyham asked.

But Huey shrugged and continued to look away.

"Hey, I'm going to do it, alright. I'm going to come out to them. Today. I am." So, get over your pissy self.

Huey had it easy. He didn't come out at all until he was in the U.S., half a world away. And even then, he only had to come out to his parents; everyone else already knew, because it was obvious. Hell, his parents probably knew too—they were just in denial. Huey had no idea what it was like to have to keep coming out, every time he met someone new. He did it once and then it was over.

Mooneyham should have come out at the bank when he first got the job, but there was always a crisis to solve: drops in the stock market, complaints from account holders. And then the office parties started, the drinks after work, weekend ski trips, and box seats for Cavs games, and coming out was no longer on the agenda.

Kevin wasn't in his cubicle when Mooneyham walked past. It wasn't quite 9 a.m. so there was still time. Mooneyham continued down the aisle to his own desk, dropped off his bag and jacket, and went to the men's room.

He fixed his hair and straightened his tie. If he was going to come out he wanted to look good doing it. His heart was beating and he was sweating more than usual. If Kevin had been at his desk they could have gotten this over with. Now Mooneyham would have to wait and anticipate, which made it that much worse.

Mooneyham pushed open the middle stall and sat down when—

"Mooneyham, that you?" From the stall on the right. Fuck. It was Kevin. "I thought I recognized those shoes."

"Hey," Mooneyham replied. Awkward. But he could get through this. Take his morning dump and then move on.

"Dude, you missed it last night. I was so wasted, I woke up drunk. Don't you hate that? God."

Mooneyham could smell alcohol, among other things, wafting in from Kevin's stall.

"I was out with Kristen and Megan, from estate planning. Megan's got a thing for you, you know. She likes the big, quiet type."

"I'm quiet?"

"That's what she thinks. See, this is what happens when you never go out with us. But now it's to your advantage. You can just sit there and let her suck your cock. You don't even have to say anything."

It wasn't very often that Mooneyham was left completely dumbfounded, but this was one of those moments.

"I can make it happen," he said. "I shit you not. Just say the word."

"Look." *I'm gay.* Just spit it out. He could save himself, and this girl, some humiliation.

"I'll tell her you're flattered, but you're shy."

"No, christ, dude. Don't tell her anything."

"No one's asking you to marry her, Mooneyham," came a voice from the left-hand stall. "Just take her out for a drink and fuck her. It'll be good for office morale." Who was this? "It's Jacob from the fraud department by the way. We met at Rodger's birthday."

Thank god Mooneyham hadn't blurted anything out. He needed to talk to Kevin one-on-one, if he was going to have any kind of meaningful conversation.

"Come on Mooneyham," Kevin said, drawing out the *ham*. "Office morale."

Seriously? What did these assholes know about office morale?

"You guys can fuck off." Mooneyham wiped his ass and flushed.

   • • •

On Friday afternoon, Ben got to Timmy's Vegetarian Bistro early because there was always a line. He took a seat on the long bench after signing in and sent Albert a quick text to let him know he had arrived. Timmy's was a keystone of Coventry Road, had been there since the seventies, along with Readmore Comix and Destruction Records. And that was the problem; it was right next door to Destruction Records, and Ben could almost feel Jeff's presence through the walls.

To have a grudge against a record store because of one person was weird. But the last time Ben went in there, at the start of summer, Jeff had looked at him with such annoyance, like there was some secret message Ben was supposed to have understood. As he walked down into the Vinyl Vault he could see in their eyes how much the other employees pitied what a sad, lonely creature he was, offering up his meager records to Jeff.

The small entrance at Timmy's was beginning to fill up. Albert hadn't responded to Ben's text. Every time the door opened, sending in a cold draft, one more person who wasn't Albert would squeeze into the tiny room.

Ben wondered if he should send another text, but then the door opened and Albert arrived.

"Sorry I'm late," Albert said. "I was next door talking to Jeff."

"Oh, that's cool." Ben forced a smile.

As they were led to their table they passed a waiter who greeted them with a "'Sup?" And a waitress, refilling a napkin holder, said, "Hey Bert."

"Bert?"

"They get that from Jeff. We come here a lot. Maybe too much?" Albert asked, but he wasn't asking Ben. He was asking their waitress, who said, "Of course not."

Ben had always thought the staff at Timmy's was rude and stuck up, too cool for everyone. But of course they would like the people at Destruction Records; they were stuck up too. Except for Albert, of course. Obviously, he was the exception.

"Where's Jeff today?" their waitress asked.

"Next door," Albert said. "In the Vault."

They were sitting in the back of the restaurant, where the

wooden tables and chairs were surrounded by potted plants with thick, waxy leaves. Sun fell through the skylights in big, heavy beams. The air was warm and humid and filled with spicy smells.

Albert looked good sitting in the sun. He still hadn't shaved, and his stubble from two weeks ago had grown more beard-like. Under the skylights, flecks of red and gold came out amongst the dark brown whiskers. Ben had never grown a beard. He'd never even thought about it because it seemed like the kind of thing only good-looking people could get away with. For Ben, there was too much of a risk that a beard would only make him look worse. Guys like Albert had luxuries Ben didn't have.

Albert shimmied out of his black hooded sweatshirt and draped it over the back of his chair. Ben noticed again the anchor tattoo on Albert's right arm.

"It was my dad's tattoo," Albert said, pulling up his shirt sleeve and bringing his arm closer for Ben to see: a black anchor with a ribbon and the words "Bub & Stew." "Bub was my dad, and Stew is my mom. Her maiden name was Stewart, but my dad called her Stew. They were high school sweethearts. They knew each other forever."

"It was your dad's tattoo?"

"Yeah, he had the same one, in the same place. I got it to kind of honor him."

"Kind of?" Ben had often wondered how his parents would react if he got a tattoo, but he'd never wanted one, so it didn't matter. "Does he not like it?"

Albert laughed, but it was a funny laugh that left Ben feeling uncomfortable, as if he'd said the wrong thing. "Am I being too nosy?"

"No, it's not that. He's dead. He died when I was three."

"Oh, shit. Sorry." Ben felt his face flushing. Of course he would find a way to turn a perfect afternoon into something awkward. "I didn't mean to, you know . . ."

"It's cool," Albert said. "I don't go into it with everybody, but obviously, I wouldn't have gotten a tattoo if I didn't want to talk about it."

"Can I ask how he died?" Ben asked. "If that's okay."

"Sure. On duty. He was a fireman, for almost twenty years, and he was in a building when it collapsed."

"Oh, god."

"It's okay, I mean, I was only three. I barely knew him. It was harder for my mom and all my brothers and my sister." Albert took a drink of his iced tea. "It's weird because I'm supposed to have this connection with someone, but I don't really feel it. Everything I know about him I learned from my family or old videos. So, this tattoo was kind of a way to strengthen that connection, I guess."

"I have a sad cat story," Ben offered.

Albert laughed. "Let's talk about something else. No offense."

So, they talked about the game instead, about Bjorndar and Flamebender, which Ben thought was such a great name. Albert mentioned how lucky Ben was with his twenty-sided die. Ben said, "It's skill, not luck."

They ate chili not-dogs and shared an order of fries. After they finished Ben excused himself to use the restroom. He couldn't believe how well lunch was going, and as he washed his hands he gave himself a pep talk in the mirror.

"You've totally got this. You're in the home stretch."

Ben returned to the table to find Albert and Jeff kissing. Albert's eyes met Ben's over Jeff's shoulder, and Albert pulled away.

"Hey," Albert said. "Jeff I think you know Ben."

Jeff smiled with his tiny teeth. "So, you *are* the Ben that Albert was talking about. What a coincidence."

"Yep, I am the Ben." Jeff was sitting in Ben's seat so Ben had to pull over another chair.

"Albert said he's gonna take a look at your used records this afternoon. That's a familiar trick," Jeff said. "For making some extra cash, I mean." Jeff stretched his arm across the back of Albert's chair.

"I thought you were at work," Ben said.

"He was," Albert said, as though he didn't want to be accused of lying.

"I'm on a break. Thought I'd pick up something to eat and see if you cats were still around."

"And what do you know," Ben said.

"We were just finishing up." Albert waved for the check.

Ben and Albert split the bill, and when the waitress returned Jeff kissed Albert in such a way as to make her say, "You guys get me hot."

Ben wanted to gag.

• • •

The cellar doors opened with a creak. Ben led Albert down the rickety stairs into the basement. At the bottom, Ben turned to Albert and said, "Welcome to my lair," and laughed maniacally. But when he saw the look on Albert's face, complete mortification, Ben could have died.

"I'm just playing with you," Albert said and broke into a smile. "Show me around."

Ben started with the records, since that was their whole reason for coming down there. On the way he pointed out his He-Man collection, the Castle Grayskull he was trying to sell, the AIBO he broke and hadn't been able to fix, and Onigiri, who jumped down from a chair to join them.

"I hope you're not allergic," Ben said.

"No, I love cats." Albert scooped Onigiri up and nuzzled him. The cat didn't resist at all, which Ben took to be a good sign. "I like how his eyes don't match. He's such a good-looking guy, yes he is."

Ben took Albert to the stereo, which was an old 1963 Motorola coffee table console, with gold-tone fabric speakers built into the side panels. Ben had rescued it from his grandparents' house, when they moved into their retirement community and threw out tons of stuff. He'd loved it at the time, but that was ten years ago. Now it served as another flat surface to hold books and board games. He'd cleared it off for Albert's visit and even dusted the top.

"Of course you have one of those," Albert said when he saw the stereo. "How does it sound?"

"Try it out." Ben had stacked his records, the ones he was looking to sell, on the floor beside the stereo.

"Jesus, some of this shit is so bad I have to hear it," Albert said as he flipped through the stack. He chose the *Mannequin* soundtrack.

Once the background music was set, Albert sorted the records into four piles—Yes, No, Maybe, and Oh-My-God-What-Were-You-Thinking. He further divided the Yes pile into near-mint, very good, and good.

"Now all you have to do is pick a starting price and post them on eBay."

After the records were sorted Ben had a brief panic that they might have nothing else to talk about and their time together was over, but then Albert saw the video games and was like, "Oh my god, Sega!"

So, Ben and Albert sat on the floor and plugged Ben's old Sega Master System into the TV. Albert chose *Altered Beast* because of the hunky werewolf transformations, and they both yelled "Welcome to your doom!" as the game started.

"Get that power-up, quick!" Albert yelled.

Ben ran toward the blue orb as it floated away and jumped for it. The power-up sank into his chest, and his muscles grew as he absorbed it. His shirt ripped open and fell away, revealing his hulking pecs and ripped abs.

"Yes," Albert said, "this game is so hot."

Ben had left out his old video games to tempt Albert into playing, but he hadn't predicted the excitement Albert would have over them.

"I used to play all these games with my brothers," he said.

The *Mannequin* soundtrack played on; Starship was rocking "Nothing's Gonna Stop Us Now," and Ben and Albert sang along as they punched zombies and kicked demon dogs in the face. It felt like they'd been friends forever.

When was the last time Ben connected with someone so deeply, and had such good, clean fun? High school? No, it couldn't have been that long ago. But he did feel fifteen again, on the cusp of a bright and exciting future.

Ben knew he shouldn't be playing Dungeons and Dragons at the age of twenty-five. He should be starting a nonprofit organization or a charity drive for Haiti. He should be showing off a new cell phone app he designed instead of the old video games he collected. But, when he was in high school, no one told him to become a computer programmer or an engineer. Everyone said do what you love, follow your heart. If you're passionate about something, you'll naturally be a success. Even his parents, who saw him every day and knew his strengths and weaknesses, never said more than go out there and find what you like. Do what you're good at.

"I'm going to major in history," he told his parents, bright-eyed and full of vigor. "Maybe focus on medieval studies."

"If that's what you love," they said.

But after graduation, he had no idea what to do with himself. Getting his job at the Cleveland Heights Public Library had been the best break. Finally, he was making over ten dollars an hour and got to talk about interesting things all day, plan cool events, all while being around books. But no one warned him that libraries were not well-funded and had constant budget problems, even good libraries with skylights and new computers and a children's annex.

He had read to the kids during the Saturday story time, and he missed those moments more than anything else. After he was laid off he went back, but even though the kids were excited and cheered when they saw him, Annabel, the children's coordinator, wouldn't let him read.

"What if one of the kids tried to sit on your lap? It would be awkward if the parents found out you don't work here anymore."

But the kids had never tried to sit on his lap. They wanted to grab the books or turn the pages, but they never tried to sit on him. He usually knelt when he read anyway. He hated sitting cross-legged; there was too much flexibility involved. Annabel was just giving him an excuse. She was probably glad he was laid off. Storytime was all hers now—she wouldn't have to worry anymore about Ben's taste in books.

Who wanted to hear about dumb princesses all the time? Kids didn't like that stuff. They wanted gore and mayhem, creatures of darkness and eyeballs on stalks. *Goodnight Cthulhu* and *A Ghoul in the Pool*. If he did have to read some stupid, regular book, like some shit about Puss in Boots, he'd hold up the pictures and ask, "Who can find the Slithering-What's-It?" and when the kids looked confused, he'd say, "That's right, the Slithering-What's-It can't be seen. Until it's too late!" And they would all squeal with delight.

He usually finished with a craft project, slime made from corn syrup and food coloring, or mini Things-That-Cannot-Be-Named from ping pong balls and green yarn. Of course, some brainiac would always want to name theirs Herman or Mildred or some other terrible name, and Ben wouldn't stop them. Why bother? Let the kids try to tame their Things-That-Cannot-Be-Named. They would learn the folly of their ways soon enough.

"What else you got?" Albert asked, signaling that they had punched their way through enough zombies. Ben took Albert to his desk and opened a drawer. It was full of rubber monster-faced puppets, with bulging eyes and tongues.

"Boglins! No way."

"I've been collecting them forever. They're too precious to sell. I keep them in there because—"

"It just feels right."

"Yeah," Ben said. "Exactly." Ben showed Albert his Power Rangers collection, and Albert knew immediately that they were the Japanese figures and not the American ones. "Because the yellow ranger doesn't have boobs. She was played by a man in Japan. I mean, he was. Whatever."

The record had moved on from Starship to something soft and instrumental, but Ben still sang, "And if this world runs out of lovers, we'll still have each other."

And Albert continued, "Nothing's gonna stop us now." Until he turned the corner, past the bookshelves, and stopped. "Holy shit. You have a water bed?"

Ben didn't know if he should be embarrassed or proud. "Yeah, it was my parents'."

Albert climbed onto the bed, and Onigiri joined him. "Come on cat. This bed is sweet. Is that a poster of Conan up there? Oh my god, is this where you jerk off?"

"What? No." Ben felt his face turn red.

"Are you sure? You've got the poster, the water bed."

"Lots of people have posters over their beds."

"When they're thirteen."

Ben stood there like an idiot. He'd never been taught how to reply to someone who'd discovered his jerk-off spot.

"I'm not saying it's a bad thing," Albert continued, lying back, as Onigiri curled up onto his chest. "I'd probably jerk off too if

I had a water bed and a poster of Conan the Barbarian." Albert bobbed up and down, stroking the cat. Onigiri's fur was a bright white against Albert's black T-shirt.

Once, on the news, a Brink's truck overturned on the highway, and thousands of dollars blew through the air. Some people stole it, others returned it, and some just stood and watched. Ben had thought that if he'd been there he would have grabbed what he could and run, but now, as he watched Albert, sprawled on the water bed like a flirting, teasing million dollars, Ben feared the truth; he would really be the one who'd stand and watch it all blow away.

"Here, move over." Ben motioned for Albert to make room and climbed onto the bed beside him. Onigiri stretched and moved from Albert's chest onto Ben's.

"He's purring," Albert said, and the soundtrack swelled. The water bed pushed their bodies together, and Ben's shoulder pressed against Albert's. The hair on their arms brushed together and gave Ben a charge that spread across his skin.

"I see what you mean," Ben said, trying to keep his voice smooth and even. "This could be a good spot to jerk off."

"Yeah, that's an awkward comment," Ben said.

Albert's blue eyes looked back at him. His scruffy jaw upon the pillows. Ben could wake up to Albert every day and fall asleep with him every night. It wasn't so hard to imagine that he and Albert could be a couple. It not only felt plausible; it was palpable. Who else knew as much about Power Rangers and video games and all the other things that made up the world?

"I'm sorry." Albert climbed out of bed. Onigiri jumped to the floor.

"What's wrong?"

"Nothing, it's just." Albert sat down on the padded frame of the bed. "I don't want to be like Jeff. I know he led you on, which is what he does. He leads people on. He would have done it to me too if I hadn't been like, 'Hey what's going on with us?' And forced him to be straight-up with me."

Ben kept his face an emotionless blank. He became an iceberg, bobbing. The piece that Albert saw was only ten percent of the whole.

"I want to be straight-up with you too," Albert said. "I don't want it to be weird or awkward every time we hang out because you don't know if I'm into you or not. I mean, I like you. I think you're cool and you're funny. But, I have a boyfriend, who I like a lot. Obviously. So, my hope is that you and I can be friends. Because, to be honest, I need friends." Albert laughed, but Ben wasn't sure if he was trying to lighten the mood or if that moment of self-realization was actually funny to Albert.

Friends. The word was a poisoned apple, and Ben didn't know if he should take a bite. Ben sat up and swung his legs over the other side of the bed. If he were honest with himself, he never truly thought he and Albert would ever be anything more than friends. He hoped for it, sure, but he knew Albert was out of his league and that he and Jeff were dating anyway. Ben began to relax. Being friends didn't feel like a concession; it felt like the jackpot.

Albert asked, "So what do you think? Is that something that makes sense?"

"Sure." Ben climbed out of the water bed. He thought he'd been gutted but was surprised when his guts came with him. "It's not like you're all that anyway." Ben was surprised by how much anger came out with each word, and he hoped Albert couldn't hear it. "You're from Detroit after all."

"Seriously, I might as well have leprosy."

"Plus you're way too hairy."

Albert's eyes hardened and the corners of his mouth stiffened. Then Ben felt like a jerk and he wanted to take it all back. Hairy was hot. It was masculine. There was nothing Ben wanted more than to jump onto Albert and rip all the clothes off his hairy body.

"I'm kidding," Ben said. "These are jokes coming out of my mouth."

Albert smiled, but it was an awkward smile.

A wave of depression washed over Ben. One after another, he was hit by all of the things that could never happen now that they were only friends. No hand holding, no cuddling as the sun set, no planning their future together, their wedding, which would have been epic, more like a Renaissance Faire than a wedding. There would have been minstrels and jugglers and jousting. They would have worn kilts and swords.

The record reached the end of side one. The needle caught in the center groove, skipping and skipping. Ben took it off.

He walked Albert to the top of the cellar stairs, and they said their goodbyes and wrapped up their afternoon together. Hanging out was fun and they'd have to do it again. Albert said he was serious after all about needing friends. Maybe Ben could show him some good thrift stores sometime? Totally, no problem, that would be great.

"And don't forget the Samuraiah Carey show on Saturday. You promised you'd go."

"Sure," Ben said. "The show. Of course." But all of their words passed through Ben without sticking to any of his bones.

The sun was still out. Ben shielded his eyes as he gave Albert one last wave goodbye. Birds sang. A breeze bent the trees. It was only four o'clock. Why did Ben expect the sky to be dark? It didn't seem right that the sun was shining, that kids were playing kickball in the neighbor's yard, that people were shopping and eating on Coventry Road, and that life as usual was carrying on.

Ben climbed down the narrow stairs and returned to his lair.

the horny homunculus

Valerie was hot and sweaty in the gorilla costume. Even on a September afternoon the suit was hot as the sun beat down on the fake fur without mercy. Occasionally, a breeze whipped through the eye holes, and Valerie would feel a tingle of cool air on her face, but that relief would be followed by a whiff of the putrid stench of the costume.

For a Saturday, business was slow at Readmore, although there were a lot of people and traffic out on Coventry Road. Valerie held a bright orange arrow that she occasionally twirled or humped, trying to be funny and attract attention. She was holding the sign gently, lovingly, in her arms and pressing the rubbery gorilla lips against it when Varnec, dressed in all black and wearing his tattered top hat, came walking up the street.

Their eyes met above the bright orange arrowhead, and Valerie let the sign slip from her arms. Varnec walked past her and into Readmore without a word. Valerie picked up the orange arrow and followed.

Varnec went straight to the rack of new titles, and Valerie stepped behind the front counter. Polly was ringing up a customer, and Kyle was watching the Book of Rare Cards II.

Valerie pulled off the gorilla head and sat it on the counter.

"Damn this thing is hot," she said. She smelled her armpits, unsure if the residual funk was coming off herself or the gorilla.

"You were only out there fifteen minutes," Kyle said.

"Felt like forever." Valerie wiped the sweat off her brow.

Across the store, Varnec stood with his back to the front counter as he looked over the racks of new titles.

"I guess someone can venture out in the daytime after all," Valerie said.

"You know he works down the street at the costume shop?" Polly said, keeping her voice low. She wore goggles on her head that she had painted gold, and there were felt cogwheels that she had stitched onto her T-shirt. She wore a holster on her hips with a toy gun on one side and a spyglass on the other. This was her steampunk look. "I went in there yesterday."

"Did you talk to him?"

"No. Talk to him about what?"

The door to the store opened with a ding, and a delivery man with a long white box came up to the front counter.

"Oh, it's for me," Polly said as she took the box from him. It was tied with a white ribbon.

Inside was a long-stemmed back rose. There was no card.

"How weird," she said, putting the flower to her nose. "Smells great, but I don't get it." She smiled in confusion.

"Why would someone send you a rose?" Kyle asked.

Valerie saw Varnec watching them through the shelves.

"A black rose? That's creepy," Valerie said.

"It's kind of romantic," Kyle said, "in a dark and mysterious way. People swoon over that shit."

"I want to swoon," Polly said with that nervous smile. "But I don't like thinking there's someone out there watching me from afar."

Varnec was still watching through the shelves, giving Valerie a strong suspicion over who sent the rose. But why was another question.

"Alright," Valerie said. "It's from me. I sent it."

Polly looked confused. "From you? Really?"

"I wanted to, you know, show you how much I appreciate you."
Kyle did not seem convinced. "But why black?" he asked.

"Why not?" Valerie leaned against the counter in a show of nonchalance.

Polly and Kyle exchanged looks. But Valerie continued to act nonchalant. It was totally conceivable to her that she could have sent the rose. In the movies, people did that sort of spontaneous thing. It wasn't so weird. It was more conceivable that she sent the rose than Varnec. He didn't even know Polly.

"Excuse me, I couldn't help but overhear," Varnec said as he approached the front counter with a stack of comics. "Perhaps I can offer a scenario that will ease your confusion. Imagine a handsome, mysterious someone who is quite smitten with you, but too shy to act. What is he to do but communicate his affection in other ways, in the grand high ways of love?"

"Yeah, sure," Valerie said, ringing up the comics. "That'll be $9.47. Did you need a bag?"

"Are you saying Valerie didn't send the rose?" Kyle asked.

Polly looked at Varnec with curiosity.

"Because I did totally send it," Valerie said.

"I'm saying you should open your heart to grander possibilities." And then to Valerie, Varnec added, "Thank you." He took his comics and left. The bell above the door chimed.

"I don't know what to think," Polly said. "Did you really send this?"

"Yes," Valerie said.

"Really?" Kyle asked. "Are you sure?"

"Okay, no." Valerie couldn't maintain the ruse any longer. Polly and Kyle obviously didn't believe her. That fucking Varnec.

"Why'd you say you sent it then?" Kyle asked.

"Because I wanted to," Valerie said. "I mean, I wanted to have sent it. When I saw it, I got jealous because I wished I'd thought up the idea."

"So, you lied."

"Oh, come on. You didn't believe me anyway."

"It was pretty obvious that you didn't send it," Kyle said, "'cause you're not that kind of person." He turned to Polly. "What'd you think?"

But Polly didn't reply. She put the rose gently into its box and looked out the window. Valerie followed her gaze, but there was nothing to see. Varnec was already gone.

. . .

Mooneyham hadn't been to O'Malley's in years, but it hadn't changed. The bar was still filled with locals. The same neon signs hung in the windows, and the same artwork hung on the walls. The TVs had been replaced with flat screens, but they still played the same channels. Soccer on one and baseball on the other. The place was dark, but homey and comfortable. A clock near the jukebox advertised Guinness and counted down the minutes to St. Patrick's Day.

"You're slipping Mooneyham," Kevin said. "Angie Barnett won the contest? What the fuck?"

"My winning streak's been broken." Mooneyham took a drink of his Guinness and licked off the mustache. "But I won three quarters in a row. I don't need to win again."

"But what about me?" Kevin asked. Anthony and Dylan laughed into their beers. "I was looking forward to those Browns tickets.

Mooneyham snorted. "Who's to say I would have invited you?"

"Come on. Who else would you invite? One of these assholes?" Kevin gave a nod toward Anthony and Dylan. "I don't think so. Or are you telling me you'd take a date?"

"I'd take a blind poodle before I took any of you fuckwads," Mooneyham said. "But alas, it was not to be." Mooneyham raised his glass. "To Angie Barnett. My only competition."

On the TV above the bar the Browns were playing against the

Dolphins. Dylan was focused on the game. Around the bar, other men were sucked into the game as well. Occasional whoops and cheers of "fuck yeah!" and "get 'em!" burst out from around the bar.

"Fuck Angie Barnett," Anthony said. "She stood me up once. Left me waiting at Dante's for nearly an hour before she finally texted me to say she had an emergency. Claimed she got salmonella poisoning and had to go to the hospital."

"And did she?" Kevin asked.

"Fuck if I know."

"You guys ever get together then?" Mooneyham asked.

"Would you get together with a girl who waited an hour before she told you she had salmonella poisoning?"

"Mooneyham doesn't get with girls," Kevin said. "Period. I've tried to set his hairy ass up so many times, you don't even know."

"'Cause you try to set me up with nitwits."

"I set you up with perfectly reasonable, readily available women. Who spread."

"Why don't you do that for me?" Anthony asked.

"You don't need the help. This guy though is practically a lost cause. I'm starting to wonder why I bother. You spend all that time at the gym getting pumped, you think you'd want to put it to good use. But no."

"Fuckin' faggot!" Dylan yelled at the TV. "Come on."

The words hung in the air like a chill breeze. Everyone turned their attention to the screen, but the offending moment had passed and the game went into a commercial break.

"What happened?" Anthony asked, and as Dylan began to explain—something about missing a goal—Kevin leaned over to Mooneyham.

"Regardless of whether you won or not, the Databing I.P.O. is still on track and set to open big, so don't worry about it."

"I'm not."

"What I'm saying is, I'm not upset about the tickets. Fuck the tickets. If we can pull off this I.P.O., then a couple of fucking Browns tickets ain't shit. But we can't slip up now. I need the Mooneyham who won the contest three quarters in a row on my team, not the guy who came in second because he lost interest and let his numbers slip. I need you to bring your A-game to this project. Don't let anything break your focus, not when we're this close to the finish line."

A roar of agony rose from the crowd. Dylan jumped to his feet. "Fuckin' cocksuckers! Goddamn!"

Mooneyham gave Kevin a curt nod, then pulled away. He took a long drink of his Guinness and wiped the foam from his mouth with the back of his hand.

. . .

Saturday night, after trying on outfit after outfit and deciding on jeans and the darkest T-shirt he could find, which was brown, Ben drove to the Beachland Ballroom. The parking lot wanted twenty dollars, so he parked for free on a side street six blocks away. He checked his hair and the collar of his yellow windbreaker in the window of his car and then checked again in the window of another car. Of course, it didn't really matter if he looked good or not, because this wasn't a date. No one went on a date at a death metal show. He and Albert were friends.

A small group stood outside the doors to the Ballroom, smoking and chatting. They were dressed all in black and Ben already felt out of place, but he paid his fifteen bucks and went in. The band had already started and the club was crowded. Ben cowered under the volume of sound, as if an air raid were going on overhead and he had to find shelter fast. He pushed his way through leather jackets and black T-shirts, tripping over boots and shoes and his own feet. He found Albert in the back, leaning against a wall near the pool tables. There was a woman with him and he was shouting into her ear.

"Awesome," Albert said as soon as he saw Ben. "I was afraid you wouldn't come."

The woman at Albert's side said something Ben couldn't hear, but it prompted Albert to say, "This is Liz, my coworker. She *hates* metal." Ben recognized her from Destruction Records. She had short dark hair and the elegant kind of neck Ben would want to have if he were a girl. "She's here with her boyfriend. She offered to keep me company in case you didn't show."

"Why wouldn't I show?"

"Sometimes people don't," Albert said simply.

Liz said something but Ben only caught the word "Ross." She smiled at Ben before walking off and disappearing into the crowd.

"She's going to find her boyfriend," Albert said. "She thinks you're cute."

"Cool," Ben said. "She has a nice neck."

Suddenly, Ben felt hot. Albert stared at him, grinning, his beer bottle poised for another swig. The club was like a furnace. On stage, the band was thrashing about, slashing at their instruments, and banging their heads in unison. Beneath the flashing lights, the lead singer, in a black samurai helmet, growled and barked into his mic. Ben tried to watch the band and Albert, and he couldn't decide who was more interesting.

Albert was wearing a black T-shirt, even smaller and tighter than the ones he usually wore. There was a screaming samurai on the front, and in a spiky font, almost too difficult to read, the name Samuraiah Carey was scrawled across Albert's chest. The shirt was short on Albert's long frame. When he arched back to swig from his bottle, Ben caught a flash of pale skin, where the T-shirt ended and Albert's jeans began. Ben glimpsed the latticework of dark hair that crept up Albert's stomach.

Ben unzipped his windbreaker, took it off, tied it around his waist, wiped the sweat off his face, and then felt self-conscious as no one else had windbreakers tied around their waists, so he put his back on again. Albert was still watching him.

"This place is great," Ben said. "Thanks again for inviting me out."

Albert nodded as he chugged down his beer. He wiped his mouth with the back of his hand. "Let's go up front."

Albert tossed his beer bottle into a trash can and led the way. Ben followed closely behind, but he didn't step more than two feet into the throbbing crowd before he was slapped in the eye by ropey hair and sprayed in the face with a beer. It splattered across his windbreaker and dripped down his chin.

"Don't worry," Albert called out above the noise of the band. "It'll wash out."

Why did Ben decide to come to this show? He couldn't name a single death metal band, let alone hum a single death metal song. He didn't even have the right clothes. His yellow windbreaker stood out like a sunbeam in a storm of black T-shirts.

"I hope it comes out," Albert called back over his shoulder. "'Cause that jacket's cute, I'm just saying." Albert grabbed Ben's wrist. "Let's get closer."

The audience was pressed so tightly together, there couldn't possibly be room any closer to the stage. But Albert pulled Ben forward, through the mob of banging heads, swinging hair, and pumping fists.

Last night, when Ben had called Celeste for advice, Celeste had said, "I can't believe you're going to a Samuraiah Carey show. They're the most evil band ever."

"How evil is that?"

"I don't know. I've never seen them, but that's their marketing slogan: Samuraiah Carey, The Most Evil Band Ever."

"No wonder Jeff didn't want to go."

As Albert pulled him through the crowd, Ben tried to make

himself as small as possible, but there were too many throbbing bodies pressed together. Ben found himself resisting, falling behind.

The crowd swayed left and Ben was forced to sway with it. Albert's grip slipped from his wrist as Ben was pushed farther away from him. Ben called out for help, in a panic, but the crowd swayed to the right and he lost sight of Albert's black T-shirt.

From behind, a body crowd-surfing above the mob fell onto Ben and pushed him to the ground. He fell hard onto his hands and knees, down amongst the spilled beer and the broken bottles. *Get up!*

"Albert!" he called again, but his voice was lost amongst the boots and shoes.

Ben had told Celeste he was afraid he might be killed at a show like this.

"You don't have to go," Celeste said. "Tell Albert no, if it's not your scene, if you're too chicken."

He wasn't too chicken. That was Celeste's manipulating reverse psychology at work. He knew her tricks. But Ben also knew things could get out of control at these shows. Someone starts a fight or there's a fire and people get stomped to death in a mad rush for the door.

His head spinning, his ears ringing, Ben pushed himself off the floor, through the writhing mass of legs and arms, as though he were digging out of his own grave. "Albert!" he yelled against the suffocating roar of the band.

Ben felt a familiar grip around his wrist, and Albert was there again, grinning, squeezing his way back through the crowd.

"Stay close," he said. "Don't stop." Moving behind Ben and putting his hands on Ben's shoulders, Albert pushed Ben through the crowd. "Just keep going."

Ben had been in crowded places before, like the mall at Christmas time, but this scene was like nothing he'd ever experienced. "Excuse us," Ben said as Albert steered him along. "Excuse us, please."

They pushed their way through until a thrashing wall of bodies, a few feet from the stage, prevented them from going any farther.

"This is close enough," Albert yelled. His unshaven chin was rough against Ben's ear and sent a jolt through Ben's body. He placed a hand on Ben's shoulder and held him back.

Ben wasn't sure if Albert's hand was there to protect him or to keep them from being separated again, but it was a comforting weight either way.

For the first time, Ben had a clear view of the stage and the band. The lead singer was bent over and barking into his microphone. He was shirtless and wore a samurai helmet over his long, black hair. To the left and right, the bass player and guitarist stood in giant coffins, and in the back, the drum kit was mounted atop a giant bat, with a glowing red pentagram in its open mouth.

The music chugged out of the speakers in such overwhelming waves, even the beat of Ben's heart succumbed to the rhythm. The crowd began to jump, wildly, long hair swinging.

"Come on," Albert said, his arm still on Ben's shoulder. "Get into it."

Ben couldn't resist, and why should he? He pressed his back into Albert's chest and they began jumping too, pumping their fists in the air.

"The best part is coming up," Albert said. "Get ready!"

Behind the lead singer, the center of the stage burst open in a ring of crepe paper flames. From within, something red with a barbed tip began to emerge, slowly inflating, growing longer and thicker.

"It's the unholy cock of Satan!"

Ben stood transfixed as it rose, dwarfing the band and the amps. The noise of the crowd drowned out all thought as the cock of Satan climbed higher. It didn't stop when its head touched the rafters; even then it grew until it was bent and looming over the stage and the mass of sweaty bodies below.

It was circumcised, which made no sense to Ben. Clearly someone hadn't thought the whole thing through very well, but before he could point this out to Albert, the crowd surged forward, roaring, hungry and lusting. Ben and Albert were pushed toward the stage, into the wall of slick, fleshy skin. Ben thought for sure he would be crushed, but unseen hands began lifting him up, pushing him higher and higher until he was above the heads and shoulders around him, surfing atop the crowd.

"No, put me down." Ben tried to push back against the hands that lifted him. "Albert!" Ben kicked and flailed as the hands passed him from one to the other, rolling him from his back to his stomach to his back again. Hands groped him and fingers probed him, crawled under his windbreaker and up his pant legs. It was like tentacle porn, like being molested by a giant tentacled creature. A hand squeezed his ass; another felt up his crotch. Ben called for help, but no one tried to save him or pull him back to the floor. No bouncers. No security. Ben struggled but he couldn't stop the hands as they carried him toward the stage, toward the thrashing band and the enormous, quivering shaft of Satan. "Help!" he shouted. "Stop!" But to no avail.

Ben rolled onto the black stage like a beached sea lion.

Quickly rising to his hands and knees, Ben searched the crowd for Albert, for some kind of support amongst the sea of faces, but Albert was nowhere to be found.

Of course this would happen. Out of all the thousands of people in the crowd, he would be the one tossed on stage before the inflatable cock of Satan.

As Ben climbed to his feet, two muscular stagehands in leather harnesses picked him up by the arms. "Welcome to the show," they said. He tried to resist but they stripped off his jacket and T-shirt to the cheering approval of the crowd. The air onstage was pulsing, hot and humid. It lapped at Ben's body like a dirty tongue. He couldn't remember the last time he was shirtless in public, but he remembered the embarrassment of his pasty skin and pointy nipples, and the three wiry hairs in the center of his chest. He wanted to run, but the stagehands had a firm grip on his boney shoulders. They took him to the bat's open mouth and strapped his wrists to the giant pentagram.

"What are you doing? There's been a mistake. I don't even like this music."

"Just play along and have fun." They passed him a heavy golden chalice, encrusted with plastic jewels. "Drink."

"What is it?"

"The jizz of Satan." They poured the liquid down Ben's throat. It tasted like the blood of Christ, like cheap red wine. It burned and he coughed it up. The wine ran down his chest in red trails. The crowd roared. The band played harder and faster, swinging their hair in circles.

"There's going to be an explosion," the stagehands said. "We'll only have five seconds to put this goat head on you."

"What?"

"And you'll need to step into these furry pants."

Before Ben could ask what the hell they were talking about, the front of the stage erupted in a showering wall of sparks. The lights went out. The stagehands shoved the goat mask over his head and yanked the pants up his legs.

On the count of five, the lights returned, dim and red. The bass player pounded out a low rhythm. Beyond the edge of the stage the crowd was hushed, but writhing under the dark lights. The goat mask fit awkwardly and Ben wasn't looking out through the eyes, but through the mouth, over the plastic teeth. Sweat ran down his back as he struggled to break free of the straps that held him to the pentagram.

How did this happen? He wasn't the right person for this. He had to get offstage. But then a spotlight fell upon him, the guitar and drums kicked in, and the lead singer screamed into his mic. The writhing mob went wild.

The stagehands released Ben's straps. He took a step forward but the furry pants were baggy and heavy. He fell to his knees.

The lead singer turned to Ben, and from under his black helmet he growled, "Rise, my horny homunculus. Rise and dance for us."

Even muffled by the mask, the sound of the music and the cheering crowd was deafening. Lights spun wildly. Thousands of shirtless men screamed and pumped their fists. "Dance!" they chanted. "Dance!" And somewhere among them, although Ben couldn't see where, Albert was watching, waiting for Ben to act.

Slowly, Ben rose to his feet. What choice did he have? He thrust out a hip, first to the left and then swung it around to the right. The crowd cheered him on. He smacked his ass and the men roared. *They loved it.* He galloped around the stage, holding up the shaggy pants with one hand and swinging an imaginary lasso with the other. The band chugged out a driving rhythm as the audience thrashed in front of the stage. Ben did the hula and the mashed potato, the swim and the funky lurch, dances that could not be named and moves that should not be viewed by human eyes. Sweat flew off his body, and his pale skin flashed blinding white beneath the bright lights, but he didn't care. Beneath the goat head, he felt liberated and free to be some other Ben. A Ben caught up in the pounding music and the energy of the moment. A Ben giddy with the jizz of Satan.

Turn to the left. Step to the right. *This was why he left the basement. This was the feeling of being alive.* Shimmy shimmy. Pelvic thrust. *Now reach!*

The unholy cock of Satan exploded high overhead, showering

silver confetti. The crowd at Ben's feet erupted, moshing and squirming, soaked in glittering sparkles. And there, near the front, Ben finally saw Albert. His was shirt off, his fist was in the air. He was shouting and leaping higher than anyone else.

. . .

After the song ended, the lights went out and the stagehands ushered Ben offstage. "You rocked," they said. "Great show." They pulled off the goat head and the furry pants and returned Ben's T-shirt and yellow windbreaker. They gave him a shiny black gift bag with chocolates, stickers, and bath salts. "If you want, you can watch the encore from back here."

"What about my friend? He's near the front, with an anchor tattoo on his arm."

A bouncer with STAFF printed in yellow on the back of his black T-shirt plucked Albert from the crowd and brought him to Ben a few minutes later.

"Un-fucking-believable," Albert said with a big grin and a hug. "You are my idol."

"Just another day in the life," Ben said, but he knew he wasn't fooling either of them.

For a moment they held each other, flesh to flesh, sweaty and panting with excitement. Ben was surprised to see that Albert had trimmed his chest. The stubble rubbed Ben's skin in the most exciting tingle. Embarrassed, Ben broke away and pulled on his T-shirt and windbreaker.

"Jeff would never do that shit," Albert said. "I don't know if I could either. You fucking went for it."

They watched the encore from the wing, and after the show they got autographs from the band. They borrowed the goat head and took pictures. They hung around outside and relived the best moments of the show. "The cock of Satan!" Liz told Ben how amazing he was, and Ross, her boyfriend, shook Ben's hand like Ben was some kind of superstar.

Ben was reluctant to say goodbye. So, when Albert finally headed off to his car, Ben said, "Wait, don't you owe me?"

"Owe you for what?" Albert asked with a grin. "I helped you price your records. I think we're even."

"Let's go to the North Coast Festival. It's like a carnival, right on the lake."

"I know what it is," Albert said. "I'll think about it."

"Let's go some time before the next game," Ben said.

"Sure. That might work, if I can bring Jeff." Albert was walking backward down the sidewalk, waving goodbye as he spoke. "We'll figure something out."

Ben walked in the opposite direction toward his car. He regretted parking so far away. He felt chilly in his yellow windbreaker and couldn't help but look back over his shoulder for one more glimpse of Albert, but Albert had already disappeared into the night.

devil horns to the ground

On her down days, Celeste spent evenings at home in her apartment. She made some tea, usually rose and hibiscus, put on some music, usually K-pop, and painted minis and terrain. She tried not to think about her body, her hormone cycles, the pain in her hips, the looks she got, or thought she got but wasn't sure.

For the game at Readmore, she had been working for a few weeks now on a forge and a smithy, carved from foam board and polystyrene in the shape of a grinning face. She cut up plastic sheets of red and orange cellulose for the flames burning in the mouth. For the blacksmith himself, she found a shirtless barbarian with a big beard. He didn't look exactly as she'd imagined. She would use some modeling clay to turn the axes in his hands into hammers. And for the rest she'd ask her players to use their imaginations, as she always did.

She knew she did a lot for this game and this club, but somehow it was never too much for her. It seemed the more time she put into it, the more time she *wanted* to put into it. And not only in the planning and organizing of the club, which admittedly was becoming less and less now that the group had filled out, but also in the building and the making of the game, plotting out her ideas in her notebook, and building whatever set pieces she could.

There was a comfort for her in the little things, in the details. In going slowly with the paint brush or the X-Acto knife. In carving each brick, placing each lick of flame, and deciding that, yes, right there, that's where a certain perfect something should be.

Her players were going to love this forge and this blacksmith.

As Celeste was applying the first coat of base paint to the forge, her phone began to vibrate. It was her mother calling to ask if Celeste planned to come home to Youngstown for the weekend. No, Celeste said, she did not. How about church? There wasn't anybody she knew that still went there anymore, and there was going to be a cookout after. Did she want to come to church? No, she said, she did not. Then how about just the cookout? It would likely be the last one of the year on account of the weather getting colder, and they were all nice people. And no one who used to go there goes anymore.

"You still go," Celeste said, surprised by the anger in her voice.

"I go because it's my church," her mother said. And didn't Celeste understand that? That some people are fine with keeping things the way they are.

"You know what," Celeste said. "Actually, I'm in the middle of something, and I don't feel all that great today, so I can't really deal with you right now. Let me call you back tomorrow."

To which her mother said alright, that's fine then.

Celeste groaned in frustration as she put down her phone. She smoothed back her braids. She turned up the music and paced around her narrow kitchen, clutching her medallion for strength.

She had nothing against her mother. The transition hadn't been easy for anyone; Celeste understood that. She had nothing against her old church either, or religion in general. In fact, she had fond memories of church, of singing in the youth choir, of sitting in the pews and writing the names of the boys she was crushing on in the back of the hymnals. Tommy, Ronny, Malcom, Jamal. And Jamal most of all, with his big eyes and his big smile. That time they hid behind the baptistery, where the shiny choir robes were stored. But of course, as quickly as she wrote

them, she crossed out the names in embarrassment before anyone could see them. And she had to cross them out; she couldn't
erase them, because those little half pencils had no erasers.

She had nothing against any of that. But did she want to go
back there? Did she want to dredge up all those old memories?
Visit all those old places, and those old pews? Walk in the foot-
steps of the person she used to be? Somehow stumble upon an
old hymnal with the crossed-out names in the back? No, she did
not.

So, Celeste dropped it from her mind. She changed the music
from K-pop to a She-Ra soundtrack. She put another dollop of
honey in her tea, because she hadn't gotten it sweet enough the
first time, but she'd been too lazy to get up and add more. She sat
down with her paint brush and her Styrofoam forge and with a
clear mind returned to the task of making something just so.

• • •

Mooneyham had never been to Chez Dante before, but he
wasn't surprised it was so crowded. The chef had made a name
for himself by appearing on the Food Network, and getting an
open table was difficult. Mooneyham had made a reservation
weeks in advance. Huey had been dying to try the place ever since
it opened, and Mooneyham thought it would be the perfect spot
to celebrate their third anniversary. The restaurant was more
trendy than formal, and while the food was expensive, the price
had more to do with the chef's name than anything else.

Mooneyham pulled Huey's chair out and kissed the top of his
head as he sat down. Mooneyham was trying to be more out-
wardly affectionate. After they ordered, Mooneyham reached
across the table and took Huey's hand. Mooneyham was still
dressed in his shirt and tie. He had picked Huey up straight from
work. Huey wore the red bowtie his sister had bought him for
Christmas.

"Three years." Mooneyham couldn't believe it had been so long. He thought for sure he'd never meet the right guy and settle down.

Then he went to that awful party his buddy Armando put on every year, each time with a different theme. Pirates one year, Vikings the next. The year he met Huey, it had been the mysterious orient. Armando's whole house was decorated like Han's fortress from *Enter the Dragon*. Lots of red caged birds, and exotic food. There was even a martial arts group performing. And there, among the crowd, sitting on the edge of the sofa, was Huey.

Mooneyham asked Armando, "Who's that Asian guy? Do you know him?"

Armando replied, "God no, are you kidding? He's with the catering." He went off to shoo Huey back to work.

Mooneyham later found Huey sitting out by the pool. The moon had risen and everyone was a little drunker, Mooneyham included.

"Taking a break?" he asked, sitting down next to Huey. He was trying to be funny and sarcastic, but the words came out of his mouth like the worst pickup line ever. Huey gave him a terrible look.

"I'm studying anatomy." Huey sipped from a large bottle of Singha beer. "This is my field research." He motioned toward the swimmers, with their slick bodies and short shorts, splashing and yelping in the pool.

"I'm Richard. But most people call me Mooneyham."

"Huey. That's my nickname, like Huey, Dewey, and Louie, Americans say."

They shook hands, Mooneyham's wide paw swallowing Huey's thin, narrow hand. They studied each other for a moment from opposite ends of a spectrum: Mooneyham, tall and broad, a patch of black hair showing at the open collar of his

Hawaiian shirt; Huey, smooth and compact in a starched white button-down and pleated black pants, his dark eyes sparkling.

"Why don't you go for a swim?" Mooneyham asked.

"You want to join me?"

A woman came out of the house, waving her fist and yelling something that Mooneyham couldn't understand.

"That's my sister, Mary," Huey said. "They need me." With a groan of reluctance, he stood.

"Wait," Mooneyham said. "Are you really a student somewhere?"

"Why? You have something to teach me?" Huey asked. He gave Mooneyham a smile and the unfinished bottle of Singha before he went to help in the kitchen.

The moment was still fresh and clear in Mooneyham's mind. After the party he'd asked Armando who had done the catering. He went to the Thai Garden for lunch the very next day and asked Huey out.

Leaning closer across the table, Mooneyham asked, "Where do you think we'll be in three more years?"

"I hope someplace happy," Huey said. "Someplace together."

"Are we not someplace happy now?"

"Sure, but we could be together more. You're always working late, or playing that game."

"That being said," Mooneyham said, pulling a small white box with a purple ribbon from his suit jacket, "I wanted to give you this." He set the box in front of Huey, whose eyes had grown wide. "Don't get too excited." He knew what Huey would be expecting from a box like that, but he didn't want him to be disappointed.

Huey slowly untied the bow. His eyes filled with surprise when he pulled off the top.

Inside was a painted metal figurine of a sorceress with dark hair and a bright red cape. She held a knotted staff in one hand and a glass orb in the other.

"Is this Marilyn?" Huey asked. "You're so funny. Not exactly what I had in mind, but . . ."

"I want you to join the game," Mooneyham said. "I'll teach you the rules and how to play and everything. It'll be fun."

Mooneyham knew this wasn't what Huey was hoping for, but gaming together was a commitment of a sort. He also knew that by inviting Huey to join the game, he was going against his previous stance that members shouldn't be allowed to date. But there had to be a way to do it properly, so that if one side of the couple decided to quit or if the couple broke up, they wouldn't take the whole club down with them. If it were possible, then perhaps he and Huey could be the ones to show people how it's done. Maybe Celeste was right. The group could aspire to something more than just being a gaming club.

Huey didn't answer right away. He turned the figurine over beneath the dim light and examined it closely. "I imagined her more slutty," he said. "But she is going to be one fierce bitch. Monsters better watch out."

"This means you'll have to walk past O'Malley's on the way to Readmore. Those guys might try something again."

"I can handle it," Huey said. "I've got some idea on what to do with them."

• • •

Ben opened the cellar door and let Albert into the basement.

"This is going to be the best music appreciation class you've ever taken," Albert said, slipping a record from its black sleeve and placing it onto Ben's stereo.

"Can't wait," Ben said, although he wasn't actually that excited. Metal still wasn't his favorite genre, even after the Samuraiah Carey show. But Albert had sent him a text, *Wanna hear some new records?* And Ben had replied, *Sure come on over*, without knowing what to expect.

"This arrived from Finland just today. I haven't even listened to it yet."

The music started with a howl, and then the chugging guitars kicked in. The pencil cup on Ben's desk shook, and the tiny basement windows vibrated.

"Oh yeah." Albert closed his eyes. "This is good metal."

Ben wasn't sure exactly what constituted good metal, but Albert's enthusiasm made him smile.

While the record played, they hooked up Ben's old TurboGrafx-16 to the TV, and they played *Bonk's Adventure*, sitting side-by-side on the floor. They listened first to Finnish death metal and then to Norwegian death metal for comparison, although the finer points between the two were lost on Ben.

The music began to build, the guitars jug-jugging to a climax. Albert sprang to his feet. "Here it comes. Devil signs to the ground." He extended his pinky and index fingers while holding the other two fingers down with his thumb. He stood with his chest out, his shoulders back, and an iron stern look beneath his brows. "Point your devil horns like you're pointing them straight into hell, straight at the devil," he said, keeping his mouth a hard frown. "That's metal."

"You don't do it like this?" Ben crossed his arms over his chest and flicked his tongue out.

"If you're a poser."

"I need a cape." Ben pulled an afghan off the love seat and wrapped it around his shoulders. "I am the horny homunculus. When do we go out and burn churches?"

Albert laughed. "Patience, my young apprentice."

They were bored with *Bonk's Adventure* after two levels, so Ben turned the TV off. They sat on the love seat and flipped through old issues of *Dragon* magazine. Their shoulders pressed together and their knees touched.

"Why does everyone like the Drow so much," Ben asked, flipping through an article on elves.

"'Cause they're half-elf, half-spider and live in the Underdark."

"I mean sure, I can so relate," Ben said. "But they're overplayed."

Albert flipped the record over and casually asked, "When did you first realize you liked guys?"

"I don't know, high school, I guess, although I actually had a girlfriend back then." Michelle Sandinski. For one awkward semester they held hands, passed notes in the hall, and played Pokémon after class. They made out at the mall and went to homecoming together, but Michelle eventually wanted to go all the way, which was exactly the same moment when Ben realized things weren't going to work out. "I told her she didn't turn me to Jell-O and maybe she wasn't the right girl for me after all."

"You actually said that to her?"

"In an email, not face to face. God, that would have been awful. Then I didn't talk to her for like three weeks 'cause I was embarrassed by the whole thing. It was high school, you know."

Ben looked back over those years with guilt. Guilt that he'd led someone on. Guilt that he'd presented himself as something he wasn't. Not that Michelle, or any girl, expected him to be Don Juan. They were lucky if he'd put down his video games and books and pay attention to them.

The reason for his reluctance should have been obvious to him as he'd spent part of almost every high school afternoon making one-handed love to the painted covers of Conan the Barbarian books, eventually moving on to mail-order clothing catalogs. But still he'd figured it was a phase. It was how he relaxed, harmless at the least, a fetish at the most. It wouldn't last. He'd find the right girl eventually and she would take him away from all of that. They'd have a giant wedding and he'd carry her over the threshold and his parents would be so proud.

"Then one night, lying in bed, it came to me. I would never find that perfect girl, because it wasn't a girl that I was searching for. It was a bare-chested barbarian, sweating, and thrusting, swinging his oversized broadsword. And no amount of girls, cute, friendly, or otherwise, was going to satisfy that quest." It hadn't been an easy thing to accept, but once he did he felt so much better and so many other things fell into place. "What about you?"

"I had it easy. I'm the youngest of five. I have three older brothers and an older sister. All of them had already explored and experimented and found themselves, bringing home boyfriends and girlfriends and various combinations of both long before I ever came out."

It had started with his sister, who ran off with a pot dealer and joined a commune. The shock for their mother was not the pot dealing or the commune, but that the dealer boyfriend was Jamaican. The commune ended up failing, the pot dealer took off with another girl, and his sister discovered her true love was reggae anyway. This need for exploration continued with his brothers. One joined a circus, learned to swallow fire and swords, and returned home broke and malnourished a year later.

"My mom fell to her knees when he walked through the front door."

Another converted to Islam, following the wishes of his girlfriend. It lasted until she met a more devout follower. Another married his high school sweetheart, became a cartographer, and found a job working for the state department.

"This wouldn't be so terrible, if the state weren't Alaska, which is just so far away."

By the time Albert's turn came around, he found his mother

had already been shocked into a dull, passive acceptance of nearly anything.

"Man," said Ben, "you make being gay seem so tame."

"Oh, totally. Being gay is nothing. I mean, when I told my mom, she was like, 'Just make sure you study hard and get a good job.' There was no drama to be stirred up by that point. Listening to heavy metal and playing D&D were far worse, 'cause they clearly weren't leading to a good job."

"Clearly."

"Man, she hated my music. So that was good."

"At least you had something. Mine were a little freaked out, but they didn't disown me or anything, obviously."

"They probably already knew."

"Maybe. I hadn't had a girlfriend since Michelle. My mom asked me one day, 'Whatever happened to that one girl you were seeing? Do you ever call her anymore?' And I was like, 'Mom, come on.' And she was like, 'What?' And I was like, 'I'm gay.' And she was like, 'No, you're not,' and I was like, 'Yeah, I am.' Then the crying started and my dad came in and he was like, 'Why's your mother crying?' But he didn't say it in a threatening way. It sounds threatening as I'm telling it, but he really just wanted to know why she was crying. So, I told him and he was like, 'That's it?' He laughed. But my mom couldn't stop crying. I think she wanted a different life for me, but what could I do? My dad said if anyone had a problem with it, then it was their problem, not mine. My mom eventually dried her eyes and that was pretty much it. I came back down here and checked my email or something."

"And the world kept turning."

"As though it didn't even know I was alive. But it's still kind of awkward, almost ten years later. They try to be supportive, but I've never really had a boyfriend, so in some ways it's still this thing that they've never had to face. None of us have had to. But I'm sure, when I do meet someone, they'll be totally cool with it. I think they'll be happy as long as I find someone I love. And I get out of the basement." Ben laughed.

His parents had yet to meet Albert. He didn't think there was any point in introducing him. If they met, his parents would ask all kinds of questions. They'd get the wrong idea and think something was going on when it wasn't. Ben didn't see any point in getting them all excited for nothing.

The album had stopped playing and the needle was bouncing in the center of the record, over and over. They sat there looking at each other, Albert on the sofa and Ben on the edge of the coffee table. Their knees were almost touching. Ben looked at his watch and saw it was almost six thirty. "We'd better get going if we wanna make it to Readmore on time."

"Yeah, I guess so," Albert said, and Ben detected in his voice a longing for something.

But Albert stood and took the record off. Music appreciation was over.

there is no escape
from the city of the dead

Albert held out his phone so the guys could see the photos from the Samuraiah Carey show, and they all huddled around.

"I shit you not," Albert said. "Ben had the goat head on and he was busting out all these moves."

"That's awesome," Celeste said. "Why didn't you tell me?"

"The goat head is a good look for you," Mooneyham said, and Huey elbowed him in the ribs.

"Huey and I have been thinking," Mooneyham said. "And we want to do something about those assholes at O'Malley's pub."

"Like what?" Valerie asked.

Ben was wondering when Mooneyham would get around to addressing what had happened at O'Malley's the week before. Everyone agreed the guys at O'Malley's were annoying at best, but no one ever considered doing anything about it before.

"Like have a kiss-in," Huey said.

"What's that?" Valerie asked.

"Where everyone kisses?" Ben asked.

Mooneyham and Huey both nodded as though a kiss-in were a simple solution to an everyday problem.

"How would we do it?" Celeste asked. "How do we organize such a thing? I've only heard about them. Has anybody actually been to one?"

"We just show up and kiss," Huey said.

"Kiss who?" Ben asked.

"Everybody!"

"I need more specifics," Ben said.

"Me too," Valerie said.

Mooneyham leaned forward and pressed a thick finger into the tabletop. "Guys, let's get serious. It's not that hard. Next week, after the game, we all head over there."

"Just us?" Ben said. "No way."

"We'll have to get the word out," Celeste said. "People will come."

"I can tell everyone at the record store," Albert said. "And they'll tell other people for sure."

"I'll invite Polly," Valerie said.

"Of course," Mooneyham said.

"Hold on," Ben said. "What are we trying to do exactly? I mean, what is the point of all this?"

"To teach those homophobes a lesson," Mooneyham said.

"And they're supposed to accept that?" Ben asked. "What if there's a fight?"

"Nothing's gonna happen," Mooneyham said. "Some people might get upset and storm out, but it's not gonna come to blows."

"On the internet," Huey said, "people just went to the place and kissed."

"Are we going to tell O'Malley's, to give them a heads up?" Ben asked.

Mooneyham looked unconcerned. "We can't. They might shut us down before we start. We simply show up and let them think it's a busy night at the bar."

"We'll outnumber any assholes," Albert said. "They won't be able to do anything." He put a hand on Ben's shoulder. "Don't worry. It's gonna be great. I'm getting stoked already."

"But you like crazy stuff," Ben said. "Am I the only one who's nervous?"

"I'm nervous," Celeste said. "It seems to me like we should tell the bar, so they can have extra bouncers on hand. What if things do get out of hand like Ben said?"

"They won't." Mooneyham was firm. "We show up, get a few drinks, have a good time, and wait until the stroke of midnight."

"Then bam—kissing!" Huey said.

"Seems too easy," Ben said.

"What am I gonna do?" Valerie asked. "I can't get in. I'm only eighteen."

"Kiss on the sidewalk?" Huey suggested.

Valerie did not seem happy with that idea, but Celeste said, "We've still got a week to figure it out. For now let's focus on getting you guys out of the necropolis."

They turned their attention to their character sheets, to the large black gate, and to the map of the underworld that Celeste spread across the tabletops.

Celeste said, "Now that Bjorndar has a living head on his shoulders, some of the other ghosts are looking at him funny. They say things like, 'Oh, would you look at him, got a head on his shoulders. What a trendsetter.' One of them says, 'A head, I'd be happy with a hand.' He holds up his ghostly arm, and you can see the hand has been cut off."

"So, with his head on, what can Bjorndar do?" Ben asked.

Celeste said, "I'll let you have some of your abilities. You can do either a move action or a standard action, but not both, and if you try to cast a spell, there'll be a fifty-percent chance it will fail, since you're only half alive."

Ben felt that was better than nothing, and the consensus around the table seemed to be that Celeste had come up with a good compromise, but Mooneyham asked why Bjorndar was half alive when it was only his head that wasn't dead.

"That would be only one fourth, not half," Mooneyham said. "If it were half, he'd be alive from the waist up."

"Technicalities," Albert said dismissively.

"I think it's important," Mooneyham said.

"Here's how I think of it as someone who has not always felt connected with herself." Celeste leaned back into her chair and smoothed down her braids. "His life force comes from a combination of his mind and his body. Both are equal contributors, fifty-fifty. His mind is alive, but his body is not. So, he's at fifty percent."

"Now we're getting philosophical," Mooneyham said, and the table erupted in argument until Celeste clapped her hands and, to Ben's satisfaction, announced the debate was over.

"The decision has been made," Celeste said.

· · ·

A low moan reverberated through the city of the dead.

Bjorndar and the rest of party stood encircled by translucent ghosts. In the distance, the black silhouette of the Hellrebus lumbered across the horizon, occasionally throwing back its three heads and bellowing flames.

"He's in a bad mood today," said a passing ghost.

"We can't let this thing stop us from escaping. There must be something we can do to distract it," Flamebender said.

"Perhaps we can throw some meat at it, and then run past while it's eating," Gunther said.

"It never eats," the ghost said.

"Maybe I can play a song that will put it to sleep," Theegh said.

"It never sleeps."

"Then we'll just have to kill it," Gunther said.

"It's already dead."

The low moan of the underworld swelled around them, but the wind died. "You are doomed." The ghost began to drift away. "All may enter, but none shall leave the city of the dead."

"Wait," Flamebender said to the ghost. "Exactly what happens when the dead reach the surface?"

"They return to life. They take on a corporeal form. They breathe and dream and dance and do all the things the living are known to do."

"Sounds great," Bjorndar said. "Can't wait."

"Then we lure the Hellrebus to the top," Flamebender said. "And as soon as it becomes a living thing, we hack it to pieces and send it back to the underworld. I have a spell that can shackle it. The shackles won't hold forever, but long enough to give us a head start as we run."

Considering the alternative—staying in the underworld forever—they all agreed it was the best plan they had.

The ghosts looked at them with pity. "Follow the wall to the western gate. There you'll find the way out, and the beast will be waiting."

With Bjorndar's head wobbling atop its ghostly body, they walked carefully through the spirit crowd, avoiding any demon patrols, closer and closer to the open gate and the giant shape lumbering ahead.

They followed the wall until they were near the western gate. Even at a distance, they could see the giant three-headed hound, the Hellrebus, pacing and snorting flames. The copper-scaled serpents flashed like writhing fire upon its three necks. When they were close enough to feel the heat wafting from it and smell its charred black fur, Flamebender knelt and whispered a prayer. Huge chains erupted from the ground and wrapped themselves around the beast's clawed feet.

The Hellrebus bellowed in fury, but the chains held it in place. Flamebender led the way as the party ran between the beast's legs. Its heads tried to snap at them, but its short necks couldn't bend enough to reach.

They ran through the gate, and then beyond. The cave wall rose before them. There was a large tunnel opening, and as soon as they reached it, Gunther yelled, "He's broken free! Don't stop!"

"Shackle it again," Theegh said.

"I can't. I can only use that spell once per encounter."

The tunnel rose up at a steep incline and the party didn't run so much as climb, scampering as quickly as they could. But the beast was following. Flames erupted from behind them as it breathed fire into the tunnel. The Hellrebus squeezed in and climbed up after them. It snapped at their legs and backs, and lava-like drool sprayed from its maws.

Gunther, with his battle axe, chopped one of the beast's burning snouts, but that only angered the other two heads more and spurred the beast on faster.

"Keep going," Theegh yelled.

"I don't think I can make it," Bjorndar said. His ghostly body, with its solid head, was top heavy and difficult to control. He couldn't run in a straight line, and every few steps he would stumble and bang his head against the sides of the tunnel. "I only have half my hit points left."

"Almost there," Theegh yelled. "I see light up ahead."

Flamebender took up his sacred sigil from around his neck, held it before the Hellrebus, and yelled, "Holy smite!" A blinding light shot forth, and the beast roared, shaking the cave, but it didn't appear to have felt a thing.

"Guys," Gunther yelled, "I hear a rumbling."

"What kind of rumbling?" Bjorndar asked. "Like the belly of a hungry dragon or something worse?"

"What's worse than that?" Theegh asked.

Dust and pebbles began falling from the ceiling as the cave walls shook.

"A cave-in!" Gunther yelled as the cave began to collapse around them.

The opening was not far, and they jumped for it, tumbling from the mouth of the cave and into the fresh air and sunshine. Rolling hills and green fields spread before them, and the sky above was blue and clear. But there was no time to admire their new setting.

The beast burst from the cave behind them, showering rock and dirt into the air. Gunther landed a chopping blow on the Hellrebus, and it bled hot, steaming blood onto the ground. The Hellrebus had become flesh.

Flamebender speared it in the side with the holy Rammaster. Marilyn raised her hands as lightning shot from her fingertips, and Theegh, wielding his magic lute, struck a note so discordant, the beast howled in pain.

But the Hellrebus wasn't yet dead. It threw back its three heads and bellowed in rage.

• • •

Albert spread out his arms to stop the game.

"Hold up," he said. "I think the honor goes to Bjorndar." He turned to Ben. "Can you get the killing blow?"

"I can try," Ben said. He only needed to roll a fourteen to hit the Hellrebus, but he wasn't sure he could do enough damage to kill the creature. "No pressure or anything, right?"

Ben picked up his golden twenty-sided die and cupped it in his hands. If there was ever a time to roll high, it was now. He sent the die tumbling across the table.

A natural twenty.

A cheer roared across the table as Albert clapped Ben heartily on the back.

• • •

Bjorndar swiftly pulled his bow from his back and notched six arrows, one above the other, and let them fly. They whistled and arched through the air, on a perfect trajectory for a critical hit. They pierced each of the beast's eyes and didn't stop until they burrowed their way deep into its brains. With a roar, the Hellrebus reared up on its hind legs. Its shadow fell upon Bjorndar and stretched beyond, across the green fields. And then, with a tremendous shudder, the fiendish creature collapsed. Lava oozed from its gaping mouths and hardened into stone. The serpents of its mane broke free and slithered into the ground as the body disintegrated into ash and blew away.

Bjorndar collapsed to the ground. His heart—he could feel it beating. His lungs pulled in a breath. He was alive again.

. . .

Ben feigned nonchalance, but around the table there was nothing but smiles and congratulations.

"See, nothing to worry about," Albert said with a laugh. "I told you I'd bring you back to life."

"I can hardly believe it," Ben said. He still half expected Celeste to pull some trick out of her sleeve, but at the head of the table, Celeste was smiling too, and not in a sinister way.

"Now what?" Mooneyham asked. "We travel back to the Cod and Piece? We still need to talk to Whistletooth and tell him about the satyrs."

"Fauns," Valerie corrected.

"Sure, makes sense to me," Celeste said. She picked up the fallen Hellrebus and folded away the gates to the underworld. "You travel a few days across hills and dales, mostly without incident. You fend off some wolves, and scare away some bandits, but you return safely to Hammervale right as the sun begins to set."

. . .

Dull light came from the windows of the Cod and Piece, and someone had painted graffiti on the front of the building. Even the sign had been vandalized. "Cod" had been painted over, and "WAR" was scrawled over top.

Two half-orcs dressed in studded black leather armor stood at either side of the doors. Heavy battle axes hung from their belts.

"They're new," Theegh said. "Has this neighborhood gotten worse since we were last here?"

As they approached, the guards sniffed them. "You smell like fire and brimstone."

"We've just come from the city of the dead," Flamebender said. "And we could use a good drink."

The guards nodded and then opened the large double doors. A cloud of smoke, noise, and laughter billowed out.

"I'll get the drinks and check in with Whistletooth," Gunther said.

"We'll get a table," Flamebender said as he and Bjorndar hung up their cloaks near the doors.

The bar was darker than usual. The fire in the hearth burned low. Bjorndar didn't recognize any of the regulars. There was a new barkeep, a one-eyed halfling on stilts. Even the serving wenches, who literally looked like hags—stringy hair, crooked noses, cackling laughs, and missing teeth—were new. They carried drinks and cavorted with customers, many of whom had horns and fangs and gripped their steins with clawed hands.

"It's odd that no one has greeted us," Bjorndar said, looking around. "This is the Cod and Piece, isn't it?"

"Maybe it's monster night," Marilyn said. "Don't judge."

Theegh was peering through the smoky darkness toward the large fireplace.

A bald, bearded man with segmented eyes and the lower body of a cricket sat on a stool by the fire. He played a slow, mournful tune by rubbing his legs together.

"I don't recognize that bard. I'll go introduce myself," Theegh said, taking his lute from his pack.

Flamebender found a spot in the middle of a long wooden table. He and Bjorndar sat down while Theegh went to the fire and Marilyn followed Gunther to the bar.

Gunther squeezed in at the bar between a tall elf and an even taller minotaur.

"Five tankards o' ale and tell Whistletooth we're here."

The halfling squinted at Gunther with his one good eye. His stilts were crudely fashioned from two-by-fours strapped onto his feet, but he clomped around on them with grace.

"The ale I can do ya for, but who's Whistletooth?"

"Are you joking? He's the owner of this bar, last time I checked."

"And how long ago was that?" asked the halfling, making no motion to pour the ales Gunther had ordered.

Before he could answer, Gunther felt a hand slip under his cloak. Quickly, he grabbed the hand before it could advance any farther. It belonged to the elf, who was looking in the opposite direction. The elf turned to Gunther with an embarrassed smile before trying to pull his hand away, but Gunther held on tightly to the elf's wrist.

"If this wasn't a gay bar, I'd think you were trying to pick my pockets," Gunther said.

"This isn't a gay bar," said the halfling bartender. "Not anymore."

Gunther and the elf locked eyes as they reached for their weapons.

"Hold on," Marilyn said as she walked up. "Was this elf flirting with you?"

"No, he's a pickpocket," Gunther said.

Marilyn slapped the elf. "How dare you lay a finger on my man. We traveled all the way from the city of the dead and brought our friend back to life. We fought demons and a Hellrebus. We've seen things you couldn't imagine. And we're not about to let a low-level thief like you waste our time."

"Wait," Gunther said. "I'm gay. I wouldn't be with some woman, not even one as amazing as Marilyn."

"What?" Marilyn looked confused. "We're not together?"

"I'm not gonna play a straight dude," Gunther said.

"You do in real life," Marilyn snapped, and a hush fell over the bar. Marilyn did not look apologetic, but she smiled at Gunther. "What if I told you Marilyn had a secret? She's not really a woman."

Now a murmur of surprise rose from around the bar.

"You're coming up with all of this right now?" Gunther asked.

"What kind of woman is named Marilyn Monsoon anyway?" Marilyn said. "That's just my stage name. My real name is Bill Jones, but that's so boring. I had to become someone else, escape my hometown, and be someone fabulous."

"How was I supposed to know all of this?" Gunther asked.

"Marilyn took you for a walk one starry night, down by the river, and with tears in her eyes, she confessed her feelings and told you everything. So, now you're in love."

"That's so touching," said the elf.

"That's role playing," Marilyn said.

"What are you talking about?" Gunther asked. "We're about to have a fight here."

"I'm talking about love. Love that transcends gender, that transcends the physical body. What would happen if everyone in this tavern focused their energies on love instead of anger and hatred? We could generate enough positive energy to change this ramshackle town for the better."

"But this is D&D," Gunther said, and he swung at the elf with his battle axe.

At the tables, Flamebender and Bjorndar took no notice of the fight starting at the bar.

"Dude, that concert," Flamebender said. "My mind's still blown away. I need to send you the pictures I took."

Gunther, struggling against the elf's short sword, called out, "If you're not going to help, at least stay in character."

"Oh, god, calm down," Bjorndar yelled. Then turning to Flamebender, he said, "I sent forth to you a magical message of text, but you never honored me with a reply."

"My apologies, but I have been busy trying to appease my liege."

"Your liege?"

"Yes, Sir Jeffery, keeper of the crypt of legendary rock."

"Ah, I believe I've heard of him."

"Perhaps this weekend we can amuse ourselves at the festival upon the north coast."

"The festival upon the north coast? Yes, that would be quite splendid."

Gunther fell upon the bar, shattering mugs and sending stools tumbling. "What the fuck are you idiots talking about? I'm bleeding out over here!"

Near the fire, Theegh greeted the cricket man with a curt nod and asked, "Mind if I join you?"

The cricket man motioned toward an empty stool by the fire, and Theegh sat down with his lute.

"I'm Theegh, teller of tales, singer of songs, and wielder of the magic lute."

"I am Krengle. That is all."

"What is the tune you're playing? I don't recognize it."

"I call it 'The Tale of Figarace.'"

"I know a guy named Figarace," Theegh said. "He often plays here, but I don't know that song."

"I'm making it up as I go along," Krengle said, and his multi-faceted black eyes sparkled in the firelight.

"To be honest, I hate Figarace," Theegh said. "He's a better musician than I am, and his voice has more range. And I can't stand the smug look on his face."

"Me either. That's why I killed him." Still rubbing his legs together, Krengle reached down into his bag and pulled out a head. Figarace's terrified face stared at Theegh from empty eyes. "If you couldn't compete with him, I doubt you'll be able to compete with me. But let's try, for the fun of it. Play a song for us." Krengle stopped his playing and then swept his arms open in a gesture that was anything but welcoming.

The monstrous patrons sitting closest to the fire turned their attention to Theegh.

"OK, sure," Theegh said with a slight wobble in his voice. Bjorndar and Flamebender were huddled over a table, talking, and at the bar Gunther and Marilyn were arguing with an elf. Theegh cleared his throat. "Have you heard the one about the paladin and the Hellrebus?"

"I have not," Krengle said. "I hope it has a terrible ending."

"We'll find out in a minute," Theegh said as he began to play.

Bjorndar climbed to his feet and withdrew his dagger. "I'm beginning to suspect this bar is under new management."

"You think?" Gunther said, his face turning red. The elf had Gunther in a chokehold and was tightening his grip.

"You leave me no choice," Marilyn said as she raised her hands. A rainbow of colors burst into the air, covering the bar and everyone in front of her in a thick spray.

"Great," Gunther said. He was coated in rainbow stripes from head to boot-tip. "Color spray. Now I'm blind."

"Me too," said the barkeep, and then he raised his eye patch and said, "No, I'm not."

The elf was blinded by the spray as well, but he didn't release his grip on Gunther.

"Can a blind creature maintain a grapple?" Flamebender asked.

"Apparently," Gunther said, his voice strained.

"I'd need to see the flow chart for the grappled condition," Bjorndar said.

"If I remember correctly, if a grappled creature turns invisible, they gain a bonus on their escape attempt. And since the elf is blind, Gunther is essentially invisible to him."

"I don't know," Bjorndar said. "That sounds like a technicality. I'd say Gunther has total concealment from the elf, but I wouldn't say he's invisible."

"Would someone just fucking stab this guy?" Gunther asked.

"Now, attacking someone while they grapple another creature is definitely something we can do," Flamebender said.

Bjorndar slipped his dagger under the elf's chin. "Someone here has made a mistake. Maybe it was you. Maybe it was us, but we don't want any trouble. Let our friend go, and we'll leave and no one will get hurt."

There came a shout from the fireplace. It was Theegh.

Theegh was being pelted by scraps of food, and some of them were quite large and painful. He raised his lute above his head as a shield. Bits of carrots and cabbage bounced off the strings with a twang.

"Not exactly the crowd-pleaser was it?" Krengle said. "Perhaps the Hellrebus should have lived while the paladin died?"

Theegh stood and made to run, but Krengle reached out a long leg and tripped him.

"You walked into the wrong bar," Krengle said. "I have heard of you, Theegh. I know how you stopped the satyrs in the forest, but we are legion. You can't stop us all."

"They claimed they were fauns," Theegh said as he crawled under the nearest table. Krengle swiped at him with a clawed hand while the monstrous patrons seated around the table kicked at Theegh and tried to pin him down with their feet.

As Theegh attempted to scramble out from under the table, two heavy hands grabbed him by the shoulders and pulled him to his feet. One of the half-orc guards dragged Theegh toward the doors as the monsters continued to claw at him and pelt him with food.

The other guard had picked up Marilyn, and more half-orcs in leather armor were coming from the back room to forcefully usher out Flamebender, Gunther, and Bjorndar.

With a grunt, the half-orc tossed Theegh into the street.

"This is our bar now," barked the guard as he slammed the door.

"Some welcome-home party that was," Bjorndar said.

A stale wind blew up the street, scattering dust and debris.

"Now what?" Theegh asked, pulling his cloak tight.

From the corner of his eye, Bjorndar saw movement at the end of the street. A cloaked figure beckoned him into the darkness.

"Lads, this way."

Unsure what other options remained, they followed the shadowy figure down narrow slanted streets, under stone archways, and across a moonlit square, until they came to the open entrance of the town smithy, where the pounding of hammers on steel could be heard even at this late hour.

"Quickly, inside." The hooded figure hurried them through the open doorway.

In the golden light of the forge, their guide dropped his cloak and revealed a broad, bearded face and a thick muscular body, covered in wiry red hair. He was naked but for a black leather apron tied around his waist. When he turned to hang up his cloak, he confirmed that his back was as hairy as his front.

The smithy was large and airy. The main hearth was shaped like a bearded giant, its open mouth belching out flames. On either side were two smaller forges, both burning brightly. Apprentice smiths, naked from the waist up, hammered in large swinging arcs. Light glistened off their muscular, sweat-slicked bodies. Occasionally, they would plunge a sword into a bath of cool water, and steam would fill the air. The smithy was infused with the intoxicating smell of smoke and metal and man sweat. There was a clanging, infectious rhythm to the pounding, punctuated by the hissing release of steam.

"I am Torgar, son of Torget. The blacksmith of Hammervale. You are safe to speak here."

"To speak about what?" Flamebender asked. "Why were you watching us?"

Gunther said, "The famous blacksmith of Hammervale. This guy's good. Not by dwarf standards, of course, but good enough for the rest of you."

Torgar said, "A fortnight ago a few of the boys and I went down to the Cod and Piece for a pint and found the place was taken over."

"Well, stoke my forge," Gunther said. "The blacksmith of Hammervale is gay."

"Of course." Torgar puffed out his broad chest. "Who do you think designs the best armor? Straight smiths? Please. They couldn't care less about shape or silhouette. They still think basilisk scale is the greatest thing ever. It's so two years ago."

The apprentice smiths began to chuckle. "Basilisk scale," they said. "As if."

"Who are these people that have taken over?" Bjorndar asked.

"As you may have noticed," Torgar said, "they're not people. We've no idea who they are or where they came from."

"But they know who we are," Theegh said. "That cricket man, Krengle, knew we saved Flamebender from the fauns."

"What happened to Whistletooth?" Gunther asked. "The barkeep claimed to have never heard of him."

"No one has seen or heard from Whistletooth in days," Torgar said. "He usually makes the rounds at the market at least once a day."

"Obviously they've done something to him," Flamebender said. "They've either killed him and hidden his body or they're keeping him captive. One thing is for sure, we can't let this group take root in our town. We've got to take back the Cod and Piece."

"But how?" Bjorndar asked. "There are only five of us and hundreds of them. Even if the blacksmith and his boys help, we're still outnumbered."

"We disguise ourselves and go undercover as cult members," Marilyn said. "It should be easy if we present ourselves as new recruits."

"Too risky," Gunther said. "If they see through our disguises, they'll kill us for sure."

"I know of a way in," Torgar said. "There is a tunnel that runs from the basement of the curio shop across the street."

"How do you know?" Flamebender asked.

"I am the blacksmith of Hammervale. I know everything about this town. I practically invented it."

"I bet it connects with the back room behind the bar, where Whistletooth always met with us," Flamebender said.

"So, we sneak in after hours and see what we can find out?" Bjorndar asked. "Perhaps Whistletooth is still alive in there, tied up somewhere."

"So, it's decided then." Flames roaring behind him, Torgar looked them all in the eyes. "Operation Rear Entry leaves at midnight."

• • •

As Ben and Albert collected their miniatures from the map, Ben asked, "So, we're still on for Saturday then? For the North Coast Festival?"

"Yeah, totally. I changed my schedule so I'm working in the morning." Albert carefully wrapped his Flamebender miniature in tissue paper before placing it into his bag.

"I hope the weather is good," Ben said. "It'd suck if we got rained out." Although, if it rained, they might have to stay inside and do something more intimate.

"I think Jeff wants to come too," Albert said. "Is that okay?"

Ben dropped his dice bag into his backpack. "Sure," Ben said, hoping that he sounded sincere.

"I couldn't not tell him about it," Albert said. "And then once I did, he got excited about wanting to go. He said he hasn't gone since he was in high school."

"Of course," Ben said. He hadn't gone since high school either, so he knew the feeling.

"Sorry," Albert said. "I know you were thinking it'd be just us. But you can bring someone too, if you'd like. We can make it a kind of group thing."

"Yeah, maybe," Ben said. But he'd almost laughed at the idea of bringing someone else.

Celeste was picking up the extra miniatures from the map: the forge and the blacksmith, she seemed especially proud of them. Mooneyham and Huey were whispering in the corner as they put on their jackets and Mooneyham slid their character sheets into his black leather bag. Only Valerie, who was slumped in her chair and texting with someone, made no move to clean up the tables. But Valerie practically lived at Readmore. She wouldn't be in a hurry to leave.

Ben tried to remain upbeat. The North Coast Festival was going to be a lot of fun. It would be nostalgic. He could have a good time with Jeff there. He shouldn't be so down about the future. Good times were just around the corner.

"Don't forget," Mooneyham said, as they all walked out the front doors together. "Next week, after the game, kiss-in at O'Malley's. Tell everyone you know."

north coast festival

The Jitterbugs Café had been a diner in a previous life and still retained the long stainless steel counter and bar stools of its earlier days, but the booths had long been replaced by frumpy sofas and low coffee tables, and the short-order cook replaced by a shiny espresso machine. The walls, which were painted in pastels, gave up their space to a monthly rotation of local artists, all hoping to be discovered by a traveling critic or millionaire patron of the arts.

Every Thursday, there was live music, usually a local folk singer or some string trio from Case Western Reserve. The last Friday of every month hosted an open mic night, an anything-goes potluck, most of which could only loosely be described as entertainment, even by Cleveland's standards.

Ben loved the place, but many Clevelanders loathed it and associated it with slackers and hippies and no-good liberals. Which was ironic to the folks who worked at Jitterbugs. They considered themselves to be a force of good in the neighborhood. They only hired the hippest and most interesting applicants, the most politically active, and the most visually compelling. The result being that every employee was some sort of local variation on David Bowie or Marilyn Manson or Janis Joplin. Although there had been a few junior Pat Benatars and a couple Buddy Hollys too.

It was a Saturday evening, and Ben had agreed to meet Albert before they went to the North Coast Festival. When Albert texted

Jitterbugs before the fest? it wasn't so much a question as it was a confirmation.

"So," Albert said between sips from his paper cup, "the Samuraiah Carey show." Albert pulled the photos up on his phone and passed it to Ben.

Ben wearing the goat head, Albert flexing shirtless, the two of them making heavy metal signs with their fingers and sticking out their tongues.

"God, that was the craziest night," Ben said. Albert looked great in the photos, shirtless and sweaty, but Ben barely recognized himself. His hair was a mess, he was grinning like a madman, and his eyes were wild and animalistic. "You gotta send these to me."

"I've been talking about the show ever since. Even Jeff was impressed."

"Where is Jeff?" Ben asked, trying to sound nonchalant.

"He's meeting us there." Albert took a big drink from his cup and then licked the foam off his stubble mustache.

"Sure," Ben said. "Of course." He sipped his soy latte and tried not to sound disappointed.

They crossed the street to the RTA station and got on the first train headed downtown. They sat side-by-side, and the train clicked and clacked as the houses and buildings passed by.

Every year the North Coast Festival rolled into Cleveland and set up attractions along the shore of Lake Erie. Tents blossomed along the water, and a giant Ferris wheel rose between the Browns stadium and the Rock and Roll Hall of Fame. For three weeks, families came from across Ohio to enjoy the rides, play games, and eat funnel cakes.

For Ben, the annual carnival signaled the passing of summer into autumn. He'd attended the fair since he was a kid, but as an adult he hadn't gone in several years.

The weather was cooler once they reached the lake. Albert was dressed in tight black jeans, but instead of his hooded sweat-shirt he wore a dark green bomber jacket with fur trim around the hood. There was a Goateyes patch on the left breast-pocket. Ben wore his yellow windbreaker, and the breeze picked up the collar and rubbed it against the bottom of his chin in the most annoying way. But he was outside with Albert, in the fresh air, and away from the basement, so he didn't care, even if Jeff was meeting them later.

Albert bought twenty tickets, but Ben only had enough money for ten.

"It's not a big deal," Albert said. "You can take some of mine."

Ben offered to pay him back later, but Albert said, "Get my coffee at Jitterbugs next time."

The late afternoon sun was low in the sky as they strolled through the crowded fairgrounds. The air coming off the lake was filled with the smell of fried dough and sugar. Ben bought a funnel cake for himself and a hot dog for Albert.

"Now we're even," he said grinning, and Albert nodded in approval.

"We never went to these things in Detroit," Albert said, as screaming kids ran past on their way to The Scrambler.

"Did your parents think it was a waste of money?"

"No, it's too dangerous."

"I think the rides are safer nowadays."

"Yeah, but there's gangs. And low-grade hoodlums."

"Oh, right."

They stopped so Albert could try the ring toss. Three rings for a ticket. Albert leaned into the booth, aiming at the bottles. His jacket rode up, and Ben could see the swath of dark hair across the small of Albert's back. If Albert bent over any farther, even just a little bit, Ben, or anyone else paying attention, would see the crack of his ass. But Albert tossed his rings and straightened up without winning a prize.

"You have a big family, don't you?" Ben said as they walked on.

"Yeah, it goes me, Sam, Kevin, Paul, and Marcy, from youngest to oldest."

"Did your mom ever remarry?"

"No. She didn't even talk about it. And I didn't want her to, at least when I was a kid. But now, of course, I wish she would. Remarry, I mean. Everyone's grown up and left the house, and I wish she had someone to retire with. I think she's lonely." They walked a little farther before Albert said, "I wish Jeff would get here already. He's supposed to text me when he arrives." The wind ruffled Albert's fur collar.

"Let's ride something," Ben said. "How about the Tilt-A-Whirl?"

They handed over their tickets and climbed into one of the cup-shaped cars. Slowly at first, the platform began to turn, and their cup started to spin. Ben held on tightly to the handrail so he wouldn't slide across the bench and into Albert. But when the car began to spin in the other direction, faster the second time around, it was Albert who didn't hold on. He slid into Ben with a slam.

"Oh, sorry," Albert said. "Am I crushing you? Sorry. Didn't mean to do that." But he was laughing and pushing against Ben harder and harder with each apology.

Ben was laughing too, giddy and dizzy from the spinning car. The lights of the midway were a blur. Albert's weight pressed into Ben, and Ben welcomed it. He could smell Albert's detergent and the exotic scents trapped within Albert's thick jacket.

"Just wait," Ben said. "I'll have my revenge." But the ride began to slow, and the spinning stopped.

They stumbled out, dizzy and using each other for support. They leaned against the low metal fence that sectioned off the Tilt-A-Whirl from the midway.

Ben said, "Let's ride something else."

"In a minute," Albert said. "I don't feel so hot." He was grinning and staggering as if he were drunk.

They regained their balance by a cotton candy cart.

"We should have invited the other guys," Ben said. "It would be fun to watch Mooneyham stumble around."

"Still no word from Jeff," Albert said.

Ben shrugged, as though Jeff's absence was no big loss.

The pink bags of cotton candy hanging from the cart swayed in the breeze. Ben and Albert moved away as a young mother with three kids came up to the cart.

"What happened between you and Jeff anyway?" Albert asked as they walked past the Tilt-A-Whirl.

"Nothing," Ben said, trying to be casual.

"But you wanted something to happen, right? It's okay if you were into him. It doesn't bother me or anything. I'm just curious."

"He really didn't tell you about it?"

"He told me you were weird and that you went out once, but that's it."

"I'm weird?" Ben stopped in front of the funhouse.

Ben had been working the information counter at the library when Jeff walked up asking for articles on anencephaly, a disease where babies are born without a brain.

"I thought he was hot, and he had this kind of helpless quality that I'm a sucker for. And plus, what an obscure thing for a guy to ask about. I mean, that's intriguing. A girl I worked with knew him and set us up. It was supposed to be a double date, but then she and her boyfriend cancelled at the last minute, so it ended up just me and Jeff."

"How was it?" Albert asked as the funhouse attendant took their tickets.

"Oh, god," Ben said. "I knew right away that he was out of my league, on a thousand different levels."

They entered the funhouse gate, shaped like the smiling mouth of a clown, and into the hall of mirrors. Ben was distorted into odd shapes as they walked, small then big, narrow then wide. In one mirror his stomach was enormous, and in another his head was lost completely.

"Did you guys have a good time?" Albert asked as they stepped into a large room with a dozen doors. Each one had a large door-knob that made a sound when either Ben or Albert pulled on it. A mooing cow. A trumpeting elephant. A barking dog. Until they found the right knob and the door opened.

"I'm just gonna come right out and tell you," Ben said. "I haven't gone on a lot of dates." He'd never even had a real relationship. "I had no idea what the heck I was doing with Jeff. I was nervous and surprised he didn't cancel to be honest."

Jeff had worn tight jeans and a gray V-neck T-shirt that showed off a tan triangle of smooth skin. He talked with a tall iced tea in one hand, condensation dripping off the bottom of the glass. Ben knew they were a terrible match, but Jeff was so good look-ing, with his blond hair and blue eyes, and there was something flattering about having Jeff's attention.

Leaving the hall of doors behind them, they continued onward. The dimly lit hallway began to twist and turn as they entered a maze. The light grew darker and darker until it was impossible to see. Ben felt his way along the walls, but began to hesitate, un-sure if he wanted to press on any farther.

"Are we going the right way?" he asked. "I think we're getting lost."

"Keep talking," Albert said from somewhere behind. "I'll follow the sound of your voice."

Ben continued through the dark, feelingly.

"So, yeah, with Jeff, I didn't know what I was doing, but I thought maybe I could win him over with some sort of awkward charm." Ben's voice echoed off the narrow passageway, and the high pitch of his voice surprised him. "We talked about growing up in Cleveland. I showed him pictures on my phone of my parents." It was so embarrassing; Ben felt himself blush in the darkness. "And I showed him my lucky twenty-sided die."

"You did what?"

Albert's hand grabbed onto Ben's shoulder.

They came to a dead end and had to maneuver around each other to make their way back to the last fork in the hall.

"Do you think that's bad?" Ben asked. As he squeezed past Albert their noses almost brushed together. "I had found that die when I moved back into the basement. It seemed fortuitous, like a good omen. I figured it couldn't be a coincidence that my old lucky die reappeared, and at the same time, I got set up with this hot guy. So, I pulled it out and showed it to him. I didn't go into all the details and do it like, 'Here's my magic die. I'm going to cast a spell on you.' I told him it was a good-luck charm and put it on the table between us while we ate. Twenty side up, of course."

"Of course." Albert was keeping a hand against Ben's back now so they wouldn't be separated in the dark as they turned left and right and left again. "I don't know about Jeff, but if some guy showed *me* his twenty-sided die on the first date, I'd take him straight home to bed."

A jet of air hit Ben in the face as they turned a sharp corner and he nearly jumped out of his windbreaker in fright. Albert laughed behind him.

The passage ahead became a dimly lit tunnel with curved walls. They were almost through the maze. But Ben realized as they approached that the tunnel was rotating. He took one step into it and slipped. Albert fell too and landed on top of him. Their bodies slid and rolled, up and down the sides of the tunnel. Ben caught another whiff of Albert's detergent as they climbed to their feet, laughing.

Then they were out of the funhouse and back onto the midway. The music and the smells returned. The wind picked up Ben's collar again, and Albert pulled up the fur-trimmed hood on his jacket.

Before they could decide on what to do next, Albert's phone began buzzing in his pocket. "Speak of the devil. Maybe he's finally here." Albert covered one ear against the noise and stepped aside to answer, but Ben couldn't help but overhear.

"What do you mean you haven't left yet? I thought you were on your way . . . You should have left when you said you did." The conversation decayed into a series of yeahs and okays before Albert said goodbye. "Sorry about that." Albert slipped his phone into his pocket. "Jeff's not going to make it after all."

"Is everything alright?" Ben asked, hoping that everything was terrible.

"Yeah, of course." But Albert's face betrayed him. Everything was terrible and Ben felt bad for wishing it.

Albert suggested they head toward the Ferris wheel and then asked, "So, what happened next?"

"Are you sure you wanna hear this? It's getting pretty awkward."

"I haven't heard any of the good stuff yet."

"Alright," Ben said. "So, we finished dinner, and then after some more chitchat, Jeff asked, 'Do you wanna invite me back to your place?' And of course, I wanted to, but I'd just moved into my parents' basement."

"You turned him down?" Albert looked shocked.

"I told him I'd just got a new place and it was a mess, which was all true. He said there was something going on with his roommates and we couldn't go over there, so we made out in the park for a little bit." The sad thing was, while Ben could remember everything else about the night, he could not remember their make-out session in any detail.

"Wow," Albert said. "He is probably still wondering how he got turned down by a guy who brought his twenty-sided die on the date."

"It's a good luck charm," Ben said. "And I didn't turn him down. Plus, I tried to make it up to him the very next day. I went to the record store and told him what a good time I'd had."

"The next day?"

"Yeah, I know," Ben said, embarrassed. "It made sense at the time. Now, I see what a weirdo I was, but in the moment, doing those things, it was hard to make a sane decision."

"How do you feel now? About Jeff I mean."

"I liked him, and I'd invested all this time and energy into getting to know him and pursuing him. So, for a while, I was really upset." As in don't-leave-the-basement-for-three-months upset. "But now?" Ben shrugged.

Thinking about Jeff was like creeping into a cave where he had known a monster lived and finding the place completely empty. If he looked closely he could find some remnants of the beast, and if he waited in that place, the creature might come back. But why wait around?

"After that, I started going to the record store to sell him the old records I found. I don't know why, but I really wanted to impress him. I was so desperate for some kind of affirmation from him that I would search and search for more and more obscure records. I must have looked so weird."

"He has that power. His charisma score is off the charts."

"How do you deal with it?"

Albert looked off into the distance, toward the Ferris wheel. "Every chance you get you knock him down a few pegs and remind him he's not so perfect."

"That's way too much work. I'm too lazy for that."

Albert laughed. "You're not lazy. You're smart."

"I don't know why I was so into him."

"Because he's cute, and he led you on."

"It's such a depressing mess. I don't know why I let myself fall into these fantasies." They walked past a group of women who were dancing with burning hoops while a bare-chested man breathed fire and juggled flaming torches. They stopped and watched for a moment.

Ben said, "There's something flattering about someone liking you, even if it's all in your head. You don't want the fantasy to end, even if it's bad for you and it's killing your soul to be in this unrequited relationship. You can't help but torture yourself because even the idea of being liked by someone feels so good. It really is a sickness." He couldn't help but laugh at the thought.

"Don't be so dramatic." Albert put his hand on Ben's shoulder. "You're only human. Besides, that's all in the past. You're not like that anymore, right? You learn and you move on."

"Totally," Ben said, but he wasn't sure Albert heard the sarcasm in his voice.

The air was colder along the shore, and Ben began to shiver. They made their way to the Ferris wheel, which sat close to the water. They handed over their tickets and climbed inside their swaying carriage.

"You're not afraid of heights, are you?" Albert asked as the Ferris wheel turned and raised them higher. The carnival shrunk beneath their feet.

Ben looked across Lake Erie as the sun sank into the west. The sky had pinkened. Gulls soared above the waves. The carriage crested the top of the Ferris wheel and stopped. It rocked back and forth as down below another couple, a man and a woman, was climbing on. Ben watched through the grate in the flooring. The woman was laughing; the man pressed his hand against the small of her back, guiding her.

Young love.

Albert was gazing across the water. His eyes were aglow. The waning light softened his cheeks and his unshaven jaw. He had never looked more handsome.

This would be the perfect moment for a kiss.

Slowly the Ferris wheel began moving, dipping toward the midway before it would rise up again, and Ben didn't know if he could bear returning to the top.

valerie and polly

Valerie was late to Polly's party, but plenty of people were still hanging around in the front yard smoking and chatting as things were winding down. Polly lived in a house off Coventry Road, with three other girls: Loren, Natalie, and Stacy. They were all vegetarian, and earth conscious, and drank a lot of tea. As Valerie made her way inside, she recognized a few people from the table of vampires at the diner. They didn't seem to notice or recognize her, and she didn't say anything to them as they passed by on their way out the door. But she thought it was an odd coincidence that they would be at Polly's party.

"Hey Valerie, Polly's up in her room." Loren interrupted Valerie's thoughts before she could dwell on the vampires too long.

Polly's bedroom, in the front of the house, had high ceilings and lavender walls that Polly painted herself. Large bay windows with long white curtains overlooked the street. Polly had put up a hammock in the windows. Valerie climbed in and warmed up under the blankets while Polly worked on a project. Through the windows, Valerie could see the vampires loitering outside and chatting with people.

"Did you know there were vampires at your party?" she asked.

Polly laughed. "I did not know, because vampires don't exist. And it wasn't exclusively my party, so . . ." Polly shrugged.

Polly's room had two workstations, one for jewelry and one for felt animals. She sold them all at craft fairs around Cleveland

and in her own shop on Etsy called Heroes in Love. She sold birdhouses too, which she painted and decorated, but she hadn't made any of those in a while. The scene was trending away from birdhouses, she told Valerie, which was too bad because her birdhouses were awesome. She'd given Valerie one for her birthday, and it was pretty sweet. Polly had what she called "decoupaged" the outside with panels from old issues of *Justice League*, and inside there were tiny figures of Superman, Batman, and Wonder Woman.

"How's a bird supposed to live in there?" Valerie had asked.

"It's for decoration, you dummy."

But Valerie was only joking with her, and Polly knew that and laughed.

As she worked at her jewelry desk, Polly filled Valerie in on what happened at the party before she arrived. Polly got into an argument with some guy because he thought women wrote boring comics. And Natalie got mad because guys were going out back and pissing in the compost pile instead of waiting in line to use the bathroom.

"You know, it was drunk people arguing with other drunk people," Polly said.

"And you don't care about the vampires?" Valerie reached over and picked up Polly's ukulele from where it sat atop a stack of books and magazines.

"I'm totally open to the idea that people are into all kinds of different things, if that's what you mean."

"I don't know, it just bothers me," Valerie said. "That night at the diner. The way they all glared at me. But I get it. You can let people be. You're cool like that."

"Maybe you shouldn't have made them mad? Or maybe you should make it up to them somehow?"

Valerie didn't reply. She strummed the ukulele while Polly soldered something together. Although Valerie had no idea how to play, she could get some nice sounds out if she gently stroked the strings.

"You know I'm a bard," she said. And she wasn't trying to sound suave or anything, but somehow her voice was smoother and deeper, maybe due to the musical accompaniment.

Polly put down her whatever-it-was she was making and climbed carefully onto the hammock. "So, you travel from town to town, singing for your supper?"

"And killing orcs." Polly was sitting on her lap so Valerie had to push out the words.

There was something about being in Polly's room, the air, her presence—Valerie couldn't put a name on it—but it felt comfortable, placid and tranquil, as if Valerie really had crossed the world and come to a place where she could settle in and spend some time.

Polly leaned over, her long hair falling onto Valerie's face, and then they were kissing and there was a hunger in it. Valerie pulled Polly in with a force that made her oomph and giggle. But Valerie was the surprised one.

Surprised when Polly took her by the hand and led her from the hammock to the bed.

"I wanna show you something." Polly opened a small box beside her bed and pulled out a hard, green tentacle. It was warped and twisted and made from a shiny resin. There were little, beaded suction marks along the bottom. "I made it," she said. "It's a kind of dildo. Do you wanna try it?"

"Hell no," Valerie said. "I'm not putting that in me."

"I meant on me, you dummy."

The tentacle was smooth and shiny, covered in some sort of varnish.

"Don't worry," Polly said. "It's safe. I'll show you what to do." She began kissing the side of Valerie's neck, and her hands slid up Valerie's T-shirt. Valerie fell back onto the pillows, and with the tentacle she gently traced the outline of Polly's breasts.

After sex, Polly laid her head on Valerie's stomach, and Valerie drove her nose down to Polly's scalp and breathed her in.

"What took you so long tonight?" Polly asked.

"To cum?"

Polly laughed.

But Valerie knew that wasn't what she meant. And she apologized for not coming around sooner. Truth was, it was all still a lot to process. The hanging out, the occasional sex. But Valerie couldn't say all that. Instead she said, "You know me, I'm a dumb ass."

the grimoire of erotic deeds

Ben spent the early part of Thursday trying not to think about the kiss-in they were planning for that night. He spent the afternoon wandering thrift stores but was unsuccessful in both finding something worth auctioning and in taking his mind off the night's upcoming event. He drove aimlessly for twenty minutes, unsure of where to go or what to do with himself before he finally thought to call Albert and invite himself over. He'd never been to Albert's place, and this seemed like as good a time as any.

Albert opened his front door, and the first thing he asked Ben was, "Are you ready for the big night, or what?" He was dressed in his black jeans, red Converse, and a black T-shirt with the name of some band across the front in an indecipherable font. "I mean, not just the kiss-in, but Bjorndar is back to life!"

"Oh, yeah, totally. How about you?" Ben feigned calm and shuffled inside.

"I mean, it's all I've been thinking about. Work was dragging on. I couldn't wait to get out." Albert led Ben through the living room into the kitchen, where the lights were on. Two overly muscled men in tank tops and spandex shorts sat at the table drinking protein shakes.

Albert introduced them as his roommates, Lou and Nino, and they greeted Ben with a hardy "What's up?" and pistoning handshakes. Then Nino said to Albert, "*Your* roommates? You forget whose house this is?"

"He's *our* roommate," Lou said with a big grin.

"They're brothers," Albert explained. "They bought this house from their mom."

"Are you guys professional bodybuilders or something?"

"Check it out." Lou nodded toward the living room.

Ben followed Albert as he turned on the living room lights. The walls were papered in yellow, with a pattern at least three decades out of style. One wall held a display case filled with trophies and ribbons. Another was filled with photos of the two brothers, flexing and posing, their bodies smooth, tan, and oiled.

"Oh god," Ben said, a realization crossing his face. "Did they convince you to shave your chest?"

Albert laughed, embarrassed. "You noticed? No, that was all Jeff's idea."

Ben nodded. Of course. Ben motioned toward the photos. "They make any money doing this?"

"Not yet, they're not actually professionals."

"Maybe someday," Lou said, as he and Nino stepped up behind Albert.

"Maybe someday we'll have our own gym and train skinny-minis like this guy how to put on some muscle." Nino gave Albert's bicep a squeeze.

"Get you a body like this," Lou said, flexing, his shirt straining against his chest.

"This is the most homoerotic house I've ever been in," Ben said.

Albert and the brothers laughed, and Albert explained, "Ben's the guy I took to the metal show."

"Oh shit, that was you?"

"He's talked about that all week," Lou said.

Albert grabbed two beers from the fridge and, giving one to Ben, invited Ben to check out his room upstairs.

"Sure," Ben said. "Show me around."

They climbed the carpeted stairs, and the wall opposite the

thick wooden handrail was filled with framed photos of Nino and Lou with their family. The brothers as boys, posing with their parents, and then older dressed in tuxedos for homecoming and prom, girlfriends on their arms in sparkly dresses. It was all so normal, and yet so unfamiliar.

Albert's room was at the top of the stairs. He didn't have much in the way of furniture, just two bookshelves, one of which he'd picked up off a street corner. He didn't even have a proper bed, simply a futon on the ground. An orange milk crate served as a nightstand. The blue desk lamp that sat on top he'd had since he was a kid, he explained to Ben. He'd brought the lamp and the crate from Detroit because he didn't want to start completely over from scratch.

"And milk crates of that quality are really hard to find in Cleveland," Ben said, sipping from his beer.

A coffee stand, raised under all four legs by more milk crates until it was nearly chest high, held Albert's record player and stereo. A pair of speakers sat on the floor nearby, with a pair of bulky headphones on top.

But most of the space was taken up by Albert's record collection. In the center of the room, in boxes still unpacked. Albert owned over a thousand records.

There were ten boxes in total, stacked three deep and three wide, with a final box on the top. He'd written on the sides A–D, E–H, I–L, and so on, all the way through the alphabet. The boxes were draped in black T-shirts and black jeans, because Albert wasn't able to access his closet very easily, and so he threw his clothes over the boxes every night.

"There used to be more boxes," Albert said. "But as you can see, I've slowly been unpacking them and moving the records over to my bookshelves."

"Are you doing that as you listen to them?" Ben asked, eyeing the mound of records and clothes.

"Sometimes, but not really, because I've already downloaded all of them to my laptop and phone. I don't really listen to most of them on vinyl anymore, although there is a certain quality that can only be captured by the record player."

"Why do you still keep them all?" But before Albert could speak, the answer came to Ben. "Oh my god, we're both hoarders."

They laughed at that, and Albert said, "Here, have a seat on the bed and I'll play you some stuff."

"The bed," Ben said, making air quotes with his fingers and looking at the futon with disdain.

"What? That's a bed. Don't mock where I sleep."

While Albert flipped through the records, Ben took a look at the bookshelves. They weren't entirely taken up by records. The middle shelf was filled with painted metal miniatures, knights and orcs, like the ones in the back room at Readmore, although Albert dusted his more often. In the center was a paladin with a pole arm—Godson Flamebender—and Albert had adjusted the pole arm so it was impaling an unpainted barbarian from behind.

On another shelf, leaning against the narrow record spines, were photos from the Samuraiah Carey show, one with Ben and Albert posing with the band, and one of Ben wearing the goat mask.

"You actually printed these?"

"Of course! No one is going to believe we met them."

"No one has ever even heard of them."

Albert scoffed. "Anyone who's cool has."

"What does Jeff think?" Ben asked.

"He thinks we're nuts. Have a seat already. I don't like you poking around."

"What is it with that guy?" Ben sat on the edge of Albert's futon as Albert put a record on the stereo. No sound came from the speakers though.

"After work I have to use these," Albert said, picking up the headphones. He pressed one side to his ear and then offered them to Ben. Furious death metal chugged out.

Ben took the headphones, tentatively at first, and then pressed one side to his ear. Albert smiled, watching, and sat down near the head of the futon. He stretched out his long legs and pressed his feet against a record box.

Ben and Albert sat, shoulder to shoulder, leg to leg, and listened together, sharing the headphones, nodding in unison to the rhythm. Occasionally, Albert would play air drums and knock back a swallow from his beer.

"Can I read the lyrics?" Ben asked. "This sounds like high Elvish."

"I think it's Norwegian," Albert said with a laugh. He jumped up and handed Ben the record sleeve.

"Is this what you and Jeff do?"

"Not quite. Usually it's Jeff playing music for me."

Ben finished his beer, and when he couldn't find a place to put the bottle, Albert took it from him and put it on the milk-crate-nightstand.

"You know," Ben said, taking his ear off the headphones and leaning back. "This is kind of awkward, sitting here like this in your bedroom."

Albert pulled away. "What do you mean?"

"It's just, I don't know." Ben looked around, imagining Albert and Jeff in the room.

"Do you wanna go back to the kitchen?"

"Does Jeff really come over that often?"

"I mean, he comes over every night."

"Yeah, I should go," Ben said. "I still gotta get ready for the game, and it's gonna be a long night."

"Hold on, I'll come with you," Albert said. "Let me just grab my stuff."

Ben waited as Albert quickly threw on his faded black hoodie. Albert tossed his handbooks and dice into his black backpack. He plucked Flamebender off the shelf, wrapped him in a crumpled tissue, and placed him in the pocket of his hoodie.

Passing the photos on the wall as he climbed down the stairs, Ben somehow felt even more jealous the second time around.

They walked out the front door together, and maybe the beer had loosened him up, but Ben paused on the porch. The light above the door was collecting moths.

"You know," Ben said, "I might play music for you, bad eighties music, but I would never ask you to shave your chest."

Albert didn't seem to know how to respond for a moment, but then he smiled.

"Let's get to the game," he said, as they walked down the front steps. "Aren't you excited Bjorndar is back to life? I mean, I am."

• • •

As Ben settled into his seat in the back room of Readmore, Mooneyham went over the plans for the kiss-in.

"We need to be there by midnight, so we'd better wrap up and leave here at eleven thirty."

"I wish we'd planned this better," Celeste said, a concerned look on her face.

"I sent out some invites," Mooneyham said. "What more is there to do?"

"And you didn't tell the bar," Celeste said.

"It has to be a surprise," Mooneyham said.

Huey nodded his head in agreement. "It's not going to work if they know we're coming. They might shut us down before we start."

"Then we'll kiss on the sidewalk and take up the street," Albert said.

"Who's we?" asked Ben. "We're like, six people. We can't take up the sidewalk."

"Other folks are going to show up," Albert said. "I invited people too. This is exactly the kind of thing that gets people amped up."

"It's not getting me amped up," Ben said.

"'Cause you're chicken shit," Mooneyham said.

"No, it's just that—"

"We know all about it," Mooneyham said. "No one's making you go. It takes balls to stand up to people, I get it. If you're not up for that then stay home and be a bitch."

Ben sat back and said nothing. There was no point in arguing with Mooneyham when he was in a mood like this.

"The worst that can happen is they kick us out," Huey said.

"I can think of worse," Celeste said. "But that's the most likely."

Ben was still not sure if he was going to go or not, but Albert said, "Come on, you have to."

"I don't know," Ben said. "Plus Jeff will be there."

"So what? You're over him. You said so yourself the other night."

But saying it and actually being in the same bar with Jeff, let alone watching Jeff kiss Albert, were two completely different things.

Valerie placed a large plate of green cookies on the table. They were oddly shaped and covered with green icing and sprinkles.

"Are these tentacles?" Albert asked as he took one.

"They're from Polly," Valerie said.

"What are you kinky kids getting up to?" Mooneyham asked as he took a bite, but Valerie just smiled.

• • •

At the smithy of Hammervale, steam rose from the smelting pools, and flames roared in the furnaces as apprentice smiths pounded steel into swords and armor while Bjorndar and the others watched entranced.

"You have your plan," Torgar, son of Torget, said gravely. "Enter the Cod and Piece from the secret passage in the basement of the curio shop and remove the monsters that have taken over."

"Can we call for you if we need reinforcements?" Theegh asked.

"You can, but I don't know how much help I'll be able to give."

"We've got this," Gunther said, slinging his great axe upon his back. "Don't worry."

With that, Torgar led them from the smithy, through the backstreets of Hammervale, until they arrived at a narrow alley behind the curio shop.

"That's the door there," Torgar said. "Knock twice three times and Mr. Gravehaus will let you in. He's an upstanding guy. You can trust him. He's one of us."

Torgar wished them luck and returned to the smithy.

Flamebender strode up to the door and knocked twice three times. The door opened a crack, and a short man with a bald head and a large mustache peered at them through thick glasses and then, with a nod of approval, motioned them inside.

"Welcome to Gravehaus Curios and Oddities. How can I help you?"

"Torgar, son of Torget, sent us," Flamebender said.

"Of course." Gravehaus pulled on his mustache as he spoke. "I knew his father very well. We worked together quite often on very special commissions for very particular customers."

Low burning candles in hanging glass lanterns cloaked the shop in flickering light. Glass cabinets with velvet-lined shelves displayed a wide variety of objects: crystal balls, crystal cubes, crystal skulls, jars of insects and spiders, jars of lubricants, and wands of various sizes, some short and thick, some long and curved, many ribbed, and most with bulbous tips.

"What kind of curio shop is this?" Bjorndar asked, peering into a cabinet of clamps and chains.

"Oh, the best kind," Gravehaus said. "Do have a look around, and tell me if anything catches your fancy."

There were whips, leather masks, finely woven silk ropes, and devices of indeterminate purpose for which it was difficult to discern whether they were meant to be used for pleasure or pain. There were books on history with titles such as *101 Positions of Prince Al'Khazar* and *The Forgotten Submissions of Ancient Massalonia*. There were high-heeled shoes that would make any man look like a woman, and a top hat that would make any woman look like a man.

"Do these shoes come in a size eight?" Marilyn asked.

"Let me check for you," Gravehaus said, swiftly moving behind the counter.

"Unfortunately, time is not on our side," Flamebender said. "We'd like to see your basement."

Gravehaus's eyes flickered with excitement. "Yes, of course. My most precious objects are in the basement."

"I'm sure they are," Gunter said.

Gravehaus pulled aside a heavy red curtain behind the glass counter and revealed a back room. Once they were all inside, Gravehaus rolled up the carpet and opened a trap door in the floor. A wooden ladder led down into the darkness. The air smelled damp and moldy, with a hint of something else that Flamebender was able to identify with a perception check of twenty-eight.

"It's man sweat," he said.

"Allow me to go first and to light the lamps." Gravehaus climbed down the ladder, and soon warm light filled the room beneath their feet.

"Come down," Gravehaus said. "It's perfectly safe."

The large underground room was filled with low leather benches. Several iron maidens leaned against the walls. Their open doors revealed that the maidens were empty and not lined with rows of spikes, but with rows of ribbed wooden pegs.

"I thought I'd never have a use for these things," Gravehaus said. "But what do you know?"

Whips and tongs and wooden paddles rested in racks against the walls, and a complicated system of ropes and slings and harnesses hung from the ceiling. Nearby sat a machine with gears and cranks and bellows and pumps. Limp hoses with curious nozzles hung from it like the arms of a dead squid.

"Never mind these things," Gravehaus said. "For now . . ." He walked toward a large wooden wardrobe sitting against the far wall and, opening it, pushed aside the leather cat suits and feather boas. The back panel opened with a click onto a dark and dusty passageway. The air was still and stale, but there were footprints in the dust.

"Whistletooth and I used this passage up until a few days ago when he disappeared. No one has been in here since, but I suspect it's only a matter of time until the fiends who have taken over the Cod and Piece find out about it." Gravehaus must have noticed the look of surprise on their faces because he added, "Yes, it's true. I know your plan. We can speak freely down here."

"Torgar was right then," Flamebender said. "You are one of us."

"I have been 'one of us' longer than you've been alive. Now, please bring my friend safely out of there."

Gravehaus wished them luck and then closed the secret door of the wardrobe behind them. They felt their way along the dark passage until they came to a small round door. Bjorndar pushed it open and stepped into a large, empty barrel. They carefully opened the lid and climbed out. They were in the wine cellar of the Cod and Piece.

Bjorndar moved silently to the thick cellar door and listened for noise on the other side.

"I don't hear anything," he said and slowly opened the door.

In the small office of the Cod and Piece, Whistletooth, cut and bruised, sat slumped over, tied in a chair. Quickly, Bjorndar motioned everyone to follow him, and he ran to Whistletooth's side.

Flamebender placed a gentle hand onto Whistletooth's forehead and whispered a prayer. The old man began to stir. He opened his eyes and said, "I knew you would come. I've been tied to this chair for days. The satyrs barged into the bar soon after you left, and they brought a gang of monstrous creatures with them, goblins, orcs, and I don't even know what. They tied me up and tortured me, seemingly for fun. They're planning an orgy or some kind of a magic ceremony. You've got to stop them."

The office was in disarray. The satyrs had overturned the desk and tables. Documents and papers covered the floor.

"Hold on. I don't buy all this," Gunther said. "It's too easy. It feels like a setup. How do we know he's really Whistletooth?"

"I don't detect anything magical in the room," Bjorndar said. "If he were an illusion or magically disguised, I would know."

"Why would they keep him alive?" Gunther asked. "Am I the only one who finds that strange? We come in here and he's tied to a chair, all beaten up. It's like something out of a bad action movie."

"I've no idea what an action movie is," Flamebender said.

"Me either," said Bjorndar.

"Whatever," Gunther said. "You know what I mean. This whole setup is suspicious. Something is off."

"You're right. Wasn't there a dog?" Theegh asked Whistletooth. "I could have sworn you had a guard dog."

"Oh, yes, poor old Scraps McGee. I won't horrify you boys with what they did to him. Let's assume he's in a better place now."

"Fucking monsters," Theegh said. "They'll pay."

"Maybe they kept Whistletooth alive because they have a diabolical plan for him," Bjorndar said. "Some future purpose that has yet to come about."

"Exactly," Gunther said. "Maybe that future purpose is now.

Maybe they left him here knowing we'd find him and that he'd tell us about the orgy so that we would go stumbling into a trap."

"And maybe you're overthinking things a bit," Whistletooth said. "Regardless, there isn't time to stand here and debate."

As Whistletooth spoke, they could hear chanting and moaning coming through the thin walls.

"We need to act now," Flamebender said, "while they're distracted by the ceremony. Let's send Whistletooth back to Gravehaus and take care of this orgy."

Marilyn untied Whistletooth, who stumbled toward the secret tunnel to the curio shop. "Good luck," he said as he climbed into the barrel. "The Cod and Piece is counting on you."

Quickly, and as quietly as possible, Bjorndar, Theegh, Gunther, Marilyn, and Flamebender slipped out from the back room and crouched behind the bar.

The Cod and Piece looked more like a place of worship than a tavern. An altar with an effigy of a many-tentacled monster sat atop the stage where drag queens once performed. The tables and chairs leaned against the walls, and the floor was a sea of naked bodies, rising and falling in rhythm. Currents of energy wafted off the bodies, swirled in the thick air, and converged upon a large open tome that rested atop a wooden pedestal in the center of the room. A hooded priest in a black robe read aloud from the book in a deep, abyssal tongue.

"What kind of magic is this?" Bjorndar asked.

"Sexomancy," Flamebender said.

"No, it can't be." Bjorndar watched the copulating bodies in awe. "No one has practiced sexomancy in hundreds of years. It's been outlawed for centuries."

"What's sexomancy?" Marilyn asked. "It sounds hot."

"Sexomancers use the energy of sex to power their spells. You can see how much energy is flowing into that book. This orgy is powering something big."

"They're trying to generate enough energy to summon the Sleeping God," Flamebender said. "That has to be their plan; it's the only thing they have ever focused on."

"Seems easy enough to disrupt," Bjorndar said. "All we have to do is steal the book."

"We might be able to do more than that," Flamebender said. "All those people having sex are straight."

"I'm not sure they're people," Gunther said as he peered over the bar. There were glimpses of green skin, gray fur, and blue scales, not to mention fangs and claws.

"Regardless, I only see straight fucking going on. That means, if we can get out there and generate some homosexual energy we might be able to counter this spell."

"No way," Bjorndar said. "You want us to join the orgy? It's too dangerous. We'll have to strip and leave our weapons behind."

"I'll do it," Marilyn said. "I'll get out there and do some sexomancy."

"I'll go too." Gunther laid down his axe and began to strip.

"That leaves us," Flamebender said to Bjorndar.

"What about me?" Theegh asked. "I'm not gonna go out there and gay it up."

"Not even a little?" Marilyn asked. "Maybe kissing a boy a little bit?"

"Dude, come on," Theegh said. "I'm straight."

"Then you've got the most dangerous job of all," Gunther said. "Steal the book."

"Oh man." Theegh peered over the bar at the book, glowing with magical energy. "You know what? I can do it. I'll need a way over there, and some way to take out the priest."

"Once you're in position, I'll cast a spell of darkness," Bjorndar said. "That should help you escape, if you can remember where the front door is."

"What if the priest grabs him?" Marilyn asked. "Maybe we should cast a grease spell on him so he can slip way."

"By the time he gets to the middle of that crowd he's gonna be so covered with lube it won't matter," Gunther said.

"Oh god." Theegh looked mortified. "You're probably right."

"All right then." Flamebender unclasped his breastplate. "Let's set this plan in action."

. . .

Ben rocked back in his chair. "I have to say, I've never considered what Bjorndar looks like naked."

"Bullshit," Mooneyham said. "Bjorndar's from the nudist colony, and you've never imagined him naked? Yeah, right. Who here hasn't jerked off while thinking about their character?"

Valerie raised her hand.

"Do people really do that?" Huey asked.

"All I'll say is that Flamebender is a fucking stud," Albert said. "He's got rock-hard pecks and an eight-pack. He wears that heavy armor around all the time, you know? That's like a nonstop workout. Plus he has a charisma score of twenty-two."

"I guess Bjorndar is good looking," Ben said. "He has a charisma score of twelve. That's above average. He's not amazing, but he's not ugly."

"Theegh's got a twenty charisma," Valerie said. "But then again, bards are charismatic, so I'm poppin' my collar."

"You didn't tell me charisma meant you are ugly or not." Huey turned to Mooneyham, looking distraught.

"Wizards don't need charisma. We put all her extra points in intelligence."

"But she's only got an eight charisma now? She's gotta be so ugly."

"Eight is average."

"Average is ugly," Huey said. "What's Gunther's then?"

"Ten."

"Oh my god, no. This cannot be happening. Marilyn is uglier than your bearded dwarf? I cannot take it. This game is so stupid. Why didn't you tell me about charisma?"

"I thought you knew. You read the core rule book."

"Oh god, the core rule book. Have you tried to read it? I mostly looked at the pictures. You were supposed to help me. Marilyn is the ugliest person at the whole table."

"Mechanically it doesn't make a difference if she's pretty or not," Celeste said.

"Mechanically whatever," Huey said. "I always picture her a certain way, and now I have to imagine that she's ugly."

"Average," Mooneyham said.

"Then here's what we'll do," Celeste said calmly. She took Marilyn's character sheet from Huey. "Instead of a wizard, we'll make her a sorceress; they're charisma-based casters instead of intelligence. We'll swap your stats around, so you'll have a high charisma but a low intelligence."

"Sounds about right," Mooneyham said, and Huey elbowed him in the side.

"I don't care as long as I'm beautiful," Huey said.

Once Marilyn's character sheet was adjusted Huey seemed happier, and with that out of the way, Ben asked, "So, how do we fake this orgy thing? I mean, what skills do we use? Bjorndar has a high acrobatics score."

"You should all make bluff checks," Celeste said, "because you're trying to fool the other members of the orgy."

"That sucks," Ben said as he looked over his character sheet. "I have a terrible bluff score. Can I use sleight of hand instead?"

"No, that's for pickpocketing."

"How about handle animal? Humans are animals, right?"

A murmur of objections arose around the table, but Celeste said, "I'll allow it."

• • •

Once they were naked, Marilyn, Gunther, and Theegh crawled into the orgy followed by Bjorndar and Flamebender, who was reluctant to leave his pole arm behind.

Bjorndar led Flamebender into the orgy and said, "Sit. Now, roll over. Good boy."

Bjorndar rubbed Flamebender's belly.

"Is this turning anyone on?" Flamebender asked.

Deeper in the crowd, Gunther and Marilyn were heavily engaged in kissing and groping; their naked bodies shimmered with pink energy.

"It's the best I can do," Bjorndar said.

"Let me try." Flamebender sat up and planted a kiss on Bjorndar's lips. "Rolled a twenty-eight on my bluff check."

"I believe it," Bjorndar said.

Waves of pink energy began to rise from Bjorndar and Flamebender and swirl with the silver energy already flowing toward the book. The pedestal under the book began to shake. The priest grabbed it with both hands but could not stop the shaking, with so much energy flowing into the pages.

As they continued to make out, Gunther and Marilyn began groping the bodies around them. Two orc women began making out, and then two minotaurs began stroking each other's horns and kissing.

"It's working," Gunther said. "We're having an effect."

The priest pushed through the crowd, pulling couples apart as he went.

Theegh, oily and sweaty, as expected, took the opportunity to step up to the pedestal. "Now," he yelled and grabbed the book.

Bjorndar spoke and all the lights were extinguished. Immediately, everything went dark, except for the book, which was glowing with magical energy, even while shut.

"Shit!" Theegh tucked the book under his arm and ran, but the floor was too crowded and he stumbled to the ground.

"Don't let him escape!" yelled the priest.

In the darkness, Bjorndar and Flamebender crawled through groping hands and unknown body parts. Once behind the bar, they scrambled into their armor.

"This is bad," Flamebender said, strapping on the Rammaster.

Bjorndar pulled on his pants and peeked over the bar. Theegh, illuminated by the book, was the only thing that could be seen, but the sounds of fighting were everywhere. And Theegh was barely hanging onto the book as he struggled to make his way through the crowd to the front door.

Then, the front door burst open and light filled the tavern again as the town guard rushed in, accompanied by Torgar, Gravehaus, and Whistletooth.

"Well done," Torgar said. "Operation Rear Entry was a success."

• • •

"Sorry," Celeste said. "I'm sure you guys could have handled that situation on your own, but it's almost eleven thirty. We need to wrap it up."

"Oh, man," Valerie said. "I was about to teleport out of there."

"You were?" Celeste looked surprised.

"Yeah, I have a scroll of teleport. I was gonna read it."

"But you're naked," Celeste said.

"It's in my bag. I was gonna ask one of you guys behind the bar to throw it to me."

"In the dark?" Ben asked.

"Sure," Valerie said. "You could have done it with your lucky d20. You always roll high."

"So, you've had a scroll of teleportation in your bag this whole time?" Mooneyham asked. "We could have used that to get out of the city of the dead, you idiot."

"I just remembered it," Valerie said.

"Anyway." Celeste folded up her screen. "Torgar and the town guard clean the place out, with your help. And thanks to Theegh you recover the magic tome."

"What's it do?" Ben asked.

"You'll have to wait for next week," Celeste said with a sly smile. "But the cover reads *Grimoire of Erotic Deeds*."

"And the priest?" Albert asked.

"Oddly, the priest disappeared in all of the confusion."

"How convenient."

Ben packed up his books and dice and began to feel a flutter of anticipation for the kiss-in. Albert must have felt it too because he turned to Ben and said, "Now we get to do it all over again. The real Operation Rear Entry begins now."

But will we still be faking it? Ben wondered.

welcome to midnight

"This is so not fair," Valerie said as she paced on the curb outside of O'Malley's. The night air was chilly, and her blue backpack dug into her shoulders. Polly stood with her arms folded across her chest.

A huge crowd had gathered for the kiss-in, and there was an anxious energy crackling in the air. Valerie had never seen a crowd like it on Coventry in all her eighteen years. Not even when the Cavs made it to the playoffs and all of Cleveland had LeBron James fever.

Every once in a while a cheer would rise up from inside the bar, and Valerie would feel a knot of envy in her gut. It sucked that she and Polly had to hang out on the sidewalk while the rest of the role playing club went inside. This was her kiss-in too.

O'Malley's wasn't some fancy nightclub; it was a local bar. But tonight, it looked like the most happening place in the world with so many people passing in and out. The front doors of the bar were open, and no one was checking IDs.

"Fuck it." Valerie grabbed Polly's hand and pulled her into the crowd of men pushing at a shuffling pace to get into the bar.

Polly said, "We're not twenty-one."

"Just act normal."

Valerie kept her head down in case someone thought she looked too young. She bumped shoulders with several people who were on their way out, and her backpack was jostled around, but she held tightly onto Polly's hand and soon they were through the doors.

O'Malley's was bigger on the inside than Valerie expected, and darker, filled with brass and ferns and antique road signs that said weird things like: *Killarney 15km, and Sláinte!* A long wooden bar took up the entire right wall, but there was no way to get close to it with the crowd so tightly pressed together. Bartenders in white button-down shirts rushed back and forth, looking overwhelmed. Valerie was thankful she didn't have their job.

"What if we get caught?" Polly asked. But Valerie could tell by her voice that she wasn't scared. She was thrilled. Valerie wanted to grab her and kiss her right then, but it wasn't midnight yet, and she should wait. Valerie pulled Polly by the hand toward the back wall, as far from the front door as possible. They passed Mooneyham and Huey, standing at the bar talking with some guy in a shirt and tie, but Valerie looked away. If she didn't see them, they wouldn't see her.

Once they reached the jukebox in the back corner, Valerie relaxed. They were in. She slid her backpack off and dropped it to the floor. The excited chatter that filled the air was so loud Valerie could barely hear the music, even standing next to the jukebox. Some of the crowd she recognized as customers at Readmore, and others she had seen on Coventry Road. Kyle and Miya were near the windows under the Guinness sign. She waved at them, but they didn't notice, which was too bad because Kyle would totally think it was cool that she and Polly had sneaked in. Celeste was up front, pressed against the pinball machine. In the middle of the mob, Ben was nervously looking around, and Albert was checking his watch.

"How long do we have?" Valerie asked Polly.

"Fifteen minutes."

The place was too noisy to have a conversation and too crowded to walk around, so Valerie leaned against the jukebox and pulled Polly into her. A motley crew of glasses and bottles stood abandoned on top of the machine, some nearly half full. Valerie took the tallest, fullest one, sniffed it, and then tossed it back.

"Gross." Polly stuck out her tongue.

"The alcohol kills all the germs." Valerie could tell by the smile on Polly's face that she didn't really think it was gross. "Do you want one?"

She shook her head, so Valerie finished all the drinks herself. Her throat burned and her face was warm, but she felt great. She felt full of courage. She pulled Polly in tight and rubbed her nose against Polly's. Eskimo kisses. Those wouldn't count.

Over Polly's shoulder, Valerie could see the guys in the role playing club still waiting anxiously for the countdown. God, she loved those guys. Who else did this kind of stuff? A kiss-in was something she imagined happened in other places, bigger cities, but not in Cleveland. It seemed too brave for Cleveland, too bold.

"I should play a song of courage for those guys," Valerie said. "Let's pick some music. That's what Theegh would do." She slipped a few dollars into the jukebox and chose some Guns N' Roses, AC/DC, and, finally, "The Warrior" by Patty Smyth. "This will put them in the mood."

In the soft light of the bar Polly looked too beautiful to be real. The colors of the jukebox glowed on her fair skin and the curve of her breasts. Valerie kissed her cheek, because she couldn't wait any longer and a kiss on the cheek wouldn't count either.

"Hold on," Polly said, smiling. "Only a few more minutes."

. . .

Jesus, this shit was too much. The kiss-in was really happening. Mooneyham tossed back shots of Jägermeister as he squeezed against the bar with Huey and Kevin. Mooneyham had no idea how he pulled the whole thing off, but in a few minutes, the countdown would begin and Kevin would learn everything. Mooneyham tossed back another shot.

"What's with all the dudes?" Kevin asked, still in his shirt and tie, and sipping a bourbon. "Is it gay night or something?" Mooneyham answered with a shrug and a belch.

Earlier, Mooneyham had introduced Huey to Kevin with a simple, "This is Huey." No explanations. Kevin asked, "How do you know each other?" But Mooneyham simply said, "We met at a party." Kevin accepted that with a nod, but his eyes had continued to scan Huey, though if Kevin recognized Huey from the altercation on the street last week, he didn't show it.

Kevin turned away to order another drink, and Mooneyham asked Huey, "Are those guys here?"

"Yeah, down there." Huey nodded toward the far end of the bar where two skinny men in hooded sweatshirts were hunched over their drinks, their backs to the crowd.

On Mooneyham's left, two gray-haired men, who must have been regulars, bantered with the busy bartenders.

"Is there a game tonight? Or a conference in town?"

Neither the men nor the bartenders had picked up on the gayness of the crowd, but they were surprised by the number of people.

Mooneyham had to give himself a pat on the back. He was good at spreading the word, posting the event online, and sending out emails. A kiss-in was the kind of protest that people could get involved with and feel good about. There was a sense of innocence to it. Everyone liked kissing.

"There she is! Hey, big girl." A hand clapped Mooneyham on the shoulder. He turned around to find his old friend Ryan with his arms open for a big hug. "I read your email and was like, oh, this bitch is pissed. And there's little Huey. Hey, hot stuff."

Mooneyham turned back to the bar to find Kevin looking at him with a curious expression on his face.

Kevin said, "Either it's your birthday or you're gay."

"It's not my birthday."

"Dude, are you for real?"

"Yep."

It was such a simple thing to say, but Mooneyham would have felt more relieved if Kevin wasn't standing there with his mouth half open.

Huey grabbed Mooneyham's hand and said, "It's almost midnight." As he spoke the crowd began counting down in one loud voice.

"Ten, nine, eight."

. . .

"Seven, six, five."

All around Ben men were locked eye to eye waiting in anticipation for the count of one. Ben knew better than to look at Albert. If he did and their eyes locked too, they would have this awkward obligation to kiss, which wouldn't be a bad thing. Ben was practically exploding at the thought of it, but Albert was still waiting for Jeff to show up. Always Jeff.

"One!"

Cheers and whoops erupted and were quickly muffled as the kissing began. Ben was knocked aside when two men fell into him, attached at the face. The shouts of "What the fuck!" and "Are you shitting me?" must have come from the regulars, not suspecting their bar had been taken over. Ben wasn't surprised, but he was disappointed to see several men storm out. The crowd booed them as they shoved by and then strengthened their cheering by shouting "Good riddance!" and "Shame!"

A chubby man in a bright green T-shirt pushed his way through, kissing everyone he passed. He grabbed Ben's face with both hands and gave him a quick peck, then turned to Albert and did the same before continuing on through the crowd. A woman in a blue sweater followed him.

"When's the last time you kissed a gal?" she asked Ben as she planted her lips on his.

A conga line of kissers danced through the bar with Celeste sashaying on the end.

"We did it!" Celeste called to Ben, blowing kisses as the line danced by.

"Hey," Albert said, putting a hand on Ben's shoulder. "We might as well kiss. Jeff's still not here."

Oh god.

"Sure." Ben tried to sound calm. It was just a little kiss.

But no, Ben couldn't fool himself. It wasn't just a kiss. It was *the* kiss. The entire reason he'd come to this kiss-in. The whole reason he'd started hanging out with Albert to begin with, perhaps even the reason he'd left the dark comfort of his basement and joined the role playing club. How could he act normal under the approach of such a kiss? Normalcy or any semblance thereof was beyond the scope of Ben's abilities at the moment, but he couldn't run and hide.

Ben straightened his shoulders. He closed his eyes. He tilted his face toward Albert and let his thoughts and fears fall out the back of his head. Their lips touched.

A sleeping dragon opened an eye. Pages in a spell book flipped. The sun rose above a towering castle on the edge of a cliff while white-capped waves crashed against the rocks below. Ben felt fingers in his hair. A shining sword slid from its scabbard. A cauldron bubbled over. Beams of sunlight fell onto the floor of a misty forest. Albert's thumbs were behind Ben's ears. Their lips parted. The dragon blinked. On a grassy hillside a bare-chested ogre stroked a large, red fox and smoked a long, thin pipe. White clouds rolled through the blue sky above. The white clouds rose higher. At the bar, men were kissing. Near the doorway, women were kissing. Albert pressed a hand against the small of Ben's back. Their tongues were touching. A record was playing in the basement. On a stage beneath hot lights, Ben danced as a thousand shirtless men cheered him on. He danced and laughed and danced.

"Bert!"

Albert pulled away at the sound of Jeff's voice. His hands left Ben's body, and Ben's feet returned to the floor.

"What the fuck are you doing?" Jeff asked, glaring at Ben as he swept Albert into his arms.

"It's cool," Albert said, his voice flat and controlled. "It was just a kiss."

Just a kiss?

"I was on a magical journey," Ben said. And then immediately wished he hadn't because Albert and Jeff gave him the strangest look, as though Ben had confirmed their every suspicion about being a weirdo.

Ben turned away from them and pushed through the crowd.

The bar was a mess, full of loud drunks and reeking of stale beer. Why did Jeff have to appear now? Did the kiss really mean so little to Albert? After all the adventures, the video games, and the Samuraiah Carey show?

Ben hadn't gone very far before Albert caught him by the arm.

"Come on," Albert said. "Where are you going?"

"I gotta get out of here." Ben broke free of Albert's grip. But as soon as Ben turned away, a burly man with a black beard grabbed his face and laid a juicy kiss on him. Goddamn. He had to get away from these people. They were closing in, suffocating him with their laughing and drinking and kissing all over the place. The front door and the fresh air were only a few feet away, but Albert grabbed Ben's arm again.

"Why are you so upset? I know you don't like him but—"

"Maybe he's not the one I'm upset with," Ben said, shocked by the anger in his voice. "For someone who's trying not to lead me on, you've done a really bad job of it."

Albert stopped, speechless.

"Look," Ben said. "I gotta go." He was done with this whole scene. Done with Albert and Jeff. Done with the kiss-in. All he wanted was the comfort of his basement.

Ben turned and found the front door blocked. By vampires.

Lord Varnec surveyed the bar as other black-clad vampires pressed past Ben and into the crowd. Varnec threw back his head and with a fang-filled smile said, "Welcome to midnight."

• • •

"Kissing is nice," Valerie said and pressed deeply into Polly's lips. She felt the weight of Polly's breasts upon her chest and the soft touch of Polly's cheeks against hers. She could do this for hours.

"Hey." Two girls with short dark hair and jean jackets interrupted them. "Why don't you share the love?"

"Yeah, why not?" Valerie pulled away from Polly.

"Not you. We mean her." The girls laughed.

"Oh, of course." Polly tucked her hair behind her ears and gave each of the girls a kiss. The three of them giggled together. "It's liberating," she said, turning back to Valerie.

"What about me?" Valerie asked the girls. "I wanna be liberated."

But the two girls were already walking away.

A blond boy in a tight black T-shirt said, "I'll liberate you."

Valerie was unsure how to answer, but Polly gave her an encouraging nod.

"Why the hell not?" Valerie stepped up to the blond and gave him a quick smooch. Their lips barely even touched.

But the blond wasn't finished. He pulled Valerie in by the belt loops and didn't break away, even when Valerie squirmed and thought she'd suffocate. The stubble on his chin rubbed her like sandpaper and static electricity at the same time.

"Liberated yet?"

Valerie fell back against the jukebox and caught her breath. "Yeah," she said. "I'm good."

The blond boy laughed and moved on through the crowd.

"That was hot," Polly said, leaning into Valerie.

"You liked that? Should I do it again?"

"Yeah." She nuzzled Valerie's ear with her lips.

Valerie couldn't believe it. Polly wanted to whore her out for her own sexual satisfaction. A wave of euphoria swept over Valerie. Why not kiss everyone in the place? What was the harm?

The crowd around Valerie and Polly continued to shift as people maneuvered around to swap kisses with any available pair of lips. Valerie kissed a guy with a handlebar mustache, followed by a young guy with a tattoo on his neck, and then a woman older than her mom with spidery wrinkles in the corners of her eyes. In between she turned to Polly and kissed her as well. It was nonstop kissing mania. It was anarchy. Freedom.

Valerie reached down into her backpack. She pulled out the gorilla mask from Readmore.

"Oh my god," Polly said. "What'd you bring that for?"

"For fun." Valerie slipped the mask on and ook-ooked around the jukebox. "How 'bout a kiss?"

Polly grabbed the sides of the ape head and pressed her lips onto its rubbery mouth. Valerie pushed her tongue through the space between the gorilla's teeth, and Polly jumped back in surprise.

"You're crazy," she said. "That mask is so dirty."

Valerie danced around, her tongue sticking out. She didn't care about germs. It was more important to make Polly laugh, but Polly turned her attention away.

"What's going on up front?" she asked, standing on her tiptoes to see over the crowd.

• • •

Mooneyham saw the awkward look on Kevin's face when he and Huey pulled away from each other, and it was satisfying.

The old men to his left, who had been so concerned about the crowd, turned away in disgust. One muttered something about a bunch of homosexuals. They quickly downed their beers and left.

"Dude," Kevin said. "Why didn't you tell me before all of this?"

"It's not the easiest info to share." Mooneyham looked down at Kevin. "Especially with a douche bag."

"You could have told me. We're supposed to be boys. You can tell me whatever. I don't care." Kevin looked around at all the kissing men and women. "What a dick move asking me to come here. You could have simply said something. Or do you think I'm too small-minded?"

"You tried to set me up with chicks."

"I thought you were straight. And you let me think that when all you had to do was say something. I'm not that big of an ass-hole. I would have set you up with dudes instead."

"I have a boyfriend." Mooneyham motioned toward Huey.

"Who I didn't know existed until now."

"Your friends called me a faggot," Huey said, pointing out the two men at the end of the bar who were trying to fend off kisses.

"What friends? I don't know those guys."

Mooneyham dragged his heavy hands down his face in frustration. "We saw you with them," Mooneyham said. "The night Huey got harassed. You really had nothing to do with it?"

"I had a cigarette with them, maybe, but I don't know them."

"Did you or did you not push my boyfriend around and call him a faggot?"

"Dude, come on."

"Did you or did you not?"

Mooneyham and Huey were looking hard at Kevin, but Kevin was looking across the bar at the Cavs game playing on TV.

"Okay, maybe I had a few too many that night and said some-thing I shouldn't have. It was just, you know, guys being guys."

"You fucking shithead." Mooneyham shoved Kevin against the bar, shaking and toppling bottles and glasses.

"What are you going to do?" Kevin asked. "Punch me?"

Rage, red and boiling, seethed through Mooneyham's body. He wanted to pick Kevin up and toss him across the room.

But Huey placed a hand on Mooneyham's arm, and that hand was cool and calming.

"I'm gonna let you wear the crown you deserve," Mooneyham said, backing away.

"What's that mean, big girl? You should've just told me," Kevin said. "This all could've been avoided. Instead you had to ambush me."

"You're a fucking dickhead. And you're a homophobe." Mooneyham pointed a thick finger at Kevin. "Homophobe, over here! Homophobe!"

Kevin's face went red. "Not cool," he said.

But his protests were drowned out as a chorus of others took up the call, pointing and yelling.

"Homophobe!"

Huey pointed out his assailants at the end of the bar. "They fucking attacked me last week."

The men looked shocked and held up their hands, as if to show they were innocent, but the crowd turned on them as well.

"Get the fuck out of here!" someone yelled.

"Fuck homophobia!" yelled another.

Mooneyham watched as Kevin and the two men pushed their way through the riled mob, which was now reacting in mass-mind. Booing and hissing at the men as they tried to pass through. The crowd had become a force unto itself.

• • •

Ben couldn't see clearly over the mass of people but some men were trying to push through. The crowd swayed left, nearly knocking Ben over, and Ben felt like he was back at the Samuraiah Carey show.

"It's getting crazy in here," Albert said. Varnec was blocking the door with a girl in each arm, the cat-hoodie girl on the right and the vampire mom on the left. Varnec leaned down and kissed one and then the other.

The crowd continued to chant "homophobe," hardly parting to let the men through, two guys in sweatshirts and Kevin, Mooneyham's coworker, who was cute, in a buttoned-up banker sort of way. When they reached Varnec, he looked down at them and said, "What's the matter little homophobes? Not having any fun?"

"Get the fuck out of the way!" Kevin yelled.

"We can't let you go so easily, can we?"

Mooneyham had followed Kevin through the crowd and called out to the vampires. "Let them out of here. We don't need these assholes around."

"These assholes harass us too," Varnec said. "They have such delicate sensibilities, you know. They take offense at our capes and find our clothes too frilly. Why should we let them go when we could have a little fun? You like playing games, don't you, little role player?"

"They've been embarrassed enough," Mooneyham said.

"Make 'em kiss," the girl in the cat-hoodie said.

"Make 'em strip," the vampire mom said.

People were riled up and shouting suggestions. A vampire next to Ben with dark hair and black eyeliner yelled, "Make 'em fuck!" The atmosphere in the bar was changing. The once-peaceful crowd was beginning to turn.

Mooneyham was not having it though. He stepped up to Varnec and tried to move him aside, but the vampire girls shrieked and pushed Mooneyham away.

Ben would not want to fuck with Mooneyham. Some other big guys stepped up as well and tried to clear a path through the vampires, but the vampires pushed back, hissing and spitting and baring their fangs.

From the back of the bar, someone in a gorilla mask came charging through the crowd. It was Valerie! She strode up and punched Varnec in the face. At the sound of the impact Ben's stomach flipped. Varnec fell to the ground with a whimper. And with a screech, the vampire girls launched themselves onto the gorilla, trying to pull off the mask.

The crowd reeled in every direction at once. One of the homophobes, in the gray hooded sweatshirt, jumped onto Mooneyham's back. Mooneyham spun and tossed him to the ground. Kevin, with his arms out, held back the crowd. The bartenders were shouting and ringing a brass bell. Ben couldn't understand what they were saying, but he got the idea—get the fuck out.

Varnec staggered to his feet. His top hat was missing and his stringy blond hair was a mess. He wiped his bleeding nose and, seeing blood, turned wide-eyed. He stumbled back against the door.

Polly was there and screaming at Valerie. "What's the matter with you? He was trying to help us."

Varnec reached out a hand to Polly. She took it, and with a look back at Valerie, she fled out the door with Varnec.

Valerie squirmed between the vampire girls, holding onto the gorilla mask for dear life, as she yelled after Polly. The girls clawed and scratched at her, and Ben couldn't watch and do nothing. He tried to pull the girls' hands off, but they were soon joined by the hands of half-a-dozen other vampires, all reaching through the mob and clawing at Valerie.

With brute force, Mooneyham grabbed Valerie around the

waist and hauled her through the vampires and out the door. Ben pushed his way after them. Albert was close behind.

The night air felt cool to Ben, after being in the stuffy bar. Valerie and Mooneyham were already running down the sidewalk. Ben ran after them. Looking back, he saw Albert right behind.

Halfway down the street, Mooneyham stopped. "Where's Huey? I've gotta go back."

"Keep going," Albert said, catching up. Mooneyham turned back, but Ben wasn't about to stop. He and Albert ran down the street, following Valerie to Readmore. Valerie unlocked the door and they slipped inside.

They sat near the front windows for a few minutes, catching their breath. Valerie kept the lights off, and in the darkness, the store was quiet and peaceful, and the shelves were still and undisturbed until Valerie threw the gorilla mask onto the front counter and began to pace. Celeste tapped on the glass door not a minute later.

"What were you thinking?" Celeste asked as soon as Valerie opened the door, a look of anger on her face.

"Fuck. I don't know," Valerie said. "They were fighting."

"What about Mooneyham and Huey?" Ben asked Celeste, but she hadn't seen them. "Never split the party. That's rule number one."

It would be a terrible irony if something happened to Mooneyham and Huey. This was their big night.

As they paced around the store, Celeste called Mooneyham's phone but there was no answer.

"Try texting him," Albert said.

Something bad was happening down at the bar; Ben could feel it.

Several figures ran past the front window, and then Kyle and Miya tapped on the front door, a frantic look on the faces.

"Thank god," Valerie said as she let them in.

"You're an idiot," Kyle said, but if Valerie was insulted, she didn't show it. "The cops just showed up. We were walking away when they arrived. Huey is still down there though. We saw him."

"They wouldn't take him to jail?" Valerie asked. "Would they?"

"For what?" Celeste asked. "He's not the one who punched somebody."

Valerie sunk her head onto Kyle's shoulder. She was an idiot, but they couldn't put all the blame on her. If Varnec and his vampire minions hadn't shown up, Ben would be home in bed by now, curled up with Onigiri.

Valerie cussed and swore, unable to get ahold of Polly.

"Why did she leave with him?" Valerie asked, but no one had an answer.

Ben sat on the floor and leaned against the shelves of board games. The adrenaline rush was passing, leaving him exhausted. Albert sat cross-legged across from him, looking at him through the darkness.

"What happened to Jeff?" Ben asked. "Did he make it out?"

"I don't know. He sent a text asking where I went, but I didn't answer yet."

Several people passed by the windows, dark and indistinguishable, but Mooneyham and Huey never arrived. The sidewalks began to clear. The bars and restaurants closed up. Cars drove by, but otherwise Coventry Road became empty. A calm tranquility settled over Readmore Comix.

At the front counter, Kyle and Miya were falling asleep. Outside, Coventry was dark and still. Mooneyham and Huey were probably home in bed by now. At least, Ben hoped that's where they were, and not spending the night in jail.

Albert was still looking at him, studying him, and it was more than annoying and awkward; it was unbearable.

"I think it's safe to leave," Ben said.

"I'm sorry," Albert whispered. "I never meant to lead you on."

"Then what *did* you mean to do?"

"Have fun, I guess."

Sure, of course, go wild with the guy who has a crush on you. Take him to a concert, hang out with him every day, and even kiss him when you have the chance. That sounds like a blast.

"I clearly misinterpreted you then," Ben said. "Or maybe I saw something that wasn't there."

"Maybe it is there," Albert said, finally looking away. "I don't know."

"You don't know?" Anger flared in Ben's chest. Of course, Albert knew. He simply didn't want to say it. Despite all the signs that Ben was a better match, Albert still chose Jeff. Probably because he was good looking, or had a job, or didn't live in his parents' basement, or some stupid reason like that.

Groaning, Kyle and Miya began to stir.

Celeste stood and stretched. "I guess Mooneyham's not showing up."

"Or Polly." Valerie approached the front window and looked out. "I think it's clear. Who wants to go first?"

"I will," Ben said, climbing to his feet.

"I'll walk with you," Albert said.

"No, that's okay."

Valerie opened the door, and Ben slid out on his own.

The air was cool, and the stars were out. Behind Ben the role playing club was saying goodbye, as Valerie let them out one by one. But Ben didn't turn back. He walked toward home, the cellar doors, and the basement.

•••

Mooneyham pulled Huey to a side street as they hurried away from O'Malley's and toward their apartment.

"What were you telling the cops?" Mooneyham asked. He was walking quickly, anxious to get away from all the chaos. He'd returned to O'Malley's just as the police arrived, and, not wanting to get wrapped up in that shit storm again, he'd hung back and watched from across the street. People were streaming out of the bar, but Huey was taken to one end of the block while the vampires, sans Varnec, were taken to another.

"I told them not to touch me, that I was innocent."

The cops had been shouting "Go home!" and "The party's over!" but that hadn't stopped people from milling around and watching.

"Why did they question you of all people?"

"Someone told them to. Someone shouted, 'He started it.' I was like, me? I didn't do anything." The tree branches hung low along the sidewalk, and Mooneyham stepped from pools of streetlight into pools of darkness. "The cops asked me did I know who organized this, but I said no. I just came with a friend. They said, 'Where's your friend now?' I said, 'He ran away, like everybody else.' 'He doesn't sound like a good friend,' they said."

A dog barked in the distance, and another dog answered from farther away.

"Whatever," Mooneyham said. "That cop's a dick. I didn't mean to leave you behind. It just got so crazy. Why didn't you run?"

"I tried, but not everyone's big you know. There was so much confusion." Huey's voice rang out, and the dog barked again. "But it's okay. I'm okay. They took my information and said, 'Go home and don't come to this bar ever again.' And I said, 'No problem.'"

The moon was bright. The Tudor homes and the brick apartment buildings of Coventry Village were quiet and still, their windows dark. Mooneyham felt as though a dampening filter had been placed over the night. The kiss-in had no impact here, a few short blocks away. Sirens in the background were the only reminder that this was a city and not the suburbs.

"God, work tomorrow," Mooneyham said. "I feel like such an asshole, but what else is new?" He ran a heavy hand through his thick hair.

"Kevin's the asshole," Huey said. "All those guys are. Don't feel bad for them."

As they climbed the marble steps to their apartment building, Huey said, "Call in sick. It's Friday."

"That'd be so cowardly." It was a tempting idea though. Mooneyham paused at the top of the stairs.

"We'll go out on the lake somewhere and get away for a while." Huey was practically begging.

"I can't, you know that. I have to face Kevin and whatever consequences come my way."

Mooneyham turned and looked toward the sirens one last time before shuffling inside.

the shambling horror

Ben stretched and groaned into awakeness. The light outside the tiny basement windows was dim, and Ben could hear rain falling onto the shrubs. At least he thought it was the sound of rain. It could have been the sound of bacon frying. Onigiri crawled across Ben's chest and curled up on the other side.

Upstairs, Ben's parents were having breakfast in the kitchen. He could hear their muffled conversation directly above him.

Conan the Barbarian looked down at Ben from the poster on the ceiling, his muscular arms and broad pecs clearly visible despite the dim light. Ben slid a hand across his own chest. He could still feel Albert's stubble against his chin and Albert's thumbs behind his ears. Ben's hands crawled beneath the waistband of his boxers, but he felt uncomfortable going any further with the cat at his side.

Ben took a shower. The steaming water fell onto his back and shoulders.

Albert's kiss.

In the dark at Readmore, Ben had felt misled.

"But maybe I'm wrong," he'd said.

"Maybe you're not," Albert said.

What a confusing purgatory to be trapped in. Ben knew that he should probably take a break from Albert. That hanging out with Albert had only led to confusing feelings and it would be best for them both to slow down. But then again, if Albert felt something too, maybe there was something worth pursuing and they should follow that path to its conclusion. Ben couldn't decide whether to call Albert or not, so he decided to let the golden die decide.

Ben finished in the shower and dressed. He opened his back-pack and dug through his player's guide and handbooks. Ben shook his golden die out of his dice bag. On a high roll he would call Albert. On a low roll he wouldn't. He set the die rolling across the scattered papers on his desk. The result was a four. Low. So, that was that. He wouldn't call.

Ben went upstairs, Onigiri hot on his heels. He fed the cat and made a bowl of cereal for himself. He wouldn't call Albert. That had already been decided, but there was no reason he couldn't text Albert. So, over his bowl of Frosted Mini-Wheats, Ben sent Albert a short text.

Hey, what a crazy night. Wanna hang out later and talk?

The reply was almost instant, as though Albert had been expecting a message from Ben.

Can't. Pretty busy coming up. Work, Jeff, etc, etc. See you Thurs?

Thursday wasn't soon enough, so Ben replied, *Wanna hang out before the game?*

Maybe. I'll let you know.

Ben put down the phone. He climbed down the stairs into the basement and checked his auctions. He thought about the kiss-in, all those annoying people and the fucking vampires showing up. Then he tried *not* to think about the kiss-in. It was not yet eleven o'clock, but he had to get his mind on other things, or he'd make himself crazy. So, he put on his windbreaker, climbed out the cellar doors, and went thrifting.

. . .

Mooneyham rushed through the lobby of the bank and squeezed into the elevator as the doors were closing. It was a slow ride to the eighth floor and filled with wet bodies from the rain. It wasn't until they reached the seventh floor that Mooneyham realized he was standing next to Kevin. The silence in the elevator became even more uncomfortable after that.

But why should he be uncomfortable? He didn't do anything wrong.

What was he supposed to say to Kevin? Sorry about the vampires? They took it too far? I only meant to call you out for being a homophobe? Fuck that. It wasn't his job to apologize for Varnec. He didn't invite the vampires. And if Kevin's stupid ass hadn't harassed Huey to begin with, none of it would have happened.

When they reached the twenty-fourth floor, the doors opened. Kevin went to the left and Mooneyham to the right.

If they were going to ignore each other, that was fine.

Mooneyham collapsed into his chair. He hadn't gotten enough sleep last night. He was running on caffeine and sugar. He felt heavy and bloated, like his body was expanding through every seam in his shirt. He loosened his collar and tie.

The porcelain turtle soap dish sat beside Mooneyham's keyboard, a reminder of perseverance and dedication to the cause, but Mooneyham wasn't sure how he felt about it now.

Just after twelve, Mooneyham decided to head out for lunch. He logged out of his computer, pulled his jacket off his chair, and slipped his phone into his pocket. On the way down the hall he passed a conference room, and through the window in the door he saw Kevin inside talking to Anthony and Devon. No doubt Kevin had called an emergency meeting and was right now describing in selective detail the asshole stunt Mooneyham pulled last night.

Mooneyham opened the door.

"What's up ass-berries? Was I not invited to this meeting?"

"Ah, no, you were not," Kevin said, standing up from his chair and looking flustered.

"Is he telling you guys about last night?" Mooneyham asked.

"I'll let you know when your expertise is needed," Kevin said.

"What happened last night?" Anthony asked.

"Maybe later." Kevin motioned for Mooneyham to leave.

"No, I wanna hear his side," Anthony said.

"So, you assholes were talking about me." Mooneyham sat down heavily in an empty chair. There was a cluster of empty coffee mugs on the table, and the white boards hadn't been erased.

"Just tell us what's going on," Devon said.

"I'm gay." Mooneyham expected an awkward silence to fill the room but instead Anthony and Devon looked unfazed.

"Yeah, he told us," Anthony said.

"It was more shocking the first time around," Devon said. "Now I kinda get it."

"What the fuck does that mean?"

"It means I've had time to think about it, and reflect back on it, and I can see how, yeah, you might be gay. Or are gay."

"You guys are fucking idiots."

"Just tell us what happened," Anthony said. "In your own words. I'm curious."

"Jesus, how do I start?" Mooneyham dragged his hands down his face. "I took Kevin to O'Malley's last night and came out to him. There was a kiss-in happening to protest homophobia. I don't know. It seemed like a good idea at the time, but things got out of hand."

"He said people went ape shit and tried to kick his ass. Like literally ape shit. That some dude was there in a gorilla costume punching people."

"Don't say it isn't true," Kevin said.

"Christ." Mooneyham pressed his palms into his eye sockets.

"Yes, there was a dude in a gorilla costume, and yes, she punched someone. The gorilla was a she. But that had to do with some vampires, not Kevin."

"It had to do with vampires?" Devon began to laugh. "What was going on at this place?"

Mooneyham sighed. "It was a crazy night, I'm telling you, and yeah it got out of hand."

"What's so fucked up to me, is that you couldn't just tell me," Kevin said. "You couldn't just come out to me like a normal person."

Mooneyham placed his big hands calmly on the table. "Believe me, it's not an easy thing to do." He didn't know what else to say. That he'd tried? That he'd wanted to come out but didn't know how? That some part of him had been too ashamed? That even now he was having a hard time looking Kevin in the eyes?

"What're we supposed to do now?" Kevin asked. "How're we supposed to be a team, even if we don't care, despite whatever happened, that you're gay. Like, how am I supposed to trust that you're being honest with me? Or that you're not going to pull some dick move again?"

Anthony and Devon agreed. Even though they wished they could have been there, just to see the look on Kevin's face when it happened, they also weren't sure what it meant now, and if they could ever really trust Mooneyham again. And Mooneyham, sitting there with them, and feeling like shit for everything that happened, couldn't disagree.

"So, I don't know," Kevin said, shaking his head, as he and the other guys filed out, leaving Mooneyham alone with the empty cups and the dirty whiteboards.

After lunch, Mooneyham joined the two o'clock meeting and sat across from Kevin, but their eyes never met.

Their boss, Bridgette, asked the two of them to work together on the Lipsky account.

"The both of you did such a good job with the Databing assignment I gave you last time."

Kevin raised a hand and said, "Actually, Bridgette, I'm still busy with the Morrisons. Do you think William could take Lipsky for me instead?"

So, that's how it was going to be then. They would avoid each other.

If Mooneyham wanted to, he could protest, but why bother? Avoiding Kevin, although less than ideal, was the easiest solution.

When Mooneyham returned to his desk he discovered his ceramic turtle was gone.

• • •

Valerie stormed into the house as soon as Polly opened the front door.

"Why are you avoiding me? Are you all team Varnec now, or what?"

Polly, who was wearing a thin black T-shirt and pajama pants with the Tardis printed all over them, gave Valerie an angry look, but she didn't say a word. And Valerie, who had started banging on the front door at 7 a.m., felt a tinge of guilt.

"I'm sorry," Valerie said, following Polly into the kitchen, where she had been making a cup of tea, apparently. "But you weren't responding to me, and you fucking left with Varnec."

Polly sighed and looked down at the kitchen counter. "I don't know what to say. You punched him."

"He's an asshole."

Polly sipped her tea. "But still. You punched him."

Now it was Valerie who had no idea what to say. She made a weird croaking noise, because no words would come out of her mouth.

Polly continued over her steaming mug, "I'm not saying he isn't weird or eccentric or whatever you want to call it. But to punch him?"

"He was starting shit."

Polly rolled her eyes. "So that justifies it?"

Valerie began to realize, standing awkwardly in the middle of the kitchen while Polly calmly sat and sipped her tea, that certain decisions had already been made, without Valerie knowing or being present.

"Are you breaking up with me? Did he tell you to dump me or something?"

"He didn't tell me anything. Well, we talked for a while. His other friends were there too." Polly stared into her mug. "Do you really think we're a good match? You and me?"

"I think we're fucking amazing." Valerie was at Polly's side in an instant, putting a hand on Polly's knee.

Polly continued to look into her mug. "What are you doing next year? Are you going to school somewhere?"

"I don't know. I still need to figure it out." The words seemed to hang in the air for a moment until they felt heavier than Valerie had intended.

Polly put down her mug and then smiled at Valerie. "I'm sorry," she said. "Did you want some tea? I should have asked you."

And then Valerie knew, officially, that something weird was happening. Whether it was because of Varnec or the kiss-in, or something else entirely, they were breaking up. It was really going to happen. And some piece of Valerie staggered back, as if struck in the chest by a two-by-four. But of course, she didn't really stagger back, and she hadn't really been struck by anything. She was still standing at Polly's side, her hand on Polly's knee. And somehow, she smiled back and said she would totally love some tea. Even though she thought tea tasted like dirty water and never drank it unless it was iced and full of sugar.

And so, they sat on stools at the kitchen counter and drank tea, and talked about their lives, or rather the lives that they wanted, someday, to have. Polly running some sort of artist's cooperative that didn't seem to make complete sense, but it was a dream, so it didn't really matter. And Valerie doing whatever she decided to do, which was probably going to involve a lot of international travel, like her sister. And then Polly's roommates, finally awake, came downstairs, and poured some tea, and talked about their dream lives too.

And when the tea was gone, and her roommates left the kitchen, and it was just the two of them again, Polly said, "I hope we can remain friends and it won't be awkward, since we still have to work together."

And Valerie said, "Of course, totally."

But she knew something would never be the same again. The piece of herself that had staggered back had yet to return. And as she said goodbye to Polly and walked out of the house into the morning sun, Valerie thought, *Fuck Varnec*. His fault or not, she had to blame someone, because she knew that missing piece was gone for good.

the die

Ben arrived at Readmore early, anxious to see Albert. They hadn't hung out since the night of the kiss-in and hadn't exchanged texts more complicated than *Hey, what's up?* Albert said he was busy all week, which Ben hoped was true and not some kind of excuse.

Ben said hello to Valerie and Kyle, who were hanging out behind the front counter, and then he pushed aside the curtain to the back room. He was the first to arrive, which had never happened before. He turned on the lamps in the corners, except for the broken lamp, which he didn't bother with.

The card tables were slightly askew, no doubt the result of some rough gaming action the night before. Ben arranged the tables properly and adjusted the chairs. He was surprised to discover that the broken chair no longer wobbled and seemed strong enough to support a person's weight. Ben thought that chair would never be fixed. He was so delighted by the discovery that he tried the switch on the broken lamp, only to be disappointed. The broken lamp was still broken.

Slowly, Ben drifted around the room, scanning the titles of the books and the dusty superhero figures that stood on the top shelves, posed for action. Superman was so gray with dust that he could be a zombie in a cape. Ben blew at the stoic figure, but the dust barely moved it was so heavy.

Arriving first and having the back room all to himself gave Ben an unfamiliar sense of freedom—not only could he explore, but he could choose any seat he wanted. He could sit at the head of the table. Curious as to what it felt like to have a different point of view, Ben sat in Mooneyham's usual seat. And the first thing Ben saw when he looked up was Mooneyham parting the curtain and walking through the doorway.

"Changing seats?" Mooneyham asked.

"We don't have to," Ben said. "I was just, you know—"

"Who cares?" Mooneyham said. "You can sit there." Without any hesitation, Mooneyham dropped his bag onto the table with a thud and sat in Valerie's chair, near the head of the table, but on the opposite side from Ben.

Huey came in soon after and said, "Oh, are we sitting on this side now?"

"Apparently," Mooneyham said.

"You can sit here." Ben motioned toward the broken chair. "It's fixed."

"Interesting," Mooneyham said. He then reached over, flipped the switch on the broken lamp, and harrumphed in disapproval when nothing happened.

"It's okay," Huey said. "I'll sit here." He slipped into the chair beside Mooneyham, Albert's usual seat.

While Mooneyham and Huey unpacked their books and miniatures and chatted about their days, Ben debated whether he should stay in his new seat. Looking at the room from a different angle was a little unsettling. There was a crack in the wall shaped like a trident, and from his new vantage point Ben could see through the part in the curtain just enough to know whenever someone walked past, and the anticipation of who would be next through the door was becoming too much. Albert could be coming through the curtain at any moment.

But Celeste was next, charging through with purpose.

"Hail adventurers. Mixing it up I see." Celeste opened her backpack and planted her dungeon master's screen at the head of the table. "I like it. I know things can get a little stale and routine week after week."

"It just kinda happened," Ben said.

Then Celeste turned to Mooneyham and Huey. "So, you survived."

"What did you expect?" Mooneyham asked.

"So, that's it?" Celeste asked, as if she expected more. "There's no drama to report? We'd imagined all kinds of dreadful scenarios for the two of you."

Huey spoke up and explained how he'd been questioned by the police and ordered to never return to O'Malley's.

"But it's fine for me," Huey said, waving his hand as if shooing away an annoying insect.

"And what about you?" Celeste asked Mooneyham. "What about your coworker?"

"It is what it is." Mooneyham shrugged indifferently. "We're not talking now, but I'm certainly not complaining. Huey can walk down the street without being harassed. We accomplished everything we wanted to. I think the night was a success."

Celeste sat quietly behind her screen, looking at Mooneyham and Huey. She did not look convinced. Ben shook his dice from their bag and they tumbled loudly onto the table.

Valerie walked into the room before things could become any more awkward. She hesitated a moment when he saw that everyone was sitting in new seats.

"And you," Mooneyham said, glaring at Valerie. "What the fuck?"

"What the fuck what?" Valerie asked. She took the no-longer-broken seat to Ben's left, and when it didn't collapse under her weight Valerie said, "I fixed it a few days ago."

"Impressive," said Celeste. She then reached over and tried to turn on the broken lamp, frowning when the light did not turn on.

"We're talking about the kiss-in," Mooneyham said. "Why the fuck did you put on that mask and start swinging? What a dumbass thing to do."

"It made sense at the time," Valerie said, and Mooneyham looked ready to strangle her. "I brought that mask because I thought it would be funny. Polly and I were playing around with it, but when I saw you guys fighting with the vampires, I don't know, I just snapped."

"Where did you come from anyway? How did you get in?"

"Through the front door. We snuck in. No one was checking IDs."

"Were you hiding somewhere?" Celeste asked. "I danced through the whole bar and I didn't see you."

"We were back by the jukebox."

Mooneyham shook his head in disbelief. "No doubt we'd all like to punch Varnec in the face, but really? Why didn't you stay outside like we told you to?"

"Are you kidding?"

"How did the vampires find out about the kiss-in anyway?" Ben asked.

"Who knows?" Mooneyham said. "People talk. Word gets around."

"I think Polly told them," Valerie said. "She wasn't trying to fuck us over or anything, I think she was trying to spread the word." Although Valerie didn't look one hundred percent certain.

The curtains parted again as Albert stepped into the room. He swung his black backpack from his shoulder and looked disoriented for a moment at seeing everyone seated in a different spot, but he recovered with a grin. "Am I in the right place?"

Albert slid into the chair next to Huey, Ben's old seat. This put

Albert directly across the table from Ben. The two of them exchanged a nod as Albert unpacked his bag. Ben regretted the new seating arrangement more than ever, because Albert was too far away to talk with easily.

"Sorry I'm late," Albert said. "I got stuck at work."

"No problem," Celeste said. "We were recapping the kiss-in."

Huey caught Albert up on what he had missed, how the cops had arrived and questioned everyone, how Huey had been banned from the bar, how Mooneyham was dealing with his situation at work, which wasn't ideal but was fine for now.

"I'm glad there haven't been any negative repercussions," Albert said, "at least for you guys."

"Has there been for you?" Celeste asked.

Albert hesitated. "Let's say I don't think it's a good idea for your boyfriend to catch you kissing another guy, even at a kiss-in."

Everyone laughed but Ben. He asked, "Really? Is that what's going on?"

"I don't know what Jeff's deal is," Albert said. "Anyway, I'm glad the kiss-in worked out for you guys. I was worried you got arrested or something and we'd have to cancel our game."

"Nope, it's game on," Celeste said, and with that she rose from behind the dungeon master screen and placed the map of Hammervale on the table. "Why don't we get started?"

But Ben wasn't paying attention. He was busy texting Albert under the table, as surreptitiously as possible: *Is Jeff really jealous?*

Celeste placed the model of the forge onto the map and stood the miniature blacksmith inside.

"The crisis is over," Celeste said. "You've saved the Cod and Piece, and you've disrupted the cultist threat for now. Also, you've recovered a book from the cultists."

"And we learned that sexomancy is a thing," Huey said.

"That's right. Sexomancy, which was supposed to have disappeared centuries ago, having been banned and outlawed and shunned by every culture on the planet, has apparently been rediscovered."

Across the table, Albert read Ben's text with a quick glance and replied: *I don't know if jealous is the right word but he's pissed at me. Was.*

Ben was about to reply, but Celeste must have seen the light from Ben's phone.

"Really? Are you two texting each other? At my table? Come on."

So, Ben put away his phone, embarrassed, and Albert did the same as he gave Celeste a sheepish grin.

• • •

The group worked with Whistletooth and the waiters to clean up the Cod and Piece. They put the tables and chairs back in place. They took down the weird altar. They scrubbed the black tar off the windows.

"It's nice doing things like this with you," Bjorndar said to Flamebender as they arranged the tables and chairs. "I feel like it's been too long."

"Since we cleaned the bar?" Flamebender grabbed a bucket of water and began scrubbing down the tables with a rough scrap of cloth.

"You know what I mean," Bjorndar said. "Now that we've returned from the land of the dead and taken care of the cultists, perhaps we'll have more free time."

"Perhaps," Flamebender said, wringing out the cloth.

From across the tavern, Theegh called out, "Hey, what do you guys want to do with this altar thing?"

They had moved the altar to the Sleeping God to a corner near the front door while they cleaned the tavern floor and replaced the tables and chairs.

"Let's take it outside and smash it," Gunther said from behind the bar, where he and Marilyn were cleaning glasses and returning bottles to the shelves.

"Are you sure that's not bad luck?" Marilyn asked.

"Why would it be bad luck to destroy an idol to a false god?" Flamebender asked.

"Because evil spirits and stuff?"

"Nah." Flamebender dismissed Marilyn's fears with a wave of his hand.

So, they opened the doors to the Cod and Piece and dragged the statue into the street. The late morning sun was high in the sky, and the merchant stalls were bustling, so it wasn't long before a crowd formed to watch.

Gunther pulled his dwarven war hammer from his belt and brought it down upon the head of the statue with a loud whack. A crack formed between the statue's eyes, but the statue held together.

"Let me try." Flamebender took the hammer and swung it hard against the statue's head. The statue shook and the crack lengthened, but still it remained in one piece.

"Maybe we need another tactic," Marilyn said. She waved her hands, and the statue flew up into the air. It soared for a moment, gracefully, and then came crashing to the ground. Several tentacles broke off, and the crowd of onlookers cheered, but still the statue didn't shatter.

"I could hit it with my magic lute," Theegh said. "But it would probably do more damage to the lute."

"Alright," said Bjorndar, "let's see what I can do." He stepped back to the edge of the crowd and notched three arrows in his bow. They hit the statue squarely but didn't appear to do any damage.

"Did I mention they were blunt arrows and do bludgeoning damage?" Bjorndar asked. Suddenly several pieces of the statue chipped off, and the crack between its eyes lengthened ever so slightly.

"That's better than nothing," Flamebender said.

"Clearly we can't break this statue by ourselves," Bjorndar said. "What if we get all these people to help us and we gang up on it?"

Flamebender turned to the crowd, arms open. "Good people of Hammervale, we have chased off the evil scourge that was tainting your fair city. The only thing that remains is this foul remnant of their archaic beliefs. Come join us as we take pleasure in smashing it to bits."

With much cheer and laughter the crowd took up what tools they had, brooms, rakes, the occasional sword or club, and with joy and determination they beat on the statue until it lay in pieces at their feet.

A grateful merchant swept the debris aside and, feeling triumphant at last, the adventurers returned inside to the Cod and Piece, where Whistletooth was waiting for them.

"You have done good work," he said. "The bar is ready to re-open. But there is one more thing." He placed the heavy *Grimoire of Erotic Deeds* onto the bar. "We need to decide what to do with this."

Marilyn took the tome and unclasped the latch that held it closed. "What do we know about this book?" she asked. "Has anyone ever heard of it before?"

"We know it contains powerful sexomancy spells," Flamebender said. "And sexomancy was outlawed centuries ago."

"Which is probably why everyone wants to do it," Marilyn said.

"It's obviously powerful," Bjorndar said. "We should study the book to see what we can learn."

"It's obviously evil," Flamebender said. "It's radiating foul energies. It should be destroyed. We don't know what power it contains."

"Which is why we have to study it. We can't let all that knowledge be lost."

"Who would be the one to study it?"

"I could do it," Marilyn said eagerly. "At least, I can see how much I can read, and then we can destroy it." But turning the pages, she found the inscriptions and illustrations to be indecipherable.

Gunther laughed at her. "You haven't put any points into your linguistics skill. Of course you can't read it. But then again, does anyone ever put points in linguistics?"

"I did," Theegh said. "I'm a bard. We have all kinds of knowledge." Theegh took the book from Marilyn, but immediately upon scanning the pages, he dropped the book in fright. "Oh, the horror!" Theegh clutched his head and moaned in pain. "I'm never putting points in linguistics again."

"See, I told you the book is evil," Flamebender said.

"But someone has to be able to read it," Bjorndar said. "The priest was reading from it last night."

"And the priest was evil," Flamebender said. "We can't risk letting the book fall into the wrong hands again."

"This is an ancient artifact." Bjorndar picked up the book and clutched it to his chest. "We need to preserve it for study, if not by us, then by someone else who can understand it. There must be a wizarding school around somewhere that can put it to good use and keep it out of the wrong hands."

"I am a paladin. I've sworn an oath to defend justice and all that is good. Evil must be destroyed wherever it is found."

"What do you guys think?" Bjorndar turned to the rest of the group.

"This book is like an evil *Kama Sutra*?" Marilyn asked.

"You don't want to know the things I've seen," said Theegh, shaking his head.

"I don't really care," Gunther said. "There's nothing I can do with the book anyway, and I pretty much already know everything there is to know about sex."

"Oh really?" Marilyn asked with a raised eyebrow.

"Maybe we should get rid of it," Theegh said. "It's already causing problems."

"That's the worst argument ever," Bjorndar said.

"You won't miss whatever knowledge is in there," Flamebender said. "And the world will be a safer place."

"I would have thought," Bjorndar said, "that erotic deeds would be something you'd all want to celebrate, not destroy."

"Are you saying we're a bunch of prudes?"

"I'm saying we have an opportunity and you're throwing it away."

"An opportunity?" Flamebender's eyes met Bjorndar's. "For what?"

"I don't know yet, but you'd rather destroy it before you've understood what it is than try to fully explore it."

"I think you're making this out to be more than it is," Flamebender said. "Just give me the book."

"No." Bjorndar stepped away. "I will not." But Flamebender reached out with a gauntleted hand and latched onto the grimoire, and a physical struggle began, back and forth.

• • •

"Enough," Celeste said. "If you guys can't make a decision, then we'll have to do this the old-fashioned way."

"A roll-off!" Valerie declared.

"That's right." Celeste stood from behind her dungeon master's screen. "The highest roll wins." She pointed to Ben and Albert. "Just you two. The loser has to give up the book."

"Really? A roll-off?" Ben picked up his golden d20. "Is this what it's come to?"

"I haven't done one of these in a while," Albert said.

On the count of three they sent their dice tumbling across the tabletop. Ben's die landed on a four, while Albert's landed on a seventeen.

"Best two out of three?" Ben asked.

"How'd I know you were going to say that?" Albert grinned and shook his die in his cupped hands. They sent their dice rolling again, and this time it was Ben's die that landed high, while Albert's rolled low. A whoop of surprise erupted around the table.

Celeste watched intently from behind her dungeon master's screen. "Last roll. Whoever wins gets the *Grimoire of Erotic Deeds*."

"What about the golden die?" Valerie asked. "Isn't that how you win the die, by rolling against it and winning?"

"No way," Ben said. "We're rolling for the book, not the die."

"Why not up the ante?" Mooneyham asked with a sly grin.

Albert looked eager to roll again, but Ben was hesitant.

"No pressure, Ben," Celeste said. "Don't let them talk you into anything."

"The die knows what it wants and goes where it wants to go," Albert said.

"Alright," Ben said. "We can do this. We can include the die. So, the winner gets the die and the book. But what do I win? I already have the die." An awkward silence passed through the group, so Ben continued. He looked Albert in the eye. "If I win, you have to acknowledge your feelings."

Albert didn't react immediately. He held Ben's gaze and with a nod said, "Sure."

They rolled their dice across the table. Albert's landed first with a five, and Ben felt a burst of excitement at the pit of his stomach. But then his own die landed with a one.

A cry of surprise escaped from the table.

"A critical failure!"

Ben sank into his chair and tried to force a smile as Albert extended a hand to him.

"Good game," Albert said.

Ben shook Albert's hand and placed the golden die upon Albert's stack of books.

"No, you should keep it," Albert said. "I can't really take your lucky die."

"What do you mean? You won it fair and square."

"I was just playing with you," Albert said. "I don't really want it."

"What are you talking about?" Ben felt himself getting angry. "You were just *playing*? You'd better fucking take it after all that."

And so, with an awkward look on his face, Albert dropped the golden die into his dice bag.

• • •

Flamebender wrestled the grimoire away from Bjorndar.

"Now to see to it that this foul thing is safely destroyed. I believe I'll take it to the smithy, and throw it in the forge." He tucked the book under his arm and headed for the door.

"He's leaving," Theegh said. "You're gonna let him get away with that? Go after him."

"No," Bjorndar said, slumping into a chair. "I don't have the energy anymore."

Flamebender walked out of the door of the tavern, and Bjorndar watched his silhouette grow smaller and smaller until the door closed.

albert

Walt and Valerie stepped up to the counter at Carmichael's Costumes and Magical Emporium. Walt rang the bell marked *Ring for Service*. The red velvet curtains parted, and a thin man with stringy blond hair stepped out. He wore an orange polo shirt with a name tag—*Bernard*—but Valerie recognized him immediately as the High Lord Varnec, Brother of Darkness, and Champion of Despair.

"Yes?" Bernard asked, as though he had never seen Valerie or even Walt before.

Walt, Valerie was surprised to see, seemed not to recognize Bernard either, because he began explaining right away that they had come to buy a new gorilla costume, and they wanted to know what options Carmichael's offered.

"A gorilla, you say? What an interesting choice." Bernard pulled a large catalogue from behind the counter. "I can show you what we have. Not all of these are in stock, of course, but we can special order whatever you might need."

"Our old costume is looking pretty shabby." Walt continued, "We've probably had that thing for twenty years. It's seen a lot of action."

"I'm sure it has." Bernard looked straight at Valerie then, and Valerie could see Bernard's nose was still slightly swollen and his upper lip too. "What a lucky gorilla."

"It's time for a new one," Walt said, thumbing through the

catalog. The pages were filled with full-color photos of people in various costumes: pirates, clowns, vampires. "We need our gorilla though if we're gonna get customers into the store," Walt said without looking up from the catalogue.

"Nothing like a dumb ape to stir up excitement," Bernard said. "Of course, there are other options. A chicken perhaps? We have a wonderful Mr. Cluckers. Comes with a top hat and cane."

"No," Valerie said. "Top hats are dumb. And capes."

"Who's talking about capes? He said cane. Here." Walt found the page with a gorilla. "This is exactly like our old one." The gorilla was posing in a barred cage with banana peels on the ground. Across the front of the cage, in red letters, was a sign that read CAUTION.

"Oh, that gorilla. That one is more likely to punch a customer than welcome them," Bernard said, and he raised a hand to his nose. He took the catalogue from Walt and flipped a few pages. "This gorilla is much more fun and inviting." He pointed to a bright-purple gorilla with a large yellow bow tie. It held a toy trumpet in one hand and a tambourine in the other.

"That looks more like a cartoon character than a gorilla," Valerie said.

But Walt seemed to be considering it. "We are a comic bookstore. That costume would be something fresh and new."

"It's even more embarrassing than the old one," Valerie said.

"Come now," Bernard said. "You can't be afraid of a little embarrassment, can you?"

"We'll take it," Walt said.

Valerie tried her best to persuade Walt to choose the other, more realistic gorilla, but Walt had made up his mind. The look of satisfaction on Bernard's face was infuriating.

• • •

On Thursday, Albert sat with the group in the back of Readmore, chatting and laughing.

Seven o'clock came and went, but Ben still had not arrived.

Celeste offered drinks and chips. They waited for ten more minutes, then fifteen. They reread their character sheets, double-checked a few rules in their *Player's Handbooks*, and clarified points on the map that Celeste had drawn.

"Should we just start?" Mooneyham asked.

"Yeah," Huey said. "Marilyn is ready to make some magic."

Albert and Celeste tried calling Ben, but there was no answer.

Since the night of the roll-off, Albert had left message after message for Ben. "I'm sorry," he said, "I didn't mean to upset you. Please call me. I wanna give you back your die." But Ben never called back. Albert sat at Jitterbugs every night, waiting, hoping Ben would show up, but he never did.

Sitting around the rickety card tables, the group was clearly getting anxious.

"Did he say anything to you?" Celeste asked. "Like, is he out of town?"

"We haven't talked since last week, but he didn't say anything about not showing up tonight. I mean . . ." Albert didn't continue. He thought for sure Ben would have forgiven him by now.

Seven thirty came and Ben still hadn't arrived. They decided to start without him. At first, they pretended Bjorndar was still among them, adventuring on. Albert made all the decisions for him, but eventually that became too difficult.

"It doesn't feel right that we brought Bjorndar back to life when he's not even here," Albert said.

"Are you saying we should kill him again?" Valerie asked.

"I don't know what I'm saying. Something doesn't feel right, that's all." Albert shifted in his seat and looked to Celeste for help, but she merely peered from over her screen.

"We wouldn't even be in this mess if it weren't for you," Mooneyham said.

"For me?" Albert asked.

"If you hadn't kissed Ben at O'Malley's, he might still be here."

"Fuck you. It was a kiss-in!"

"It's not his fault," Celeste said.

"How is it not?"

"Are you kidding me?" Albert asked. "This is ridiculous."

"You knew Ben had a crush on you. It's as obvious as shit," Mooneyham said. "You should've seen something like this coming a mile away."

"Come on, no one could have predicted this," Celeste said.

"And you shouldn't have allowed it to happen," Mooneyham said, turning to Celeste. "I told you, ever since the group broke up the first time, that members shouldn't be allowed to date."

"How was I supposed to know this would happen?" Celeste asked. "I've got my own life to worry about."

"And fuck you for saying that as you sit next to your boyfriend," Albert said.

"My fiancé," Mooneyham corrected. "That's different. We're practically married."

"Are we?" Huey asked.

"If we're not gonna play, I've got other stuff to do," Valerie said.

"Like some tentacle porn," Mooneyham said.

"Whatever. Just forget it then." Albert threw his books into his backpack, thanked Celeste for the game, and walked out. Celeste and Mooneyham called for him to calm down and come back, but he ignored them. Partly because he knew he wouldn't have as much fun without Ben at the game, but also because he knew Mooneyham was right. He had fucked everything up.

Albert continued to leave voicemails for Ben, but Ben never returned them. Not a text, nothing. Finally, Albert went to Ben's house. He walked around to the back and knocked on the cellar door. But it didn't open, and Ben didn't appear on the other side and whisper, "Just go away," like Albert had thought he might. Albert knocked louder and harder, and when there was still no answer, he tried the handle. It was unlocked. Albert pulled open one of the heavy wooden doors and called down in a hushed voice.

"Ben, are you in there?" There was no reply. The cellar was pitch dark.

Slowly, Albert climbed down the steep stairs into the darkness. Albert had been down these stairs before. He knew it was silly to get creeped out, and he laughed at himself for feeling so spooked. But he couldn't help thinking that perhaps Ben's mind had snapped after he lost his die and he was now living in the dark basement eating dead cats.

Albert slipped quietly through the storage area to the part of the basement where Ben lived, and the place looked mostly the same. Ben's normally cluttered desk had been cleaned and organized. The records were still stacked against the record player, although the ones Albert had helped sort through were gone. Ben's white cat, Onigiri, jumped down from the water bed with a meow and rubbed against Albert's legs.

Albert considered the best place to leave the golden die. Ben's desk, recently cleaned off, had a spot there where the die would stand out. Or, he could leave it on the water bed, on Ben's pillow, but that seemed super cheesy and more romantic than Albert was intending. On top of the record player might be good though, or the coffee table.

Albert's decision was interrupted when the basement door opened, and Ben's mom walked down the stairs. At least Albert assumed she was Ben's mom. She looked like Ben anyway, or Ben looked like her: auburn hair, pink cheeks, slight build, and something familiar in the mousey way she reacted when she saw Albert. He must have looked suspicious hunched over Ben's desk, the cat still between his legs.

"Hello," she said tentatively. "Is Ben here?"

"He's in the bathroom." The lie slipped out before Albert could even think about the fact that there were absolutely no sounds coming from the bathroom.

A million thoughts seemed to flash through the mind of Ben's mom before she said, "Tell him I'm leaving his mail here with his other mail." She placed some letters on top of a bigger stack already sitting on the bookshelf. She turned to climb up the stairs and asked, "Who are you?"

"Albert."

"And which one are you?"

"From the role playing club."

"I meant which character."

"Flamebender. The paladin."

"Oh, of course." She smiled and shut the basement door quietly as she left.

Albert left the golden die on top of Ben's pillow and slipped out the cellar doors.

That night, as they were draped over each other in bed, Albert told Jeff he was going to quit the role playing club. Ben had stopped coming, and the game just wasn't that fun anymore.

"Cool," Jeff said, dragging his fingertips up and down the hairs on Albert's chest. "That group was for dorks anyway."

Albert laughed. But then he realized Jeff wasn't joking.

He wanted to tell Jeff how cool the group was, how Jeff would have liked those guys if he gave them a chance. But he knew there was no point.

"Did I tell you Goateyes is coming to town?" Albert asked, changing the subject. "You've gotta go with me to see them. They're amazing live."

"Sure," Jeff said. "Maybe." And then, "Let's shave your chest. It's getting out of control again."

But Albert took Jeff's hand from his chest and turned away.

"Oh my god, are you pissed about that?" Jeff asked.

Albert turned off the light atop his milk crate and tried to sleep. But all he could think about was Ben. What was Ben doing? Why hadn't he returned to the game?

The next day at work, while they were restocking the incense, Albert told Liz, "I'm an idiot. I shouldn't have pushed him."

"It's not your fault," she said. "You didn't know he was going to react like that." They were keeping their voices low.

"Yeah, but I could've guessed." Albert hated to admit it, but Mooneyham was right.

"Why do you care about Ben anyway when you've got Jeff?"

Albert didn't answer. While they worked, they kept their heads down and didn't make eye contact with any customers to maintain an air of unapproachableness.

"I don't get why you're so into him," Liz said, tucking her hair behind her ears. "I think he's cute but he's a total geek."

"What's wrong with liking geeks?"

"You'll have to explain it to me, 'cause I'm not into guys like that."

Albert laughed. "How can I explain it? That'd be like explaining root beer or something. I mean, you like root beer, right? But could you say why? Could you describe what it tastes like?"

"Tell me you're not breaking up with Jeff because you prefer the taste of root beer or some hokey shit like that. Do you know how many girls here, and guys too I bet, would love to go out with Jeff? You're the perfect couple. He's blond and beautiful, and you're dark and surly."

"I'm surly?" Albert had been called many things, but never surly.

"I meant swarthy," she said, but that didn't sound any better.

"Oh my god, I figured it out," Albert said. "You're right." Liz had gotten to the root of his problem, whether she knew it or not. Jeff was hot and fun and knew a lot about music; although he preferred to tap his foot and bob his head more than get into the pit and rock out. But whatever. Just because two people didn't like the same things all the time, it didn't mean they couldn't be together. But sometimes it was impossible to know if you liked the taste of something until you'd tried it.

...

Celeste wished she wasn't a creature of habit as she walked into Readmore on Thursday night. She knew no one was coming to the game, so she didn't even go through the curtains and into the back room. Although she did glance in that direction, hoping that, somehow, she was wrong. But she was not. The curtains were closed; the back room was dark and empty. She stood in front of the new arrivals rack and tried to be interested in the titles. She tried to act like she was in the store because she wanted to be, not because she had nothing else to do.

But she wasn't fooling anyone. It was only a moment before Polly came around from behind the front counter and touched Celeste on the arm.

"Hey," Polly said, with an awkward smile. She was dressed in her green Poison Ivy outfit, with fake leaves and vines stitched around the arms. "Did Valerie text you? I don't think she's coming tonight."

By the time Thursday rolled around, Celeste had received a message from every member of the group, except Ben, telling her that they weren't going to make it. Albert had been the first, followed by Mooneyham and Huey, and finally Valerie on Wednesday night. By then Celeste had already resigned herself to the fact that the group was falling apart. And try as she might, Celeste couldn't get anyone to change their minds.

"She did, thanks. I'm just here hanging out."

"Oh." Polly's smile widened. "Sure. That's cool."

But Polly didn't walk away or leave Celeste alone to peruse any comics. She continued to stand there, as though she had something else to say.

So Celeste, trying to avoid an awkward moment, nodded in

understanding and said, "I know, the group is done. Or taking a break, maybe. That's what I'm going to call it."

"Sorry to hear that," Polly said.

Celeste picked up an issue of *Batgirl* and flipped through the pages. "Perhaps not being in the group is what people need, at least right now anyway. They've got their own dramas right now."

Polly's smile faltered for a moment, but Celeste continued on, saying, "I did what I could to keep it going, but I can only do so much."

She couldn't help feeling like she'd failed somehow or made the wrong decisions. Maybe if she had told Albert he couldn't join or told the group they shouldn't organize the kiss-in, things would have gone differently. But then, so many good things wouldn't have happened either.

In the comic, Batgirl was riding on a purple motorcycle and leaping over a police car, its sirens flashing.

Celeste chuckled to herself and put the comic back on the rack. "I'm going to have to find something else to do on Thursday nights. That's my biggest problem right now. Guess I could always read more comics."

Polly gave Celeste another smile and said she was always welcome to hang out at Readmore, and then she was called away to help someone at the front counter. Celeste lingered for a while, took a look at some RPGs, and bought a new set of dice for herself. She gave the dark doorway of the back room one last glance before she left.

　　　• • •

Albert was off the following Saturday, and the weather called for rain, which meant staying indoors. Albert had been waiting to visit the Cleveland Museum of Art with Jeff, and a rainy day seemed like the perfect opportunity.

The museum sat on a small lake near University Circle, in an old, neoclassical building made of white marble. If it hadn't been for the rain, Albert would have liked to walk around the lake and the gardens. But as it was, they shuffled inside, shook the water off their jackets, and left them at the coat check.

Jeff had been there before, but not since middle school, and the museum had been remodeled since then. He pointed out all the differences and laughed at how big and mysterious the museum had felt back then.

They walked through the Asian art, the Egyptian art, and then the Armor Court, around all the polished breastplates and gleaming helms. Large tapestries telling the story of Dido and Aeneas hung on the walls high above them. It was hard for Albert to be surrounded by medieval weapons and armor and not think of the game and the role playing club.

"This is exactly the kind of armor my paladin would have worn," Albert explained as they stepped up to study a suit of plate mail.

They moved quietly from display to display, noting all the details on the armor, and speaking in low voices even though that wing of the museum was empty at that time of day. They could hear the rain falling upon the skylights overhead.

"What are you gonna do now that the game is over?" Jeff asked.

"I don't know. I saw something about a sci-fi book club. It's only once a month, but I might start going to that."

"And you're absolutely sure the group is done?" Jeff inspected the embellishment on a silver breastplate.

"Until everyone decides to get together again, I guess. Celeste doesn't have the energy to look for new people and start the whole group all over."

Walking through the halls with Jeff, taking in the paintings and sculptures, Albert found he could relax and focus his thoughts. He felt connected to a bigger story. His problems seemed small and manageable.

"Yeah," said Jeff. "Sure." But he was looking down at his cell phone and punching out a text message with his thumb. "Sorry," he said. "I just got a text from someone. It's kinda funny."

Albert's body slumped along his long thin frame. "No problem," he said. "I'll just be over here. Thinking."

Albert stood in front of a large landscape painting, a dirt crossroads meeting in a golden sea of wheat. Weathered telephone poles retreated along the road into the distance. Above the yellow field, storm clouds gathered in the sky like large gray bundles of wool. Despite the realism and the attention to detail it was impossible to know for sure if the scene was taken from real life or from some foreboding dream.

Albert couldn't say why he was drawn to the painting, but there was a familiarity about the scene, as though he'd been there, to that very place, but he couldn't remember when or why. Maybe it was the gold in the wheat field, but for some reason Albert thought of Ben and his golden die.

"To be honest, I still can't believe the group is over," Albert said. "It hasn't sunk in yet. I guess I thought it was going to last forever. I feel like we only just started."

"Everything ends at some point," Jeff said, sliding his phone into his back pocket and walking over.

Albert turned away and looked to the high ceilings, to the skylights dimpling with raindrops. "You know, you do things, you try something new, and you try different ideas. You try to keep things going. You give it your best, and still, it all falls apart."

"Hey, don't be upset about it. Not everything is destined to work out. That's just how it is. It doesn't mean it was a waste of time though." Jeff took Albert by the shoulders and turned him around. "Come here," he said and pulled Albert forward until their hips locked together. They looked at each other for a moment, until Albert turned his face away. Jeff leaned into him and then tucked his head beneath Albert's chin. "That's just how it is," he whispered.

Albert pressed his nose into Jeff's hair, nuzzling, and they breathed together, in and out. The rain fell upon the skylights. Albert's arms slid around Jeff's waist to hold him, and then, finally, before the golden wheat field, and the crossroads, and the darkening clouds, Albert let go.

the thing in the cellar

After losing his golden die to Albert, Ben came straight to the basement and stayed there, first for one day, and then another. When his mother knocked on the door, he said, "I'm sick, go away." When she offered to call a doctor he said, "I'm fine. Just go away." When his phone rang, he didn't answer. When a text message beeped, he didn't check it. He didn't shower. He didn't shave. He didn't jerk off, whether the cat was on the bed or not. He survived on chips, old beer, stale popcorn, and whatever else he had in his room. When Thursday came and the club met again, he stayed in bed with a pillow over his head.

All strength and motivation left him whenever he thought about facing Albert. His feet wouldn't step into his shoes. His arms wouldn't reach for clean clothes. His brain wouldn't settle itself around slaying goblins or rolling dice or solving riddles. Ben only wanted to sleep, to drift away into a void and not think about anything.

But even that couldn't last.

Partly motivated by hunger and partly by boredom, Ben, scruffy and hollow cheeked, emerged from the cellar doors and into the gray afternoon light of Cleveland Heights. He had dwelt in darkness for days, and he had dwelt on certain realities too. That he lived in his parents' basement. That he didn't have a real job. That he was single and twenty-five and hadn't found love yet. That he spent most of his time either selling old toys online or playing fantasy role playing games. And if he didn't get up and get moving none of that was ever going to change.

The fresh air cleared his mind as he stretched, breathing deeply through his nose. He rubbed the sleep-sand out of his eyes. He bent over and tried to touch his toes, but he was too stiff. He left the cellar doors open while he went to shower, to let the air circulate through his room and free any bad smells or dark thoughts that were still lingering.

He began finishing up the cleaning job he had started weeks ago. He took all his dirty dishes upstairs to the dishwasher, and he vacuumed the basement floor, much to Onigiri's displeasure. He did a load of laundry and folded his clothes as he dressed in something clean for the first time in days.

Ben returned to the surface world, making his rounds thrifting, checking out books at the library, and avoiding Coventry Road.

When Ben returned home and found the golden die on his pillow, he immediately wanted to send Albert a text, but he knew he shouldn't.

Ben paced across his bedroom. Of course, he was happy his lucky die was back, and there was something romantic but also vaguely creepy about Albert sneaking in to surprise him. He wanted to tell Albert to come over, to bring some records, and hang out. But he knew that would put them back into the same painful place again.

So, Ben put his phone in his pocket. He sat at his computer and checked his auctions. He played some video games. Finally, he pulled out his phone again and wrote: *I need some time to think.* But he didn't send it, he let the message sit there.

The following afternoon, Ben arrived at the Cuyahoga Discount Thrift to find a madhouse, even worse than usual for a Saturday. Shopping carts and overflowing baskets filled the aisles. High school students with bad posture scouted around looking for vintage clothes. Old people shuffled by, inch by patient inch.

Moms dragged their kids and spanked their kids and forced them back into strollers. The store needed a good airing out. It smelled of dust and disinfectant.

Every item had a colored price tag, and each week a different color was fifty percent off. The new color was chosen on Saturdays. Ben and all the regulars knew this. Saturday was the day to go. On this Saturday, the color was yellow, the most common color. A bonanza for everyone.

Ben was not having much luck though. He found a unicorn belt buckle that he might be able to get a few more bucks for, and there were a couple paint-by-numbers that looked interesting, but nothing that was so exciting as to make him drop his basket. He was about to give up and go home, when a flash of pink caught his eye. On a bottom shelf, between two stacks of tattered board games, was a pink Furby. One of the original pink-and-yellow Furbies with the blue eyes, not the black eyes— those ones came later and weren't worth anything.

Ben cupped it gently in his hands. It was in good shape. Someone had obviously cared for it and brushed its fur. It was still so fluffy. Ben checked underneath for the price. Seven dollars and a yellow tag! Clearly the person pricing these things had no idea what they were doing. In the Furby heyday of '98, this thing could have gone for three thousand dollars. He still might get over a hundred for it if he wrote the auction right. That would be amazing. He could do so much with an extra hundred dollars, like buy a new windbreaker to replace his old yellow one. It was getting so worn out.

He headed for the registers, clutching the Furby to his chest. A group of schoolgirls giggled and pointed when they saw the pink fur between his hands. *Yes, look and laugh you simpletons.*

As he neared the checkout and stepped to the back of the line, Ben saw a familiar blond head near the front. It was Jeff. Oh god.

He couldn't let Jeff see him with a Furby. Quickly, he stepped from the line and tucked the Furby on a shelf between two white coffee mugs.

Ben had no idea that Jeff even came to the Cuyahoga Discount Thrift. Jeff never mentioned thrift shopping, and Ben had never seen him wear anything vintage or even used.

As Ben walked past the line, he caught Jeff's eye.

Jeff said, "Hey."

"I didn't know you were into thrifting."

"I wasn't but I heard they have good records here." Jeff flashed the stack of records he'd found, but Ben didn't recognize any of the covers.

"And who could have told you that?" Ben asked, but Jeff just laughed in response. Which was actually a relief, because Ben wasn't trying to be a jerk or anything; he was trying to be funny.

"Where's Albert?" Ben asked but instantly regretted the question when he saw the awkward look on Jeff's face.

"I dunno," Jeff said.

"He doesn't tell you what he's doing?"

"We broke up," Jeff said. "Like, days ago."

A cold shock washed over Ben.

"He dumped you?" Ben asked.

"No, are you kidding? It was mutual," Jeff said. "Obviously. By the way, you've got something pink stuck to your face." Jeff reached out and pulled some pink fuzz from Ben's unshaven chin. "Got it."

Ben stood stunned, not knowing what to think as Jeff said goodbye and moved up the line. If they had really broken up, why hadn't Albert told him?

Ben returned to the shelf, but there was no flash of pink between the mugs. The Furby was gone.

In the minds of Clevelanders, certain things are inevitable and must be accepted as the unknowable workings of fate or destiny or Mother Nature. If someone has a job they enjoy and brags about it at a party or picnic, they will surely find themselves laid off within a week. If they have a pretty house, it will catch on fire or be infested by termites beyond repair. If someone is whistling and smiling and generally enjoying the day as they walk down the street, they will be victims of some random act of violence. New shirts attract spills and stains the first time they're worn. New cars are crashed as soon as they're driven off the lot. Outdoor weddings are ruined by rain, or snow, or hail, or all three at once. That is life, Clevelanders say, and Ben would agree.

So, it made sense to him that the complicated machinations of the universe would send Jeff to the thrift store at the same moment that Ben would be there. It made sense that Ben would find out about the breakup through Jeff, and not through Albert. It even made sense that the Furby would be gone. And most of all, it made sense that somehow used records would be involved.

When Ben arrived at Destruction Records, Liz, the girl with the nice neck, was organizing silver rings in the jewelry case. Ben didn't see Albert anywhere. But the door to Vinyl Vault was open, so Ben climbed down the stairs.

The Vault had a low cement ceiling with flickering fluorescent lights and row after row of records lined up in wooden bins. A few customers stood around silently and shuffled through the records as heavy metal chugged out of the speakers. And there, behind the counter at the far end of the room talking with a customer, was Albert.

Ben's courage faltered when he saw Albert. Rather than step right up to the counter, Ben drifted between the record bins, scratching his scruffy chin, pretending to look for something to buy. When Albert's customer left, Albert looked over at Ben, and their eyes met.

"I thought I recognized that windbreaker," Albert said.

"I considered doing a dive roll and hiding beneath the recent arrivals," Ben said. "But I don't actually know how to do dive rolls."

Ben had tried to imagine what this moment would be like, and where it would take place. In front of Readmore? At Jitterbugs when he ran in for a soy latte? Wherever it happened, he expected it to be awkward. But he felt surprisingly comfortable, even relieved that the moment had arrived.

"I ran into Jeff," Ben said. "Why didn't you tell me you two broke up?"

"I don't know." Albert sorted cash in the register and then slid the drawer shut with a clang. "I was embarrassed I guess."

"About what?"

"Who knows? I mean, probably a lot of things," Albert said. "Did you get my texts? You never responded."

"I meant to, but . . ." Why was Ben having such a hard time saying what he wanted to?

"That's too bad," Albert said. "I've been wondering about you. Celeste said she hadn't heard from you either."

"Yeah, I've been trying to lay low."

"Look, I've gotta pick up my food at the Chinese place," Albert said. "I'm about to take my lunch break. You wanna walk with me and we can catch up?"

"Sure," Ben said.

The weather was perfect for a walk; the air was crisp and dry. Fall was ending and winter would soon begin. The air already smelled of ozone and metal and all the other scents that reminded Ben of snow. Coventry Road was changing its clothes, putting on its festive wear. Wreaths were hanging on the streetlamps, and soon there would be colored lights strung around the shop windows.

As they waited at a corner for cars to pass, Albert said, "I know how you haven't been showing up to the game because of me, and I want to say I'm sorry."

They crossed the street, and as cars passed Ben said, "I've been wondering for a while now what I would say if I ran into you."

"Yeah?" Albert shielded his eyes from the sun. "And what was that?"

"I still don't know. Actually, that's not true. I do know. It's more a question of how to say it."

"You can just say it." Albert shrugged with his usual nonchalance. "I don't care."

"Yeah, maybe."

They stopped outside the Chinese restaurant, and before going in, Albert turned and said, "Look, even without the group, I'd still like to get together and hang out some time, if that's possible."

A handful of kids ran past, laughing and squealing on their way home from school. A large service truck was beeping as it backed out onto the street. Ben swallowed.

"Okay," Ben said, and his eyes met Albert's as he stepped up to him. "You've gotta know, and here's the thing, this is what I'd tell you, I guess. You've got to know that I'm really a dork. I mean, really. You've seen the basement, all my posters and stuff. I have no job. I make all my money selling stuff on eBay. I'm twenty-five and I haven't even had a real boyfriend yet."

"It's okay," said Albert. "I work in a record store. Who cares?"

"Yeah, but I spend most of my free time trolling the internet and reading Doctor Who fan fiction. Erotic fan fiction. What I'm trying to say is, I understand why you'd choose Jeff."

Albert held up a hand as if to stop a ten-course meal at the second dish. "But I didn't choose Jeff."

Another group of kids ran by, screaming louder than the first. Albert continued, "I wanna hang out with you."

"Okay." Ben waited. The truck had stopped beeping. "Is that it?"

"That's it. Actually, you know what?" Albert snapped his fingers. "Goateyes are playing at the Agora, this Thursday. You wanna go?"

"On a Thursday?"

"Come on, it's not like you're doing anything anyway."

"How do you know?"

"I know. We both know. The group is dead. What else is there to do on a Thursday?"

Ben couldn't think of a single thing.

So, they made a date. A real date. Albert said, "I'm gonna remind you and hold you to it." Then he went inside to pick up his food.

Ben watched for a moment through the window as Albert waited to pay.

Could happiness really be so easy? Could it really be a matter of saying yes instead of no? As simple as running toward something instead of running away?

Ben turned from the window. He closed his eyes and stretched out his mind, as though looking for lost dice. His fingers crawled through the air, seeking. But he wasn't looking for lost dice. He was looking for something else. Love, happiness, both together? Could he summon into being this unnamable yet desirable thing? It felt so close and so tangible, Ben could practically visualize it, but he didn't dare speak its name, lest the thin magic connecting them should break. Ben concentrated. *Manifest, manifest!* And then, on the count of three, he opened his eyes.

peering through the oculus

The usual gray gloom never arrived, chased away by a pink glow that washed over the trees, the houses, and the sidewalks. It seeped through curtains and across windowsills and fell onto fluttering eyelids. There it stayed, flickering, ready to break, like the breath-held moment before the orchestra begins. All was buttery and rose-washed then. Even the palest of complexions looked healthy, the gauntest of cheeks like peaches.

Then the sunbeams arrived, and everything was golden.

Ben peeled his arm from across Albert's hairy chest and climbed out of bed. He pulled on his boxers, and, not being able to find his own, he put on Albert's T-shirt instead. It was too small and too black. The moment had seemed impossible a few weeks ago, but, as he looked at himself in the mirror, in a T-shirt so tight he could hardly lift his arms, the proof was undeniable. He had become that guy who wakes up and puts on his boy-friend's T-shirt, and he couldn't help but smile.

Downstairs, Albert's roommates were already watching TV. It must be nice to have roommates who are not your parents, Ben thought, to sleep in a bedroom above the ground, several stories in the air, to look out the window and see the sky, the clouds, the stars at night.

He quietly padded over to the shelf of lead figures. Surrounded by a mob of angry goblins, the painted figurine of Flamebender stood beside the miniature Bjorndar, fighting side-by-side.

Albert stirred. Ben leaned over and laid upon him the sort of kiss that no one could sleep through. Which only inspired more kissing and further touching. Albert opened his eyes, reached up, and pulled Ben back into bed.

...

A little before six o'clock, they went to Ben's house. They climbed down into the cellar, and Ben left the doors open behind them. Ben turned on the lights in the storage room, which he and Albert had spent the week cleaning out. In the middle of the room, where boxes and Christmas decorations used to be, now stood an old dining room set, a thick, dark wooden table, with contoured beveled legs and six high-backed chairs in dark-red leather upholstery. Halloween decorations hung on the cinder block walls. A skeleton strung with lights leaned against one corner, holding a plastic broad axe. Tall electric candelabras flickered in the other corners, draped with fake cobwebs. Near the table, a black mini-fridge hummed, filled with beer and drinks. A Teddy Ruxpin in a purple wizard hat sat on top of the fridge between bags of chips and popcorn.

This was a proper gaming den.

Mooneyham and Huey were the first to arrive, followed by Valerie "The Ape" and Celeste. They wasted no time pulling out their books and character sheets and placing their miniatures on the map Celeste had drawn and unfolded.

Ben readied his golden die with a grin and gave a nod to Albert.

Celeste looked at them from over her dungeon master's screen. "So, where were we then?"